Praise for

ANTIPODES

"Michele Bacon's writing expertly plunges us into a captivating New Zealand setting and Erin's journey as she learns how to whole-heartedly live her life rather than simply accomplish it. *Antipodes* is a must-read."

—Natasha Sinel, author of *The Fix* and *Soulstruck*

"*Antipodes* is an engrossing read about being right side up when you're upside down, and finding yourself when you didn't even know you were lost. When you read Michele Bacon's richly-detailed, fully-realized New Zealand, you'll want to visit. When you meet Hank, you'll want to stay."

—Katie Kennedy, author of *What Goes Up*

"*Antipodes* is a love story, yes, and as much one about loving ourselves for who and what we are. It's wise, compassionate, and bursting with the bittersweet complexity of adolescence."

—Martha Brockenbrough, author of *The Game of Love and Death*

Praise for

LIFE BEFORE

"A gripping story about a shattered family and one boy's journey to begin again. Bacon takes on the subject of domestic violence with skill and compassion in this fast-paced, suspenseful, and thoroughly enjoyable novel."

—Kirsten Lopresti, author of *Bright Coin Moon*

"Xander is a believable protagonist who triumphs over fear and trauma. Michele Bacon adds a new, honest, and strong voice."
—Cheryl Rainfield, author of *Scars* and *Stained*

"*Life Before* is a thought-provoking and engaging read, which beautifully illustrates that anyone could be striving to overcome difficulties—no matter what you see on the surface."
—Mindi Scott, author of *Free Fall* and *Live Through This*

"A riveting story told in a voice that will resonate with teens. . . . A great read-alike for teens who enjoyed Alex Flinn's *Breathing Underwater*, Laurie Halse Anderson's *Speak*, or Sharon Draper's Hazelwood High trilogy."
—*School Library Journal*

"Both a coming-of-age story and a nail-biting thriller, this debut novel will appeal to a wide range of readers."
—*VOYA Magazine* teen reviewer

ANTIPODES

Also by Michele Bacon

Life Before

ANTIPODES

MICHELE BACON

Sky Pony Press
New York

Sky Pony Press books may be purchased in bulk at special discounts for sales promotion, corporate gifts, fund-raising, or educational purposes. Special editions can also be created to specifications. For details, contact the Special Sales Department, Sky Pony Press, 307 West 36th Street, 11th Floor, New York, NY 10018 or info@skyhorsepublishing.com.

Sky Pony® is a registered trademark of Skyhorse Publishing, Inc.®, a Delaware corporation.

Visit our website at www.skyponypress.com.

10 9 8 7 6 5 4 3 2 1

Library of Congress Cataloging-in-Publication Data is available on file.

Cover design by Kate Gartner
Interior design by Joshua Barnaby
Map by Karen Rank

Print ISBN: 978-1-5107-2361-0
Ebook ISBN: 978-1-5107-2364-1

Printed in the United States of America

for Heather Booth
because she's the best

ANTIPODES /anˈtipədēz/

noun

1. Direct or exact opposites. *Erin's months studying abroad were the antipodes of her previous life.*
2. (often capitalized) Australia and New Zealand, The Antipodes

ONE

Last July, Erin had studied astrophysics at Harvard's Pre-College Program. Even Astrophysics at Harvard was easier than this.

July as Erin once knew it was over. Here, in the Southern Hemisphere, July was the dead of winter, and Erin Cerise was in limbo. Twenty-four hours prior, she'd departed her childhood home, boarded a flight in Chicago, flown across her own country, and traversed the vast span of the Pacific Ocean. In a mad panic, she'd edited the third draft of her personal essay for college applications and tried in vain to sleep on the plane next to her snoring, fetid seatmate.

Erin was eager to end her journey and begin her exile halfway around the world. Her fellow passengers, however, possessed no comparable sense of urgency as they disembarked in Christchurch, New Zealand.

Erin flexed and released her fingers, an unconscious signal she needed to lay hands on her cello immediately. Her Suzuki teacher insisted she practice daily and, until this little excursion, she'd held a streak of 2,243 consecutive days. She'd reached the twenty-four-hour point mid-flight, and crossing the International Date Line had forced her to miss Friday entirely.

Erin was starting over at Day One.

With cello, that is. If only she could start over at Day One with everything else, turn back the clock twenty-four hours to summer in Chicago, or a bit further to when Ben loved her in early May, or to when she was assured the swimming captainship, or back to summers in Michigan.

Any one of those would suffice. She wanted to turn back the clock to a time—any time—when she'd been happy.

Today, she was not happy.

Mid-July was winter in New Zealand, so Erin felt upside down already. Departing sunny, humid Chicago to endure a second winter Down Under felt more like punishment than a clever ploy to augment her college applications.

Just two months prior, she'd had excellent college prospects, complete independence, a supportive swim team, and a great boyfriend in Wheaton, twenty-six miles west of Chicago.

But one tiny cosmic shift had ruined everything, much like lollygagging New Zealanders were ruining her first morning in Christchurch.

Kiwis. New Zealand people called themselves kiwis. She knew that much.

Sidestepping a family of five, Erin dashed past a wall of windows that would have offered her a first glimpse of Christchurch's vast azure sky, unmarred by clouds. Tourists snapped photos, but Erin was ready to meet her host family and establish her new schedule.

Her loss of swim team captainship left a huge—gaping—hole in her college applications, to say nothing of the voids in her weekly calendar.

Voids, vacuums, and black holes had mesmerized Erin for most of eleventh grade. Where voids in the universe kept planets and solar systems at peace, however, voids in her schedule and résumé were devastating.

Her mother, Claire, hoped studying abroad might fill that void and make Erin an attractive Ivy League candidate. Attending Columbia—or any Ivy, really—would establish her trajectory toward a great medical school, a great job, and a great life.

But first, she must endure five months in New Zealand. Squaring her shoulders, she walked down the escalator toward baggage claim.

TWO

Felicity, Erin's host mother, had promised to wear a yellow shirt for their meeting at the airport, but there were no yellow shirts. There was no host family. Erin walked through the crowd, studying every woman of the appropriate age.

She tried not to panic as the luggage parade began. One guy had spray painted his carry-on. Easy to find, yes, but completely ruined. Erin's new suitcase was black and enormous. Thanks to her father, it boasted a bright orange bow of yarn, a nice complement to the construction orange duct tape that marked his own luggage. Erin spotted her suitcase and yanked it off the conveyor belt.

Still no Felicity.

Erin wrestled her luggage into a restroom stall, peed, washed her hands, splashed water on her face, and assessed her reflection. As a final parting gift, Chicago's humidity had frizzed her carob curls; she tried her best to tame them before emerging from the bathroom.

Still no host family.

Everyone from her flight had departed with their luggage, deserting Erin and her enormous suitcase. Was she in the right place?

In a cute kiwi accent, which fell somewhere between British and Australian, a man paged Vienna Galagher with increasing frequency and urgency. Erin expected to hear her own name and an explanation for her desertion, but it was only Vienna Galagher, over and again.

In a foreign country where she knew literally no one, she had no Plan B.

Stalling for time, she wheeled to a snack counter that carried strange candies and something called chocolate fish. She bought a Picnic candy bar, which seemed safe. Refilling her water bottle at a fountain, she calmed herself.

I will not cry. I will not cry.

She was in way over her head, but phoning her host family would expose her unworldliness. Felicity must perceive her as confident and self-sufficient, which she surely was in all moments.

Except this one.

Instead she texted her best friend, Lalitha.

Erin: They're not here.
Litha: What do you mean they're NOT THERE?
Erin: I've been standing alone at baggage claim for
        20 minutes. Everyone else from my flight has left.
Litha: Are you at the right airport?
Erin: I'm not an idiot.
Litha: Maybe call a cab?

She'd never done that before. She studied the airport signs, all of which were in English and a second language she couldn't decipher. Searching for taxi stand indicators, she looked north and south before spying a flash of yellow moving toward her from the far end of baggage claim.

Erin relaxed. It was definitely Felicity.

Erin: They're here. Text later.
Litha: ❤

She drew a deep breath. No turning back now.

THREE

Erin's host mother had brought her partner and a small girl who carried a poster with Erin's name in lopsided multicolor letters. The girl, who Erin figured for the promised little sister, was *far* littler, perhaps eight. Bright gratuitous patches dotted her jeans, and her shoes were worn within an inch of their life.

"Felicity?" Erin said.

The precocious pigtailed girl thrust her hand toward Erin. "I'm Pippa, your new little sister."

It sounded like *sista*.

"She has been so excited to meet you. I'm Felicity." She hugged Erin loosely. "Nice to meet you, Erin."

Ear-in. The adorable kiwi accent got her name wrong: Ear-in. In middle school, when Erin's mother hired her Suzuki instructor, she had warned him about Erin's listening skills: *If you don't look her in the eye, everything you say will be ear-in, ear-out.*

That's how her name sounded in Felicity's mouth: Ear-in.

Felicity's partner said, "Hamish Wakefield. Good to meet you, Erin."

Ear-in.

"Easy flights?"

"Yeah."

Pippa bounced. "Did you gedda look out the window?"

"No. I worked on the way to L.A., and for some of the big flight. Otherwise, I tried to sleep."

Pippa's shoulders sagged. "Oh."

On their way to the airport exit, Pippa peppered Erin with questions about America: Had she been to New York? Had she been to Los Angeles? Had she been to New Orleans?

Hearing that Erin had been to all three put Pippa in awe.

"And the States are like Australia, Pippa," Felicity said. "So that's like traveling to Cairns *and* Melbourne *and* Perth."

"Do you get to Australia often?" Erin asked.

Felicity laughed. "Haven't been since she was seven. But she hasn't stopped talking about it."

Erin smiled. "Maybe we'll go while I'm here."

"Not bloody likely," Hamish said. "It's two thousand kilometers away."

"No kidding." Australia had seemed a lot closer on Google Maps.

"All right then?" Hamish asked.

He pulled Erin's suitcase into the sun and thanked a woman greeting them at the door. In response, she said, "Cheers!"

People in New Zealand—kiwis—were awfully chipper for 7 a.m. Lalitha would be appalled.

FOUR

Erin inhaled Christchurch's crisp, clean air and detected no aroma—not the smog of L.A. or the grease of Chicago or the distinct earthy scent of her grandparents' lake house. New Zealand air was so fresh she wanted to eat it . . . and so chilly she pulled her striped sweater from her carry-on.

In the small parking lot, Hamish lifted Erin's suitcase into an ancient blue Nissan. "What's this? Twenty kilos?"

A kilo is 2.2 pounds, so a pound is .45 kilos. Fifty pounds is: "About 22.6 kilograms."

"Just one bag, then?" Hamish asked.

"That's all I was allowed. My dad shipped another box. It should get here Friday."

Felicity squeezed into the backseat with Pippa so Erin could sit up front and enjoy the best view. Erin had anticipated driving on the left but hadn't imagined the unsettling feeling of being a passenger on the left side of the car; she checked the rearview mirror repeatedly, but it faced Hamish on the right.

She studied the Nissan's buttons and dials; everything was in Japanese. "Do you speak Japanese?"

"Whazzat?" Hamish asked.

"Your car. Everything's in Japanese. Are you fluent?"

Hamish guffawed. "Nope. Don't read it, either, but when you have a car going on fifteen years, you figure it out."

Fifteen years. Erin figured her parents had owned at least eleven in that time, plus her own Fiat, which was just a year old.

The Wakefields must be broke.

The host-family dossier had noted Hamish's occupation as "construction" and Felicity's "secretary." Suspecting a blue-collar family was a bad fit for Erin, Claire had spent two weeks lobbying unsuccessfully for a Scottish experience. Foreign Study Network insisted it was too late to swap; Erin could have New Zealand or nothing.

"You all right, Erin?" Hamish asked.

Ear-in.

She nodded, staring down the long, flat road, which ran between squat buildings and construction projects. Road signs—in two languages, again—sat propped in brown grass. Only speed limit signs stood on posts: 80 kilometers per hour. Fifty miles per hour. On the highway. Hamish motored among sedans and tiny vehicles—not an SUV in sight—all of which obeyed the speed limit.

Short and slow and small.

Christchurch was less the promised Garden City and more like . . . Parma, a nearby suburb where Erin and her ex-boyfriend, Ben, had enjoyed drive-in movies. That vintage venue stood among lots cluttered with road garbage, overgrown wildflowers, and vacant industrial buildings.

Hamish pointed to a shopping center featuring stores called The Warehouse and PAK'nSAVE. "At's the Hub, closest shopping center and grocery."

Pippa said, "On special occasions, we get ice cream sundaes at Wendys."

Erin twisted to make eye contact. "American Wendy's doesn't have sundaes. Just burgers, fries, Frosties, and boring salads."

"That stinks," Pippa said.

After three uninspiring strip malls, Hamish said, "This is us."

He turned onto a quiet residential street where, without exception, houses were small ranches reminiscent of Wheaton's old rental-house neighborhoods. Stickers on each mailbox read NO JUNK MAIL.

Unusual plants bordered meticulously manicured lawns. Fences and walls of all sorts—tall and short, wood, brick, and stone—separated properties from one another and the road. Huge bulbs of leaves sat atop skinny, bare tree trunks, as if conjured by Dr. Seuss. Not a mature tree in sight.

Erin spun Grandma Tea's ring around her finger and wondered whether she was being punked.

I hope I'm being punked.

Hamish pulled into a narrow driveway sandwiched between two peeling wooden fences. At the driveway's end sat a tiny gray ranch boasting a single front window. Hamish parked facing the baby-poop green front door. An attached garage to the left created an L-shaped house.

L for *Loser.*

She needn't turn back the clock to happiness; a mere twenty-four hours would suffice.

BEFORE SHE LANDED IN CHRISTCHURCH

BEFORE SHE LANDED IN CHRISTCHURCH

Erin's flight from Chicago to Los Angeles was a piece of cake, but she had only ninety minutes to locate her connecting flight.

And she was famished.

After grabbing a Chipotle burrito, she caught the world's slowest shuttle to the international terminal, where the world's longest security line awaited her. She spun her ring around her finger, counting the minutes until her flight was due to depart. She'd flown plenty, but never alone and never halfway around the world.

"Passenger E. Cerise for Air New Zealand flight 2 to Christchurch. Please proceed to your gate immediately. Doors close in five minutes."

Shit.

Though she would rather stay in America, missing her flight would only postpone the inevitable. And Erin's mother would berate her via phone until she boarded the following day's flight. Shouting and waving her arms wildly, she appeared enough of a security threat to entice three TSA employees to her side.

"They just paged me. E. Cerise." She thrust her passport at them. "They said my gate is closing in five minutes."

A squat, blonde TSA woman crossed her arms. "Were you delayed getting here?"

"Yes."

"Flight delayed?"

"I—I'm on my own here. I didn't know about the shuttle, and I had to eat dinner, and I'm traveling alone, and I'm freaking out. If I miss that flight, my mother will kill me."

A male agent took her passport. "Erin?"

"Yes."

He unfastened the stanchion and pulled Erin out of line. To the blonde woman, he said, "She's seventeen, Shannon. Cut her some slack."

Gate agents paged Erin again as she removed her shoes and tossed her computer into a gray bin. When her luggage emerged from the other end of the X-ray machine, Erin slung her carry-on over her shoulder, tucked her laptop under her arm, grabbed her shoes, and ran to her gate barefoot.

The door was closed.

Panting, she yelled, "I'm here!"

Two women in purple paisley dresses, black jackets, and snug hats assessed her.

Erin's dad, Mitchell, would wield his power, money, and witticism in this situation, but Erin could only plead. "Please help me."

"Ms. Cerise?" one agent said.

Wiping tears from her eyes, Erin tried to catch her breath. "Yes. It's me. I heard you call. I'm sorry I'm late."

The agent lifted the phone next to the door. "We're so pleased you're traveling with us today."

Traveling. Today.

In that cute kiwi accent, the phrase was magical.

More terrified than thrilled, Erin boarded the plane and departed her country alone.

FIVE

"I'll get your things from the boot. You go ahead in." Hamish unlocked the trunk with his key.

Pippa opened the garage door to reveal towers of boxes, boats and metal shelving suspended from the ceiling, and wall hooks supporting a hodgepodge of junk. Near the door, a single cleat hung from the wall.

Between the garage and the fence, cinder blocks supported a huge, dented RV in the grass.

The Wakefields were hoarders. Or slobs. Or Erin didn't know what.

Hamish hoisted Erin's bag from the trunk. "Got it."

Erin said, "It has wheels."

"Driveway'll kill 'em."

Felicity unlocked the front door. "Welcome home, Erin."

Sapphire carpet welcomed her entry. Everything slowed as Erin realized she wasn't in Kansas anymore. She was nowhere near Kansas.

"Erin?"

Ear-in.

"Erin? Welcome home? Shoes there, dear." Felicity

pointed to a neat row of shoes next to the front door *outside* the house.

Erin studied her shoes. "They're ECCOs."

Felicity cocked her head sideways. "No worries, the overhead keeps them safe from rain."

Felicity might be insulted if she admitted being more concerned about theft, so Erin kicked off her ECCOs and followed Felicity, hoping the house's exterior belied a spacious, beautifully decorated interior.

Nope.

Closed French doors stood to Erin's right. The entryway—which actually put Erin in the middle of the house—gave way to a dining room where a heavy mahogany table sat six. A cluttered peninsula separated the eating space from a modest kitchen. Over the peninsula hung a small oil painting of a naked child nuzzling her mother's neck.

Erin's house in Wheaton boasted a six-burner stove, immaculate double-sized island, breakfast table for eight, and formal dining room for entertaining. This New Zealand kitchen barely had space for two caterers.

Small.

Papers cluttered one counter; magnets and photos covered the fridge. A pail of what looked like rotting food sat next to the sink.

The air hinted at smoke, but not the way Erin's house had when her dad chose to work in front of a winter fire. Erin turned to discover a genuine woodstove in the corner of the Wakefields' dining room.

Incredulous, she said, "Do you cook on that?"

"Of course not!" Felicity smiled. "We use it to heat the house."

No HVAC. Squeezing her eyes shut, Erin drew a deep, calming breath.

"Soon we'll have so much sunlight, we won't have use for it." Felicity fanned her hand across two walls of windows, through which Erin spied a large backyard complete with a single tall swing, a sturdy wooden picnic table, a wooden playhouse that Pippa would outgrow any second, a giant trampoline enclosed in netting, and a paltry brown garden.

More brown fence encircled the backyard. Fenced backyards of four other houses shaped the property like a keyhole; the narrow driveway was her only access to the outside world.

Erin texted Lalitha.

Erin: I have made a huge mistake.

Hamish said, "Want to see where you'll be bunking?"

No, she did not, but following him distanced her from the awkward not-dining room and cramped living quarters. Hamish opened a door adjacent to the kitchen. "We keep this closed during winter."

Erin hardly had a second to wonder why before stepping into a frigid hallway. It was as if she'd stepped outside.

The short hallway dead-ended into a longer one, where Hamish pointed to the left. "Over there's a bedroom and toilet. Felicity's mum lived with us until she died, and we haven't emptied it yet."

Erin flinched at his candor.

"Laundry and garage are that way, too."

Garage rhymed with *carriage* in New Zealand.

He headed the other way and pointed as he went. "Toilet room. Shower room."

Erin peeked in to find the bathroom split into three tiny spaces: one for the tub, one for the sink, and one even smaller for only a toilet.

At the end of the hall, Hamish said, "Felicity and I are straight ahead on the right. You're with Pippa in here."

Hamish flipped the switch to reveal a cluttered room with two twin beds. "Everything you need here: hired cello in the corner, bed, wardrobe."

Erin surveyed the room in one fell swoop: juvenile posters over a twin bed, a single window, a second twin bed, a cello case, and two sliding closet doors.

No chest of drawers. No desk. No mirror. No space. Nothing.

I worked my ass off to get here?

Hamish stood at the threshold. "You all right, then?"

She couldn't speak. Her room back home had a walk-in closet, two upholstered chairs, and a cherry desk. And there was light for days, even in winter. How could she share this tiny, dark room? And a closet? Down the hall from a shared bathroom?

"Is there a reason I can't use Felicity's mother's suite? I don't want to crowd Pippa."

"She won't be crowded. She's over the moon you're here."

"It's just . . ." *Be diplomatic.* "I'm used to more personal space, and if no one is using that room . . ."

Hamish lowered his voice. "Felicity isn't ready. She and her mum were very close, and the loss hit her quite hard. The room is out of bounds."

Erin studied the rough blue carpet.

"You want to unpack?" Hamish asked.

Erin wanted to un-travel.

"I'll, uh, leave you alone for a bit," he said.

Christchurch wasn't as advertised. It wasn't a Garden City. Study abroad wasn't an answer to her Columbia problem or a respite or a cure.

Getting into Columbia wasn't worth five months in this cramped, freezing house surrounded by strip malls.

Erin rifled through her suitcase for her warmest wool sweater and seized the box of host-family gifts she'd packed, her return ticket to the warm half of the house.

SIX

The carpet was rough over hard concrete. Erin had never given a second thought to her plush bedroom carpet, but she now longed for it. Or the hardwood of the first floor. Anything but this.

In the warmer half of the house, the now-open French doors revealed a living room with two droopy sofas and more blue carpet. The whole family was inside.

"I have some . . . things for you?"

Hamish muted the television so Erin had their full attention. Felicity admired bath bombs and massage bars from LUSH, a Canadian company Claire had deemed "close enough" to America. Pippa declared the Chicago skyline *cool* and dug into the travel-worn bag of Garrett's popcorn. Hamish pulled on the Chicago Bears jersey over his polo.

"The rest of this is food that's specific to my state, Illinois: Vosges chocolates and Frangos minty chocolates, maple syrup from southern Illinois, though Canada's is better. Oh, and chocolate chips, because I read somewhere that people outside America don't really have chocolate chips. My mom wanted to send you her favorite wine, but I couldn't travel with it because I'm too young." Erin didn't mention that

Claire also had opined a construction worker and a secretary probably preferred beer.

"Thank you so much, Erin." Felicity's arms were full of stuff. "Did you find everything you needed in your room?"

"I did, thanks," she lied, staring into the empty box in her hands.

"Is that cello okay?"

"I'm sure it's fine." Erin's last hope for a reprieve in New Zealand was an inability to find a cello for rent, but Felicity magically had found one for the duration. Erin hoped it was within the Wakefields' budget.

"I cleared out a drawer for you in the bathroom," Felicity said. "At the top. Pippa's on the bottom. Shared items in the middle."

Pippa said, "One more day of winter hols. Are you keen to swim tomorrow? Mum says you're a brilliant swimmer."

Brilliance had nothing to do with it. "I'm on the swim team at home. Here, too, I hope?"

Felicity said, "They're keen to have you."

"Thank you."

"And Erin needs to do some school shopping tomorrow, Pippa."

Hamish said, "Cello in an orchestra and competitive swimming and studies, Erin? Sounds a little intense, even by American standards."

Intense was the perfect word for it. "It all fits together."

"But how?" Felicity asked.

"Orchestra is only Saturdays, year-round. In summer, I take two or three intensive courses and compete in a summer swimming league to keep in shape. During the school year, I swim before and after school."

"So Sundays are free."

"To study, yeah."

"And your parents? Are they just as busy?"

"Yeah. My dad was the youngest lawyer to ever make partner at his firm. My mom is the first ever female managing partner at hers."

Felicity was not appropriately impressed. "How do you ever find time together?"

"At night, except if Mom has a case that keeps her late. Saturday afternoons in winter. Summer Saturdays, they usually sail on their friends' boats. But, yeah, we're all busy. I think, maybe, life is a lot faster at home."

"That's one word for it." Hamish un-muted the television.

Felicity walked Erin toward the bedrooms. "Thought you might like to settle in this afternoon. Tomorrow, as I told Pippa, we'll buy your school things. Monday I'll get you to school and you can choose your classes."

Erin nodded.

"This all must be a little unsettling for you. How can we make this feel more like home?"

Erin bit her lip. "I'm fine. Just jet-lagged. I should lie down."

Felicity gave her a loose hug. "Tea at half six."

Tea wasn't really her thing, but she nodded to her host mother and retreated.

SEVEN

Alone in Pippa's room, Erin texted Lalitha again.

Erin: I tell you I've made a huge mistake and you say nothing?
Erin: I'm all alone in a frigid country. What are YOU doing?

Illinois was seventeen hours behind Christchurch, but Erin thought of it as seven hours ahead and a day behind. So it was 8 p.m. yesterday there. Friday. Lalitha should be out of swim practice.

Erin connected her phone and computer to Wi-Fi using the password Hamish had given her: @llBl@cks.

That's offensive, right? All blacks what?

She pulled on her gloves and zipped into her down jacket before lying on the narrow twin bed. Still freezing, she crawled under the covers—a thin down comforter and low thread count duvet—and rubbed her feet together to warm them.

This was the warmest time of day. She was so screwed.

No. She'd focus in the freezing cold and remain hyper-vigilant. Perhaps she could go home after the national swim meet. A national title would prove she deserved admission to

23

Columbia and her legacy status would seal the deal. Columbia would propel Erin into a great medical school, a great job, and a great life. Her future still was within her grasp.

Winning the national meet would be her unique factor.

Her focus was crystal clear.

Until the jet lag pulled her under.

BEFORE SHE FLEW TO LOS ANGELES

Erin grabbed her passport and—on second thought—her favorite striped sweater before rejoining her parents in the car. "Sorry about that!"

"All set?" Mitchell asked as he eyed his daughter in the rearview mirror. "I hope you get to explore while you're down under."

Claire stopped tapping on her phone. "No, Mitchell. Exploring is not unique. Sightseeing is not exceptional. Erin needs to appear exceptional."

Claire twisted in her seat and waited until Erin made eye contact. "Sweetie, if you start thinking you can't win at Nationals, you find whatever it is that's going to make you seem unique. I know you are exceptional, but we have to prove it to Columbia. The *unique factor* will make you an exceptional candidate. If it weren't for those Quigleys, you would look exceptional already, but now we'll take a different tack." She faced forward again. "Drive, Mitchell."

Erin pressed her fingers into her tiniest pocket to feel the indent of the treasure she'd put there. The panicked crescendo of the previous months reached full frenzy on the ride to the airport. Claire had looked up New Zealand's butterfly records, so Erin knew she would do well in swimming, but could she win? Would her team welcome her?

How difficult was the transition to driving on the left? Would she like her host family? Would they like her? Would her Wheaton friends miss her? Could she make new ones?

Would she find her unique factor and get into Columbia? What if she didn't?

At the airport, Erin unloaded several items from her suitcase and weighed it three times before it met weight requirements. Attempts to shove her toiletry kit into her carry-on were futile, so she tucked it under her arm and headed for security.

"Once you're inside security, buy some Garrett's cheese-and-caramel popcorn for the construction-worker father," Claire said.

Mitchell shook his daughter's hand before wrapping her in an awkwardly snug hug. "I'll miss you, kid."

There were no tears.

"I'll be home for Christmas, Dad."

———

For the length of the security line, Erin's parents walked next to her, Claire tapping on her phone and Mitchell offering last-minute travel advice: keep your eyes on your carry-on at all times, put your computer in a gray plastic bin, stay hydrated in flight, call upon arrival.

At the turn, where they could no longer hug over the stanchions, Mitchell said, "I guess this is good-bye."

And there were the tears.

"Keep it together, Mitchell," Claire said. She made a kiss sound to Erin. "Find your unique factor. We'll keep in touch."

"I promise this will work," Erin said.

Mitchell leaned into the line for one last hug. "Love you, kid."

"Love you both," Erin said.

Claire held Mitchell's elbow with her left hand and continued texting as they walked away. They disappeared and Erin counted to one hundred before pulling Grandma Tea's ring out of her pocket and slipping it onto her finger.

EIGHT

Felicity knocked quietly before opening Pippa's door.

"Erin? It's nearly seven."

Sea-vin. Even numbers were turned on their heads in a New Zealander's mouth.

Erin's eyelids were lead. *Tungsten. No, platinum. Or whatever was heavier than platinum. That new metal.* She couldn't remember the name. With jet lag as her drug, she could have slept for the entire five months.

Felicity flicked the lights on. "Erin? Time for tea. You'll be wrecked tomorrow if you don't start moving."

Erin was wrecked either way and tea wasn't her thing, but eating on a schedule was the quickest way to shake jet lag. She threw off her blankets, experienced two seconds of chill, and covered right back up again.

"Why is your house so cold?" Erin couldn't look at Felicity's face.

"The table is plenty warm. And the whole family is waiting for you."

Had Claire known about the frigid house, Erin wouldn't be here. Surely the family couldn't help being poor, but Erin could hardly endure a cold, tiny house on the ugly side of town.

Erin hoped this was the ugly side of town. What if all of Christchurch was one huge strip mall?

She raced to the bathroom where towels hung in disarray over a slick floor, as if the tidy house had been a mere illusion projected for her tour earlier. The toilet paper was a sad surprise: thin and rough like in public restrooms.

She splashed her face and gave a little pep talk to the girl in the mirror: *You can do this. And if you can't do this, you are one phone call away from securing a flight home.*

Still in her down jacket, Erin opened the door to the other side of the house. It smelled like a bakery. Her host family sat around the table, talking easily and all at once.

When he spotted her, Hamish uncovered the serving dishes. "Sweet as!"

Six little pot pies circled one dish, green salad filled a beautiful red bowl, and fresh sliced bread steamed on a cutting board. *Tea* in New Zealand meant dinner.

"Beer with your tea?" Hamish asked.

Erin glanced from Hamish to Felicity. "I'm seventeen."

Hamish's rough, calloused hands flourished his beer in Erin's direction. "You're also in New Zealand now. Can't buy alcohol, but you can drink it."

Felicity was drinking wine.

Alcohol had never been good to Erin, and she hadn't drunk anything since her last birthday party, which she was trying to forget. "No, thanks. Maybe another day."

Pippa, who was ten, had missed gymnastics to fetch Erin from the airport, but had spent the afternoon riding bikes with friends. Pippa was in year six—not sixth grade, mind you—at Ilam Primary and she was having Kapa Haka and wanted to know if Erin wanted to come.

Felicity jumped in. "She's been here eight hours, Pippa."

Pippa blushed.

Erin peeled off her socks under the table. The room had become downright toasty while she napped. "I think I need to recover from travel before I make any plans. Maybe we can talk scheduling tomorrow?"

Pippa's smile was unconvincing.

Erin raised her eyebrows. "It smells like heaven in here."

"A day of cooking will do that to a house. I made a chicken stock and chopped the chicken for enchiladas tomorrow night, cooked a lamb, and made lamb pies for tonight. Are you vegetarian?"

Erin was not in any way a vegetarian, and lamb was a meat she knew. "You made these?"

Felicity nodded, her mouth full of food.

Erin hadn't imagined people made pot pies from scratch. Her parents sometimes bought frozen pot pies. Valentina cooked for her family when she cleaned twice a week, and Erin's grampa used to cook delicious and creative dinners, but neither of them had made anything as tricky as this.

Felicity's lamb pie was cupcake-shaped and almost the exact size of Erin's mostly empty stomach. Erin dug in with her fork, but the oozy center she expected never materialized. It hung together really nicely. And it was delicious.

"So, Erin? What kind of weird stuff do Americans eat?"

Felicity almost spat out her bite. "Pippa!"

"Mum, I waited all day!"

Felicity grinned. "It's true, actually. Pippa has been on pins and needles waiting for you to wake up. She has some questions for you."

Pippa held up a notebook. "Sixty-one questions. The weird food stuff was number fourteen."

Four-deen. The accent was particularly cute out of Pippa's mouth.

"Let's start at number one: do you own a gun?"

Erin squinted. "Of course not."

"I heard America has more guns than people."

Erin bit her cheek. "Well, I heard New Zealand has more sheep than people."

"'at's true," Hamish said.

"Question two," Pippa said. "When is your birthday?"

"May nineteenth."

Pippa squealed, "Mine is November nineteenth!"

Confused about Pippa's enthusiasm, Erin feigned her own. "That's . . . exciting?"

"We're like half twins: our birthdays are exact opposites. May/November. June/December."

"Oh. Right." Erin imagined it was a kiwi sentiment.

"Okay. Next question: Your accent is neither Southern nor Boston nor New Jersey. I know all of those. So what's yours?"

Ten minutes later, sated, warm, and bemused by Pippa's intense questioning, Erin felt slightly less regret about her plight.

Felicity said, "I'm afraid we don't have a pudding prepared. I meant to bake a pavlova for your first night, but time got away from me. Another day, perhaps."

Pippa said, "Can we have Hokey Pokey?"

"I suppose," Felicity said.

Pippa leapt to the freezer and returned with a container of Hokey Pokey ice cream. Felicity scooped some into a bowl and offered it to Erin. "Hokey Pokey?"

Hokey Pokey looked like vanilla ice cream laced with suspicious candy.

"Sure. I actually prefer ice cream to pudding anyway."

Felicity scooped ice cream for Pippa. "*Pudding* just means whatever sweet thing you eat after tea. Ice cream is pudding. Pavlova is pudding. Your pudding might be biscuits."

"We call that *dessert*," Erin said before taking a timid bite. The Hokey Pokey bits hung in suspension of thick, rich ice cream. For ice cream, it was totally decadent.

Maybe the Hokey Pokey is what it's all about. Erin's brain leapt from the ice cream, to the bumper sticker on her ex-boyfriend's car, to Ben, and her brief happiness deflated.

Disappointment and agony wrapped around her stomach and she couldn't eat another spoonful.

After inhaling her ice cream, Pippa scampered outside to play in the dark. Hamish loaded the dishwasher while Felicity cleared the table.

"Erin? I'd love to hear your cello," Felicity said. "I've never heard one in person."

Hamish laughed. "She's lying. The very day it arrived, she pulled it out of the case and dragged the stick across it. Pure hell on the ears."

"You can't blame me for having a go! I'm sure it sounds much better with you in the musician's seat, Erin. You can practice out here. In winter, we usually don't go to the bedrooms until we're ready to sleep."

Though the house felt like it was no larger than her smartphone, Erin wanted to find her own corner and have some time to herself. Her journey had broken that 2,243-day streak of cello practice, so what was another day off?

She treaded lightly. "Actually, it probably needs to warm up. Cellos don't do well in the cold. Maybe tomorrow?"

"Or maybe as a birthday prezzie," Hamish said. "Felicity's turning thirty-seven Saturday next."

"That might work," Erin excused herself to Pippa's bedroom, where she crawled under the covers in search of heat. Rubbing her feet together like a mad grasshopper, she tried to create enough friction to spark some semblance of warmth.

NINE

Erin pulled her computer onto her lap. Her mother had sent several frenetic emails: Had Erin finished a new draft of the essay? Had she landed? Was the family okay? How did the presents go over?

Had she landed? If her plane hadn't landed, the entire world would know. Erin closed her email and snuggled further down in her covers. A moment later, Felicity knocked on her door.

"Your mum's on the phone, love."

On instinct, Erin covered her grandmother's ring with her right hand before accepting the phone from Felicity. "Hi, Mom."

"You're alive!" Claire sounded happier than Erin had expected, which meant she hadn't yet discovered Erin had stolen the ring.

"I'm fine, Mom."

"How is the cello? I hope it's okay."

"I'm looking at it." Erin glanced at the case. "It's fine."

"How does it sound? Is it suitable for a player of your caliber?"

"It's great, Mom," Erin lied. Anything could be inside that cello case. She wasn't in the mood to play it.

"I sent several emails. They do have Wi-Fi, right?"

Felicity waved to indicate she was going back to the living room.

Erin gave a wan smile. "Yes, Mom."

"Good. You know, I'm glad you chose New Zealand. It's a lot like home, so it's study abroad without the hard parts—no language barriers, no culture shock, no weird cuisine. This is going to be great for you."

"Right."

"I haven't seen your essay come through. Did you work on it in flight?"

"Yeah."

"Yeah?"

"Yes, Mom."

"And did you—"

Claire's voice disappeared and Mitchell boomed. "Hi, darling."

"Hi, Dad."

"We've been waiting all day to hear from you."

"I'm jet-lagged, I just woke up."

"Of course you are. We just wanted to be sure you were settled. Did you forget anything?"

"I don't know yet."

"I thought you might want a little care package in a couple of weeks. Some Vosges or those little Mensa Mind Puzzles you take on vacations. Or those pens you couldn't get enough of last summer. Just let me know what you need—anything at all—and I'll send it."

"Okay."

"So, how is it? Is New Zealand as gorgeous as everyone

says? Two of my partners say they'll pay you to go on the Lord of the Rings tour and take photos. Is the landscape as sublime as the movies?"

No. Just no.

"Dad, I literally came back to their house and crashed and then Mom called five seconds after we ate dinner."

"How is the family?"

"Fine."

"How is the house?"

She didn't want to get into it. "It's fine, Dad. Everything is fine. I'm just tired. It was a long trip."

"I'll bet. Hey, I've been tracking the big box, and it should be there right on time. New Zealand Friday, not American Friday."

Claire commandeered the line. "I'm emailing you a list of ideas for significant winter volunteer opportunities to pad your résumé."

"Mom, college applications will be over and done with by then."

"But you need to get a jump on actual college. Volunteering in your senior year can only help your med school application. You'll be ahead of the game. This is all going to work out. Don't you think it's all going to work out? Volunteering this winter plus a BS with honors in biochem will look really good to med schools."

"Right." Erin had expected a break between college applications and actual college. "Mom, I'm pretty tired. Can you just email me?"

"We can communicate via email you if you will actually respond."

"After I sleep."

Claire sighed. "Okay. Get some sleep, but be sure your phone is on."

"Okay, Mom."

"Is the phone having trouble with international?"

"No. Just forgot. I'm so tired."

"Call me tomorrow when you're over the jet lag."

"I'll try, Mom."

"No, Erin. Do it."

"Okay."

"And focus on your unique factor."

"Yes, Mom."

"Good night."

"Night."

Erin peeled back her covers and returned the phone to Felicity in the living room.

"Everything okay, Erin?"

Erin nodded, because speaking might make her cry. Everything was decidedly not okay.

"Did you want to move the cello out? Pippa will head to bed here in a minute."

"Sure." Erin hauled the cello case to the living room and propped it in a corner.

Felicity said, "Bring whatever you'd like out here so Pippa's not disturbed."

Erin felt disturbed. "I'm pretty exhausted. I think I'll go to bed, too."

Without brushing her teeth or unruly hair, Erin climbed into bed and under the covers again. That nap earlier hadn't put a dent in her jet lag.

In their shared bedroom, Pippa bounced around for several minutes before Felicity calmed her enough to tuck her in. Erin listened while Felicity snuggled close and read a book to her daughter.

Erin faced the wall and rolled her eyes. She'd learned to read at four, so no one had needed to read to her at bedtime—or ever—for well over a decade.

Felicity whispered, "What will you dream about tonight?"

Erin felt like an eavesdropper, though she clearly had nowhere else to go. She imagined her own nightmares would continue here; she still woke in tears some mornings, but perhaps being eight thousand miles away would help.

Pippa's dreams were better. She squealed, "Lamb pies and spring holidays and sisters!"

Erin twisted to wish Pippa good night.

Felicity smiled at Erin before turning out the light and singing about a Wonky Donkey. He had three legs, one eye, and he liked listening to country music, and he was quite tall and slim, and he smelled really, really bad. He was a stinky-dinky, lanky, honky-tonky, winky wonky donkey.

Erin conjured an image of him and fell right to sleep.

TEN

Midnight in Christchurch was 7 a.m. in Wheaton, so naturally Erin was wide awake.

Restless, she checked her phone every ten minutes until a burst of air resonated from Pippa's bed. Erin's eyes shifted left and right in the black room as she pondered what was next.

She flinched when the stench of gas reached her. How could a sweet, small girl make such a massive, foul fart?

Erin surfed Reddit on her phone. She caught up with Good-Time Girl, a seventeen-year-old Christchurch chick who never showed her face but constantly posted about parties, fashion, and sporting events. She tried counting laps in her head, which usually triggered sleep.

But her brain was no match for jet lag.

After Pippa's third gassy spell, Erin stealthily climbed out of bed and crept into the hall.

She opened the door to the warm side of the house to find it no longer warm. Shivering on the living room sofa, Erin felt bone-cold, as though she never would be warm again.

Wheaton winters were far colder than Christchurch's and often buried under feet of snow, but her house—the whole thing—was always comfortable.

Erin knew nothing about building fires, so she returned to her suitcase for merino socks, a second sweater under her jacket, and gloves. Suspecting she couldn't get any colder, Erin slid open the back door and wandered out into the night.

The Wakefields' picnic table beckoned her. Lying on it, she dared to look up at the sky.

Blessedly overcast. Just as well. Spying the moon would reopen her Ben wound again.

When they started dating—when Erin tried desperately to bond them together in meaningful ways—she enthused about her astrophysics course at Harvard. Ben was interested until she tried filling his brain with the most fascinating stuff: how amazingly fast Jupiter rotates or that orange dwarfs can stay stable for thirty billion years. Thirty billion years was enough time for life to spark and evolve and a whole host of things to happen in a different solar system. Erin hyped herself into a frenzy of possibilities, but when nothing sparked Ben's interest, she backpedaled to popular astronomy like constellations and moon phases.

Erin loved the moon. Ben often said she had given him the moon, and after he'd dumped her unceremoniously, the moon no longer felt a part of her. She hated him for taking the moon from her. Even more, she hated herself for giving it away. Before Ben, it had been hers and hers alone.

That wasn't true, of course.

Before intensive study consumed Erin's summers, July and August had belonged to her grandparents on Michigan's Upper Peninsula, the U.P., where Erin immersed herself in Lake Michigan and old music. Her grampa taught her new ways to play guitar chords. They played board games and hiked late into the night, always with a promise never to tell Mitchell and Claire they'd slept until noon.

Constellations and the moon had interested her then, because her grampa was the best storyteller she'd ever known. Together, Erin and her grandfather had studied planets and read about other galaxies.

Ben had stolen all of that from her.

Why was I even with him?

She could pretend to forget, but with her eyes closed, she imagined his warm breath behind her ear as his lips tugged lightly on her earlobe. Her heart still leapt at the thought of rolling around during marathon make-out sessions on his parents' alabaster rug. Or in her bedroom when she snuck him in. Or in her Fiat when they were desperate.

He'd said she was amazing and that he loved her.

Erin was pretty new to love, but she believed love should outlast a little embarrassment. If Ben had really loved her, he would have stood up for her amid rumors.

He should have.

Erin wasn't getting Ben back. She didn't want him back, except when she did. She missed their private jokes and sharing stories, and how much he loved her body. She had loved so much about him, until he'd broken her heart. Then she'd hated him. And still loved him.

Regardless, she would never get him back.

She caressed Grandma Tea's ring through her glove. Claire hadn't mentioned the ring.

Just as well. Claire wasn't getting that back, either.

BEFORE SHE GRABBED HER PASSPORT

Erin buckled into the backseat of her dad's silver Mercedes. Mitchell grabbed the passenger seat so he could reverse out of the driveway.

Claire said, "I need you to drop me at the office after the airport. The McKinsey deal is going down today and I have to prove a worthy managing partner. A smooth deal will prove I was the right pick."

"No doubt," Mitchell said.

Erin took a deep breath and steeled herself. When they reached the end of the driveway, she gasped. "Oh! I forgot my passport! I'll just be a sec, promise."

She unbuckled, ran back into the house, and sprinted upstairs to her parents' room. Like a cat burglar, she tiptoed into her mother's walk-in closet. Digging into the ornate wooden jewelry chest, Erin slid aside necklaces and a diamond tennis bracelet to find a small satin ring box. She opened it and memories of Grandma Tea flooded her mind.

A wide, flat, silver ring with channel-set diamonds and sapphires scattered light on the ceiling. It was too large for her ring fingers but fit her left middle finger perfectly. Erin had loved the ring and its history for years; her grandparents' great love story made the ring precious. It was personal. It was unique. It was hers.

She stared at Grandma Tea's ring for another moment before stowing it in the tiniest pocket of her jeans. Satisfied, she snapped the ring box shut, replaced her mother's jewelry, and headed toward her room to grab her "forgotten" passport.

ELEVEN

Erin: I am lying on a picnic table on the other side of the world.
Litha: What time is it?
Erin: Three in the morning.
Litha: Yay for one day down!
Erin: I guess.
Litha: How's New Zealand?
Erin: Don't know. I've been in the airport and at this house.
Litha: Cool house?
Erin: I don't want to talk about it.
Litha: ☺ Practice last night was cuh-ray-zee. Be glad you missed it.
Erin: Glad. Check.
Litha: I saw Ben at the pool last night.

Erin's stomach lurched. Imagining Current Ben was more painful than remembering Historical Ben. She couldn't ask about him. She didn't want to know. She didn't want Lalitha to know she desperately wanted to know everything.

Litha: He asked how you were, and I told him he was not
privileged enough to know.

Erin: Thanks.

Litha: Said he deserved to know since he still had feelings for
you, and I told him to fuck right off.

Ben still had feelings for her, but which ones? The lovey, half-naked feelings of the eleven months they'd dated? Or the vile hatred of the last two months? It was a vital distinction.

Erin: What did he say to that?

Erin: What kind of feelings do you think he has?

Litha: Who cares about his feelings?

Erin: I just wonder whether he's missing me.

Litha: Of course he's missing you.

Litha: And now he has to start a relationship from scratch.

Erin's breath caught in her throat. Ben was starting over.

Erin: With whom? With whom?!?!?!

Litha: Claudia Quigley told me he called her Monday night.

Litha: She had a million questions about him.

Erin: What did you tell her?

Litha: The truth.

Erin: Which truth?

Litha: That you're awesome and Ben sucks. She asked if she
could call you.

Erin: HELL NO

Litha: That's what I said.

Erin: I mean, yeah, she can call if she wants, but why would
she want to talk to me?

Litha: He told her he was interested in her brain.

Erin: Are you shitting me?
Litha: Nope.
Erin: Worked on one swimmer, guess it'll work on them all!
Litha: She thought it was weird.
Erin: It was weird, except he's so charming that it works.
Erin: I cannot believe I fell for that.
Litha: You were enamored.
Erin: You misspelled horny.
Litha: HAHAHAHA
Erin: You tell her that Ben is all talk.
Erin: He will LOVE her and FOREVER her and SOLID her, but he's all about Ben.
Erin: Tell her if one thing goes wrong, he will bolt.
Litha: Will do.
Litha: Hey, I'm headed to North Beach. Catch you later?
Erin: Yeah. Miss you. ❤

Lalitha disappeared, leaving Erin alone again with the clouds. Thousands of miles away, America was awake. But here, Christchurch was sleeping. Or most of Christchurch was sleeping. An hour ago, Good-Time Girl posted snaps of a party on a beach. In winter.

Erin had been stalking Good-Time Girl for weeks; she now thought of her as the closest thing she had to a friend in New Zealand.

Erin could create a parody account, Sad Lonely Girl, for snaps of the cloudy night sky.

She couldn't help thinking there was no room for her on this huge planet, spinning rapidly as it circled the sun.

In this vast world, she had only one friend. But then, Lalitha was always exactly the friend she needed, so she couldn't complain.

BEFORE SHE RECLAIMED HER RING
BEFORE SHE RECLAIMED HER RING

Lalitha swooped into Erin's bedroom wearing the white Steven Rosengard dress Erin had coveted from the June issue of *Marie Claire*. Lalitha's dress was only half-white, though; the back was a million shades of green, the letter L stamped in a hundred different fonts.

Erin couldn't keep her mouth shut. "That dress!"

"You like?" The dress flared as she twirled.

Erin nodded, but no. You do not take a seven-hundred-dollar designer dress and stamp it to make it your own. It was like a high-end bumper sticker, and Erin didn't do those either.

Lalitha's face fell. "Have you been drinking?"

Erin didn't move. "Uh. Maybe never again. Lalitha, I can't do this."

"Then don't go."

"I don't want to go, but I have to go. And I meant the packing."

"Yeah, I thought you'd be done by now. I brought you a parting gift." She handed Erin a cardboard poster tube.

"Oh, Li. I found one." Erin pointed to her suitcase, where a tube protected a poster of Sol Gabetta and her cello, a group photo from last summer at Harvard, and a Chicago skyline.

"Open it."

Eagerly, Erin unfurled a poster from *Catch Me if You Can*. She grinned at Lalitha, who had taken her to see the musical in New York. They both had their posters signed backstage, but Erin's mother had recycled hers. Claire had final say on all art in the house and had chosen for Erin's room framed impressionist oils, family portraits, and a pencil drawing of Yo-Yo Ma. Yo-Yo Ma's audio was amazing, but his photograph did not inspire.

But, for five glorious months in Christchurch, *Catch Me if You Can* would be Erin's again.

"You're the best," Erin said.

"Tell me that after we pare down your luggage. Preparing for life abroad is a life skill."

"It is a skill I do not possess."

"Yeah, but I do." Lalitha upended the FedEx box and dumped the contents of Erin's suitcase. "Eleven summers in Bhiwandi. Three Indian wedding trips. I have a system. You don't even need FedEx."

Erin pulled herself to sitting. "New Zealand has winter, Li. Right now. I'm doing winter in the suitcase and summer in the box."

"You are so not a traveler."

"I've traveled plenty."

"You vacation," Lalitha said. "You don't travel. Try spending months at a time in India. Be practical: take five pairs of pants that go with everything and ten interchangeable tops. You can layer for winter or dress up as needed. Choose lightweight stuff so you don't go over weight."

"I have really pared down." Erin pointed to a pile of clothes on the floor. "Winter is the problem."

Lalitha tapped on her phone. "First off, Christchurch winter isn't Chicago winter. See this? Coldest temperature ever: 43 degrees Fahrenheit. You need three sweaters, max. And you want all your stuff to go together. You'll always look put together, but you can mix up your outfits so no one thinks you're wearing the same five pairs of pants all the time."

Lalitha clutched Erin's spare toiletries. "Holy crap, Erin. You know actual people live in Christchurch, right? They use lotion and nail polish and shampoo. They have stores."

"But they don't have CND Palm Deco. I checked."

"Take the nail polish then. Skip everything else."

"Li, just let me have this one thing."

Lalitha rummaged in the bag. "It is literally twenty-three things."

Erin was near tears.

"It's your trip," Lalitha said, pulling a box from the bottom of the suitcase. "What's this?"

"Host family presents: books, Frangos, a framed Chicago Skyline."

"Claire's picks?"

"Yeah."

"Tell her to choose lighter stuff next time: clothing, coasters, ornaments. Garrett's popcorn looks like a substantial present, but weighs next to nothing."

"That's on the list, too. I'm buying it at O'Hare."

Lalitha rolled up a gray cashmere sweater and nuzzled it next to the host box. "Saves loads of space. Roll everything." She held up a multicolored striped sweater from the Gap. "But not this one."

"It's my favorite."

"It stands out, so you can only wear it every two weeks or more. It's wasted space."

Erin rolled her remaining sweaters as Lalitha tucked coiled socks into her shoes.

———

Two hours later, they sealed the FedEx box. Lalitha studied the room once more. "Where's George?"

George was Erin's cello. "My host family rented a cello so I can play in the school orchestra." Cello was the only thing going right in her life. She hoped her record as fifth chair with the Chicago Youth Symphony Orchestra would encourage admissions boards to overlook five months in a tiny school orchestra.

"It kind of sounds like life down there will be a lot like life up here."

"Yeah." Wanting to believe it, Erin changed into travel clothes.

Lalitha stacked the last of the rejected items in the closet and teared up. "So, we're done. And you're really going to New Zealand. All alone. For half a year."

"It's only five months."

They called it five months, but returning the instant school ended in New Zealand would keep her away five months, two weeks, and two days. A lifetime.

Erin said, "Send me texts. Tell me everything."

"I promise." Lalitha wrapped her arms around Erin, swaying dramatically as if her friend were never coming back.

Erin surreptitiously dropped her passport on her nightstand and wheeled her suitcase into the hall.

TWELVE

Sunday, her first full day in Christchurch, Erin leapt out of bed, pulled on her jacket and gloves, had the world's fastest pee, and jumped into the shower.

Afterward, she couldn't make her hair dryer work. Even though she'd plugged it into both the converter and transformer, it was dead. Heat from her shower disappeared through the bathroom's enormous frosted window as Erin leaned against the towel rack, which stung her bare back.

Heated towel racks. Enveloped in her towel, Erin leaned against the warm metal to soak in its heat. *Heavenly.*

While Pippa showered, Erin pulled on her warmest pants and layered several shirts on top. Cashmere looked bulky over multiple layers, and wool was almost too hot. Almost. She settled on a solid parakeet-green V-neck sweater, with one base layer peeking beneath it. She hoped yanking the base layer around the top of her pants would keep her midsection warm without making her look frumpy.

Pippa had allotted exactly half the closet space for Erin. On one side, shelves were built in like cubby holes, and Erin filled the top three. She hung as many items as she could on her half of the closet bar but still had half a suitcase of clothes needing space. She jammed her open suitcase into the floor of the closet; clean underwear and socks could live there, out of sight.

Erin tacked Lalitha's *Catch Me if You Can* poster near the head of her bed, then photos of her former swim team, her astrophysics study group, Chicago's skyline, and herself at the beach with Lalitha. She unfurled her poster of Sol Gabetta, which she loved more for Gabetta's gorgeous dress than her cello aptitude, and tacked it near the closet.

Fresh from the shower, Pippa said, "You're decorating?"

Sheepishly, Erin flashed two thumbs up. "I hope they're okay?"

"Sweet as!" Pip mimicked Erin's thumbs up and pulled a paper from under her bed—the ERIN sign from the airport. "This too?"

Pippa's eyes were so hopeful, Erin couldn't refuse her, though hand-drawn signs weren't at all to her taste. She hung it above her study group.

"Are those your best friends?" Pippa asked.

"Friends, yes. I spent three weeks at Harvard last summer. These guys were in my study group. They're from New York, India, Canada, and Japan."

"What were you studying?"

"Astrophysics, like science about planets and space and black holes."

"What's a black hole?"

I'm living in it.

"It's a place in space so dense, and with such a strong gravitational pull, that nothing can get out of it, not even light particles."

"If light can't escape, how do you know it's there?"

"Great question. Scientists use special tools."

"Cool."

Erin smiled and scanned her inbox on her phone. "It *is* cool. I need to run. Your mom is taking me school shopping."

"I want to hear all about it later," Pippa said.

Claire had emailed to inform Erin that a professional college admissions essay editor was reviewing her fourth draft. She also suggested Erin crusade to save the kiwi or yellow-eyed penguin to show she was immersed in New Zealand culture.

Erin dashed off an email: "Thanks, Mom! Off to buy school supplies."

After a quick breakfast, Felicity and Erin set off in the Nissan, like a mother taking a young child back-to-school shopping. *So much for independence abroad.*

Back out in the city, Erin focused on her surroundings.

"Is this the way I'll drive to school in the morning?"

"You'll probably take the 81," Felicity said.

So there were real highways in Christchurch. "Is the entrance around here?"

"I'll point to one when I see it."

They stopped at an enormous two-lane traffic circle. It was complete chaos: two speedy lanes of traffic circled clockwise and exited just as quickly. A truck carrying panes of glass zoomed past. Three buses in a row ringed the circle. Erin gripped her door handle; she couldn't fathom getting through this spinning circle of death without, well, death. There were no accidents, but drivers waited at every exit—entrance?—of the circle. No signals governed traffic flow.

When Felicity accelerated, Erin squeezed her eyes shut and ducked her head like a turtle hoping to protect itself.

A minute later, Felicity asked, "You all right?"

Erin had missed the circle completely. "That was terrifying."

"What? The roundabout?"

"Yes, the roundabout. How do you even get into the inside lane? And why is it there? How do you get out?"

Felicity smiled. "Some exits have two lanes. If you know where you need to exit, the inner lane makes sense. The inner lane is sort of express if you need the fourth or fifth road. You'll get used to it."

Dubious, Erin focused on the scenery. Houses with painted wooden fences lined the street, and several sets of traffic lights hung ahead. Tall trees filled the nature strip on both sides of the road. Finally, something felt a bit like home.

Felicity turned on the radio and music burst into the car. Christchurch was playing the song of summer from four years ago, when Erin had learned every summer *had* a song of summer.

"This is Riccarton Road in Riccarton," Felicity said.

"So Christchurch is behind us?"

"Ahead of us, actually. Riccarton is an inner suburb. We're heading to Mainland first. I'd like to set you up for school, but we can't very well buy stationery without know-ing your courses."

"I'd rather not take calligraphy if I can help it."

Felicity squinted at the road. "Is calligraphy a course in the States?"

"Oh no. I wanted to say I don't need stationery."

Felicity said, "Stationery here is pencils and pens and notebooks and things."

"Oh. Everything is different here."

Felicity laughed. "Isn't that the point?"

"Sort of." Erin couldn't reveal to Felicity she was min-ing this experience for college-application gold. "It's both very similar and very different. I mean, we're speaking the same language, but everything feels a little off. Driving on the wrong side of the street."

"Wrong to you."

"Yeah. Opposite, I guess. Different. And your music! This isn't even on our radio anymore."

Felicity turned it up a bit. "I love this."

"It's catchy, but it's four years old."

"It's not four years old here. And I'll still listen to it in another four years. Why throw out a good thing?"

"Because everyone's listening to new stuff now." Erin pointed to a road sign. "And all your signs have another language below the English. What's that about?"

"That's Māori. We have three official languages: English, New Zealand Sign Language, and Māori. The Māori are our native people who lived here hundreds of years before Europeans arrived."

"Like Native Americans?"

Felicity furrowed her brow. "Yes. Native New Zealand people. Europeans arrived and renamed the country New Zealand. Māori people still call it Aotearoa, which means 'long white cloud.' You'll hear a lot of Māori: *kura* means 'school,' *mahi* means 'work,' *kai* means 'food.' I've always thought the language is quite beautiful."

Felicity pulled into a gravel parking lot.

"Let's get you some new things, shall we?"

Erin followed Felicity into a small, quiet shop. Her mouth hung open as she studied racks of plaid wools and bulky V-neck sweaters.

Felicity said, "Hi there. We need uniform for Ilam High. Erin here is on study abroad from the States."

THIRTEEN

She had no words. Well, one word: *uniform*.

"Happy to help. I'm Charlize." The sunny woman sized up Erin. "What are you, about an eight in the States?"

"Six," Erin said.

Charlize hummed as she slowly pulled pieces from shelves all over the store before leading Erin to the dressing area.

"Sizing here is a bit different than in the States," Charlize said. "I've brought you rough equivalents of the things you'll need. Have a go and let us know what works."

Erin nodded.

"You all right, love?"

Another nod.

"You sure?"

"I'm great, thanks."

Just outside the dressing room, Felicity chatted with Charlize, though they clearly didn't know each other. For several minutes, Erin negotiated her way through the pile of clothes. An itchy wool kilt in navy, dark green, and royal blue hung below her knees. She buttoned a starched white blouse before pulling on a navy V-neck sweater vest with royal stripes around the arms and neck.

Through tears, she studied her frumpy reflection.

"Let's see, then," Charlize said.

Erin wiped her eyes and threw the curtain aside.

Charlize clasped her hands together like a fairy godmother. "A perfect fit. Now, can you tie a proper tie, love?"

"I'll do it." Felicity wrapped a tie around Erin's neck, looped the ends around each other, and tied it gently.

Charlize slipped a royal blue blazer over Erin's shoulders and instructed her to button the middle button.

"You must be kidding me," Erin said. "This is a joke, right?"

Charlize smiled. "Of course you'll have a few options in summer, but this is the winter uniform, love."

Erin wanted Charlize to stop *love*-ing her. "Is Ilam a Catholic school? I'm not Catholic." She looked from Charlize to Felicity.

Felicity touched Erin's upper arm. "It's a state school. And all state schools in New Zealand require distinct uniform. I guess you don't see as many movies of us as we see of you. Everyone knows Americans don't generally wear uniform."

"All mufti all the time," Charlize said.

Erin closed the curtain to her dressing room and eyed her reflection again. An embroidered navy-and-white crest on her blazer read ILAM HIGH.

If anyone back home saw her like this, she would die.

I can't do this.

Tears welled in her eyes. If she pulled the exit cord, no Columbia. Staying was the only viable option. Perhaps surviving without ripping her uniform to shreds would be her unique factor. Erin steeled herself. Five months. She could do anything for five months.

She dressed quickly and emerged from the dressing room to find Felicity had already paid.

"I could have bought my own clothes," Erin said.

"Nonsense. Pippa will need Ilam uniform eventually. I'm merely buying early. Off to the grocery, then home?"

They passed a lovely fountain that was inexplicably home to a half-dozen grocery carts.

"Your school's just over the road, there." Felicity pointed in a general direction, but Erin spied only trees. Felicity pulled into a parking garage. "And this is Riccarton Mall."

Erin could endure no more surprises. "What's next? Hair bands and school-sanctioned earrings?"

Felicity forced a smile. "No jewelry at school."

Erin spun her grandmother's ring around her finger.

"Erin?"

"This school. It sounds a little like prison."

"I found life easier when I didn't have to decide what to wear every day."

Erin was ambivalent. "I really, really love clothes." *Clothes I've chosen myself.*

BEFORE SHE LEARNED TO PACK

BEFORE SHE LEARNED TO PACK

Beneath her middle school track shorts and what was supposed to be her senior class T-shirt, Erin wore her ugliest underwear. All other clothes were candidates for her suitcase. She carried with her all the emotional baggage of her birthday and breakup with Ben, but her actual baggage—everything she would need for five months abroad—would not fit in her allowed luggage.

Foreign Study Network's list of essentials included a camera and film, so that list couldn't be trusted. A thousand websites' suggestions for study abroad included hats and "cultural toiletries," whatever they might be. No one suggested true necessities: gummy bears, Sephora, and fluffy towels in case her host family owned short, thin towels like at the gym.

From the center of her enormous bedroom, Erin eyed stacks of clothes, toiletries, and sundries. Pastel sticky notes indicating the weight of each stack fluttered as the AC kicked in.

"Dad saves the day!" Mitchell dropped a huge box on Erin's carpet. "FedEx says it'll get there in a week. Sixty pounds, max. Problem solved, and you know what I say?"

Erin wasn't sure which Dad quip was relevant in this situation.

"If you can fix it for under a thousand dollars, it's not a problem."

Erin appreciated both his optimism and his wallet.

Mitchell hugged his daughter before regarding her with pity and longing—he had been almost unbearably sappy for weeks—and left her to pack.

Erin lay on her floor staring at the ceiling, willing herself back to a time when everything was okay. She couldn't even remember when that was. To stimulate her resolve, Erin checked her phone. Her new favorite follow, Good-Time Girl, was a seventeen-year-old Christchurch girl who never showed her face but constantly posted about parties, fashion, and sporting events.

Good-Time Girl's most recent snaps were of skiing over winter break. Images of a gorgeous lake at the foot of a mountain appealed to Erin. Good-Time Girl couldn't fill the void of all the former friends Erin had unfollowed after her fall from grace, but she was a start.

Good-Time Girl seemed . . . normal. Maybe Erin could find normalcy half a world away.

FOURTEEN

Still without warm pajamas, Erin followed Felicity through the garage into the house, where she dropped her bags in Pippa's room and scrolled through her photos.

After seeing several odd fashion choices, Erin had snapped a photo of a woman in black stretch pants that stopped mid-shin, a cropped Lycra top, and a lacy bright blue shirt that was practically a poncho. She texted it to Lalitha.

Litha: What the actual fuck?

Erin loved Lalitha in this moment more than ever.

Erin: I just got back from the mall.
Erin: She was one of MANY.
Erin: I saw eleven barefoot people.
Erin: A mannequin in an unironic three-piece suit.
Erin: in CAMOUFLAGE.
Erin: practically transparent T-shirts and many hideous prints.
Erin: A lot of pleather, and even more lace.
Erin: Remember Desperately Seeking Susan?
Litha: Never forget Susan.

Erin: It's just exactly like that.

Litha: Come HOME!

Erin: I DID accidentally spend over $700 on a sweet pair of white leather pants.

Litha: Who are you, and what have you done with Erin?

Erin: No, they're cool. I swear.

Erin: Also, teen kiwis wear one-piece costumes as pajamas. Like, with whole animal heads as hoods. All sorts of animals.

Litha: Did you choose a piggy?

Erin: No, I spotted them after the pants, and decided $700 was about as much as Mitchell's Visa could take.

Erin: Also, kiwis get very excited about wool/possum blends.

Erin: I swear I am not making this up.

Erin: What are you up to tonight?

Litha: My cutest-ever blue shirtdress.

Litha: Drinks at Claudia's house.

Erin: Claudia . . .

Litha: Quigley, yes. She's cool.

Litha: And her mom feels super guilty about the divorce.

Erin: So?

Litha: So, she's buying the beer.

Erin: Sweet

Litha: And I have a new love.

Erin: SPILL

Litha: Teddy Kozel

Erin: That's old news.

Litha: The new news is he might be interested in ME.

Erin: If he's not, he's a fool.

Felicity knocked. "Afternoon tea, Erin?"

"Isn't it early for dinner?"

"Yes. This tea is a wee snick."
Erin considered that for a moment. "Snack?"
"Yes."
"Absolutely. Give me one minute."

Erin: Li, I need to know all about that date.
Erin: Right now, I need to eat so I can get on Christchurch time.
Erin: (My host mother called it a "wee snack." How cute is that?)
Litha: Super cute. Don't buy any lace.
Erin: Okay. Don't do anything I wouldn't do.
Litha: So, the sky's the limit, then?
Erin: ❤
Erin: Call you in a few.

In the living room, Pippa intently wrapped her fingers around a guitar neck, desperately reaching for the upper frets. A tattooed Asian guy in a torn green T-shirt guided her: "First fret on the G string. Yup. Go."

Pippa strummed an E chord and spotted Erin. "Hi sista!"

The tattooed guy turned and smiled. His deep umber irises were so dark near the middle she couldn't tell where his pupils began. His eyes were spectacular.

"Hank is teaching me to play. He says I have to learn my chords first."

Hank's hand brushed a metal clip of keys attached to his belt loop as he reached to greet Erin. "Hank. And you're the American sister."

"I am. Erin." She gripped his hand firmly, and let go a second after Hank's hand relaxed, just as Mitchell had taught her. "Why the chords first?"

Hank grinned, revealing wildly crooked teeth. "Easy to sing along when you've got chords, innit? Learn eight chords and you can sing nearly everything. Fingerpicking, you have to learn one song at a time, slowly."

He was right—she knew he was right—but he had missed the point. "If you teach Pippa to read music, she'll be able to learn any song for herself."

"We'll get there. All in good time."

"Got your uniform today, Erin?" Pippa asked.

"I did."

Pippa told Hank, "She's going to Ilam, too."

"Sweet as," he said.

"Do you go to Ilam?" Erin asked.

He smiled widely again. "I left school at sixteen. Have a carpentry apprenticeship with Blakely."

That explained his huge biceps and forearms, but learning he was a dropout fizzled the dreaminess of his eyes.

"Want to join us?" Hank asked.

Erin eyed her cello case. What was another day without practice? "Need to have a quick snack and get ready for school tomorrow," she said dismissively. "Happy practicing, Pippa."

After a few crackers and slices of cheese, Erin retreated to her room, where she pulled up Ilam High's website to see girls in her exact uniform. Boys wore shorts and knee socks in warmer weather, so perhaps she'd gotten off easy? She texted photos of the uniform to Lalitha and settled in bed to call her oldest friend.

"I'm no Superman!" Lalitha said when she picked up.

"There's no Superman here, either," Erin said. "I do, however, have a tattooed high school dropout in my living room."

"No!"

"I do. He is teaching my little sister—who is ten, she'll have you know—guitar chords."

"Did you step in and show him what's what?"

"No. I—" Tears welled in Erin's eyes. "I don't . . ." Her voice was a whisper.

Lalitha's voice was calm and quiet. "You okay, Erin with an E?"

Erin shook her head, unable to speak.

"Did I lose you?"

Kind of.

"I'm here," Erin whispered through her tears. "I just don't know what I'm doing here. You saw the photos."

"Oh, I did. But I'm guessing it's too soon to ridicule?"

"Much too soon. Their food is weird. Everything is slow—slow traffic, slow talkers, slow walkers. I almost trampled kiwis at the airport."

"Dillying and dallying and dallying some more?" Lalitha said.

"Exactly. No sense of urgency. So, probably because everyone is so slow, instead of traffic lights, they have huge, terrifying roundabouts. What if I wreck their car?"

"Well . . ."

"Say nothing. That accident was not my fault. And their car, catch the singular? They have only one."

"How does that even work?"

"I'm afraid to ask."

"Maybe they carpool?" Lalitha said.

"I don't know, but today, my host mom drove me to buy my uniform. We went to the mall. Oh my god. Lalitha, they have Kmart and McDonald's, but no Banana Republic. The clothes are mostly terrible." She gasped. "Oh, my god. Lalitha, my white leather pants are to die for."

"Who are you, and what have you done with my girl?"

"No, they fit me like a glove, and it's a beautiful matte leather. I promise they are cool. At least something is cool. Li, they have an Aldi-caliber grocery store in their *mall*. And people dress like it's 1987. And I'm sharing a room with a ten-year-old who has the stinkiest farts in the world."

"Worse than Peter McQueen the Pooty Machine?"

"Worse." Erin cracked a smile remembering their gassy elementary classmate. "But thanks for that."

"I'm sorry you're there. I wish you were here."

"Yeah. Hey, is that Quigley going to call me, or what?"

Lalitha didn't answer.

"What?" Erin said.

"She's not that bad."

"Traitor!"

"I know, right? She's kind of quiet, really smart. She wore a periodic table of nerds T-shirt yesterday. I sort of think under other circumstances you'd be friends."

"I'm not sure whether I feel better or worse."

"Her sisters are hankering to go back to L.A., but she likes Wheaton because it's quiet."

Erin scoffed. "Tell her she should transfer to New Zealand. There's no place quieter."

FIFTEEN

Monday morning, the last social media posts were hours old—and that was Saturday night in Wheaton.

Good-Time Girl had posted at midnight: "Farewell, winter hols. Back at it tomorrow."

Maybe she's at Ilam too.

Claire had sent a to-do list for Erin's first day of school and reminded her to be in the office fifteen minutes before school started.

Erin checked the weather for a respite from the cold. Her computer knew she was in New Zealand, but she couldn't bring herself to reset her Google Maps home to Christchurch.

It was zero degrees Celsius. Lalitha had been wrong: six degrees Celsius, or 43 degrees Fahrenheit, was Christchurch's *average* July low. That would be all well and good if her house weren't the same temperature.

After a quick breakfast, Felicity drove Erin and her still-nameless rented cello to Ilam High. They were ten minutes late.

"I'll fetch you at half two and take you to the pool?"

Erin nodded.

Felicity waved to several students and greeted more by name. "Jade, this is Erin. She's staying with us until Christmas.

Erin, Jade used to mind Pippa when we went out. It's Erin's first day at Ilam."

"Hello," Erin said. It was a very strange sensation, meeting someone dressed in the same frumpy kilt, the same white blouse, the same tie. Jade wore a ponytail and, despite a questionable complexion, absolutely no makeup. No foundation. Nothing to widen her slightly small eyes.

Jade said, "Want me to show you in?"

"I need to talk to a counselor about my schedule first."

"I can wait."

Erin left Jade leaning against the gray exterior and entered Ilam High.

Halfway around the world, Erin's New Zealand guidance counselor was just as scatterbrained as Mrs. Brown in Wheaton. Their offices were practically identical: multicolored piles of papers, books shoved into every available shelf space, and almost no space for students, let alone Erin's poor cello.

In bold black ink, a huge poster read:

INTEREST

+

ABILITY

+

CAREER

=

SUBJECT CHOICE

"I'm Penelope. How do you do Erin?"

Erin relaxed immediately; Penelope wasn't kiwi and hearing *Erin* pronounced correctly felt like home.

"Based on your records, Erin, you are welcome to our entire curriculum. I'll walk you through the same as I do with most students near the end of term four. First, let's talk about what you enjoy."

Penelope took copious notes as Erin spoke. "I do well in all my classes. I'm through Calculus in math, physics in science. I've finished my high school literature requirements. I've taken six years of Spanish. Science and literature are my best subjects."

"And are those your favorite courses?"

"They're my best."

Penelope squinted at her. "The way we approach course selection here is to start with your interests first. Once we know what you enjoy, then we consider your ability. We wouldn't do well to have you doing things you loathe just because you excel at them. Why would you do something you're good at if you don't enjoy it?"

Erin didn't have an answer for that. Penelope's words repeated in her head.

"So, Erin, which courses do you like best?"

"Math, for sure. Science. I took astrophysics last summer and loved it."

"We don't have astrophysics, but we do offer physics. Do you enjoy other sciences?"

"Chemistry, yes. Biology, no."

She wrote more. "And do you enjoy language and literature?"

"English classes, if it's creative writing. Deconstructing literature trips me up."

"And the arts?"

"Music. I play cello and used to play guitar."

"And do you enjoy both of those?"

"Well, I love guitar—I started playing when I was five. I gave it up for cello in fifth grade."

"And do you enjoy cello?"

"I play with the Chicago Youth Symphony Orchestra."

"But do you enjoy it?"

No. No, she didn't. But Erin was diplomatic. "I prefer the guitar, but that's not available in American schools."

"Would you enjoy our orchestra?"

Felicity had rented a cello for five months. Five months without playing cello would seriously derail seven years of intensive practice and lessons. Five months without cello would leave Erin with a lot more time holed up in a freezing bedroom all by herself.

Five months without cello might feel like vacation.

"Erin? Does playing in our orchestra sound like something that interests you?"

Almost imperceptibly, Erin shook her head.

Penelope smiled. "No orchestra then."

Just like that, Erin was free. She glanced toward the cello case. "May I leave that cello here for the day?"

"Of course. Now, what about visual arts?"

"I couldn't fit both music and art into my schedule in Wheaton and I always had to choose cello. I haven't taken art since middle school, so I probably would be far behind everyone here. I'm not very good."

Penelope pressed so hard with her pen that her paper bowed slightly around each loopy letter. "Foreign language?"

"Didn't Wheaton forward my records?" Erin sighed loudly. "You should have all my grades."

"I do have your marks, Erin. I'm trying to get to know you, which is easier in person than parsing how your teachers have rated your work. You study Spanish, you said?"

"It's the most practical language."

"You've had six years of Spanish, including some university courses, which surpasses our courses here, I'm afraid."

"I did that to comp out of foreign language in college."

Penelope smiled. "Of course. We do require students to enroll in foreign language every term. Would you prefer Italian, Mandarin, Japanese, Māori or New Zealand Sign Language?"

"Wouldn't I be starting with freshmen?"

"Many Ilam students dabble in foreign languages instead of pursuing proficiency, but yes. Some of your classmates would be quite young."

Pippa was more than enough young person in Erin's life.

"Which language most appeals?"

"Italian, I guess?"

Penelope beamed. "Italian it is then. Now, have you thought about careers that interest you?"

"I'm going to be a doctor."

"So of course you plan to go to university."

Obviously. She'd been raised to believe everyone went to college, unless they weren't smart or driven enough. Or poor, she guessed. Erin had heard of a woman who applied for a job at McDonald's, and wasn't hired because other applicants had college degrees. Without a degree, Erin's future was bleak. Without an Ivy degree, she believed her future was bland.

Penelope finished her notes. "Students from abroad are always special cases, aren't they? Mathematics, foreign language, statistics, and English literature are compulsory. You will choose three other subjects. For university entrance, you will want science. I would recommend visual arts for you. For music, our ensembles do not accommodate guitar, but I can recommend some fine teachers in Christchurch. I'll find you some names."

Penelope passed Erin her schedule and a Pupil Handbook. "Read this tonight. The most pressing matter is that we don't allow makeup. No jewelry. Wear your ring for today, but tomorrow you'll need to leave it home. For now, remove all the makeup before your first class."

"Is there a reason for that?"

"It's unnecessary. And it's a distraction. You should be focused on your studies. Your classmates should be focused on their studies. No jewelry, no makeup, no visible body art. Shoes are required."

Erin stared. "So it's not my imagination, right? Is bare feet a religious thing or . . . cultural?"

"Cultural, absolutely. Shoes are constraining. Some of us go barefoot year round. If I'm being honest, I wear them only at work, and if I'm the last in the office, they come off immediately."

Instead of career advice, application strategies, or a long checklist, Penelope had given Erin only food for thought.

BEFORE SHE FOLLOWED GOOD-TIME GIRL

BEFORE SHE FOLLOWED GOOD-TIME GIRL

Wheaton's head guidance counselor, Mrs. Brown, monitored the emotional ebb and flow of two thousand students. After Grandma Tea died, Mrs. Brown had left a little purple note with Erin's first-period teacher. When Erin started fighting with her boyfriend freshman year, Mrs. Brown had sent a flurry of purple notes inviting her to talk.

Erin had ignored all the purple notes and visited the stuffy office only to discuss college strategy.

One of Mrs. Brown's chairs housed a sloppy pile of paperwork in an array of colors. In the chair usually reserved for students, Claire sat pursing her lips and tapping on her phone.

Everything about Mrs. Brown—smile, eyes, arms, body—sagged in pity when she saw Erin. She caught herself and tried to smile. "Miss Cerise. I'm so glad you're here."

She closed the door behind Erin, and Claire stood so Erin would sit.

Claire crossed her arms and glared at her daughter. "I talked to Principal Drouin about cyberbullying and this weekend's fiasco; she's handling it. Mrs. Brown and I have a solution to the other problem. Getting into Columbia—or any Ivy, really, at this point—requires something unique.

Chicago Youth Symphony Orchestra makes you different, but we must show breadth of interest and uniqueness. Did you know that only a fraction of one percent of high school students study abroad? That will make you unique. There are spots available."

Erin picked the cuticle of her left thumb, parting it from her flesh.

"And you can choose where you go." Mrs. Brown navigated between several websites and her inbox. "There are maybe ten options left. Let's see. Moscow. How's your Russian?"

"Spanish," Claire said.

"I *know*," Mrs. Brown said. "Unfortunately, everyone has been pushed into Spanish when we really should be learning Mandarin. Soon the whole world will need Chinese."

"So, China?" Erin said.

"No. I was saying that everyone and his brother takes Spanish. So, Spain and Mexico go first. You passed on Moscow. We have Jordan."

"Absolutely not," Claire said.

"The Netherlands, Russia, Brazil, Greece."

"Even with the best tutors, she can't learn any of those languages in time," Claire said.

Mrs. Brown returned to her computer. "The only English-speaking countries we have are Nigeria, New Zealand, and Scotland. That one's Edinburgh."

"She's not going to Nigeria," Claire said.

"Okay. Scotland and New Zealand."

"Your choice!" Claire raised her eyebrows in expectation.

Senior year somewhere else. Erin could barely catch up, let alone choose. Though everything was broken in Wheaton, she didn't want to *flee*.

"How long will I be gone?" she asked.

Mrs. Brown said, "One semester, either way."

Near England or Near Australia?

Erin had visited London three years ago two weeks before the PSAT, so her memories were of flash cards and root words. She wracked her brain for anything about either country. Australia was hot and England was chilly. New Zealand and Scotland both were full of sheep—or perhaps that was Ireland?

"Do I have to go?"

"You should *want* to go," Claire said. "Studying abroad will make you an appealing candidate. Almost no one does this."

Mrs. Brown clicked her pen as Erin pondered her options. "You should know that New Zealand is kind of wonky because the seasons are opposite. You'd be starting in the middle of the New Zealand school year and would have to leave in mid-July."

Mid-July was less than two months away, and she already had math at University of Chicago and summer swimming to fill those weeks. Her departure, however—from that viral video, from Ben's sphere of gravitational pull, from her horrid new nickname—couldn't come soon enough.

"New Zealand."

Claire grabbed the doorknob. "Great! I am very late for work. I'll send you a check and completed paperwork tomorrow."

Erin stared blankly at Mrs. Brown. Her life had changed in an instant. Again.

SIXTEEN

Students—all of whom wore the same blue blazer—poured past Erin as she walked out the front door of her new school. Jade was waiting in the light drizzle. "All set then?"

Erin nodded slowly.

"Where's your first class?" Jade asked.

Erin scanned her schedule. "M5?"

"Can I see?" Jade studied Erin's schedule as they walked around the administrative offices.

Erin had expected the school to loom down a corridor beyond the administrative offices, but Ilam High had no corridors, no metal detectors, and no roof.

Like a tiny college campus, discrete buildings housed specific subject areas. Jade identified the languages building, the literature building, the maths building—all of them circles of classrooms with doors on the outside.

Ilam High was inside out.

A sea of royal blue blazers congregated around doorways and between buildings.

In what seemed like the middle of campus, Jade said, "This is the commons. Tea and lunch here. Toilets there. Fields are just on the other side of the arts building. What's your sport?"

"Swimming."

"Oh. Shall I walk you back to M5 then?"

"I can find my way, thanks. I need to stop in the restroom. Toilets." The word *toilets* felt ugly in her mouth, as if uttering it invited an image of her sitting to pee.

"Cheers!" Jade disappeared into the sea of blazers and Erin was alone again. No one noticed her because she had become part of the sea. And why introduce yourself to the new girl if you didn't know she was new?

The patina of mourning marred Erin's uncertainty. She was here to mourn Ben. And her swim team captainship. And her sense of belonging.

And her skin. Removing makeup with New Zealand paper towels was like exfoliating with sandpaper. No Boscia. No Make Up For Ever for her eyes.

When the bell rang, she called it good enough and retraced her steps to M5, where her tiny, perky calculus teacher wore a synthetic mock turtleneck and pleated slacks.

She handed Erin a textbook. "I'm Donna Weiler. Have you been studying calculus in the States?"

"I have. This year I'm supposed to take a second calculus course at the community college."

A smile. "Well done. Lovely to have you, Erin. Take any seat you like."

There was precisely one empty chair: in the center of the front row. Some things are the same in either hemisphere.

Ms. Weiler said, "We have a new student today, from the United States." A pause. A long pause. "What was your name?"

"Erin. Erin Cerise."

"Right. Everyone introduce yourselves after the second bell. Now, before the term break, we were discussing the fundamental theorem of calculus. I'd like to move on to separation of variables on page two-nine-three, but wonder whether anyone had any questions about the fundamental theorem before I do that."

No one did. Separation of variables it was. Erin opened her book and felt comfortable for the first time in days.

———

Lunchtime hiccupped blazers into the open air again. The drizzle had stopped sometime during Erin's Italian class, but the benches and concrete weren't yet dry so she leaned against the math building.

Ilam had a little to-go window with hot lunch options, but most people were eating sack lunches. And they were eating them everywhere—standing in clusters or sitting on damp benches in the commons. Just like in Wheaton, bookworms pored over novels and outcasts stood awkwardly alone.

But at Ilam, musicians played guitars and sang in groups. A gaggle of girls sat in a semicircle comparing bracelets they had hidden under their sweater sleeves. No one was squealing over a new dress or admiring nail polish because there was no nail polish. Except on Erin, of course. Everything felt less frenetic.

On the other side of the earth, everyone would tease these people about what they were wearing. Erin was embarrassed about her wool and equally embarrassed about their wool. But they all were in the same boat.

Erin followed a herd around the art building to discover an enormous unmarked field with nary a goalpost or sideline. People, still mostly in blazers, played Frisbee and soccer. Three different games of Erin didn't know what—played with a football—were underway.

No adults supervised. In Wheaton, security guards ensured students stayed where they belonged—in class or in the cafeteria—or weren't smoking in the bathrooms between periods.

Ilam High's campus was one giant picnic.

She caught a rogue Frisbee a fraction of a second before it beheaded her.

A lean, blonde guy jogged toward her. "Sorry! I'll take the disc." He was easily a head taller than she and lanky like a basketball player. She handed over the disc and he lobbed it toward a girl in the field.

Just beyond him was a group of people—guys and girls—playing cricket. Erin could scarcely believe it. Cricket. Her first night in London, after her parents had gone out for the night, she sat in her hotel room doing homework to the sounds of cricket on the TV. The sport was complicated: wickets and bowlers and overs.

These guys were in school uniforms and not the bright whites of the cricket . . . field? Court? Diamond? She didn't know.

"There you are!" Jade said. "I've been looking for you. How was your morning?"

"Good," Erin said.

"I usually sit over there." Jade pointed to a threesome playing guitars. "I want to introduce you around, though."

She walked Erin around the courtyard, introducing her to so many people Erin would never remember their names. Jade introduced her as "Erin from America." Erin appreciated the clean social slate.

"Summer swims, too" Jade said, standing next to a girl who'd tied her school blouse into a knot at her waist.

"Good to meet you, Erin," Summer said. "Need a lift to swim?"

It seemed juvenile to admit Felicity was driving her around Christchurch. "I have a ride today, but maybe tomorrow?"

"Sweet as."

Jade introduced other students, including a pockmarked guy named Jackson, who wore a badge reading HEAD BOY.

He said, "You have the cutest accent ever."

"Thanks, you too." Erin blushed.

Introductions finally over, Erin and Jade settled atop their school bags in the grass near the guitar threesome. Erin opened her hastily packed lunch. At the last possible second, Felicity had told her to throw something together, so lunch was ten pounds of fruit.

"We spent the winter hols in the States. Beautiful beaches," Jade said.

"What were you doing in America?"

"Cousin's wedding, but it was really just an excuse to get a bit of sun. Bunch of my mates skied at The Remarkables, and I would have rather done that."

The Remarkables. That's where Good-Time Girl had skied two weeks ago. Perhaps she was one of Jade's *mates*. Erin suspected Good-Time Girl could show her the best of Christchurch; perhaps Jade was the lead required to track her down.

BEFORE SHE CHOSE EXILE IN NEW ZEALAND

BEFORE SHE CHOSE EXILE IN NEW ZEALAND

Even her disastrous birthday celebration hadn't been as isolating as Monday morning in homeroom. Amid video announcements for sports results and study abroad, morning briefing provided prime time for gossip.

Erin caught two words: "Gag reflex."

In her peripheral vision, she caught a classmate making a lewd gesture and tonguing his cheek. Another guy gagged and pretended to vomit on his desk.

Heat swelled in Erin's chest and crept up her neck.

She looked around the room, then turned to Ben's best friend, Jamie. "What are they talking about?"

He laughed.

Erin stood. "What are you talking about?"

Someone behind her made a vomiting sound.

What had Ben told everyone? She hadn't gagged on anything but her own vomit. Erin whipped out her phone and texted him: "What did you tell people about Saturday night?"

She texted Lalitha the same thing.

Aaron, who Erin had dated just before Ben, laughed. "Now I know why you said no to oral. Glad I didn't push you any harder to do it."

"That is not what happened," Erin said.

The PA popped and rattled: "Erin Cerise to the guidance office."

She gathered her things and stomped to the hall.

"So long, Gag Reflex," she heard before the room erupted in laughter.

She would never live this down. *Gag Reflex* would follow her forever. Someone would write it in her yearbook. Next year—senior year—someone would spray it in shaving cream on her Fiat or Sharpie it on her locker.

SEVENTEEN

Felicity was chipper as she helped wrestle Erin's cello case into the backseat. "And how was your first day?"

"Fine." Erin rested her head against the seat back.

"Really? A totally different school on the other side of the world, and all you've got for me is 'fine'?"

Erin stared at blue blazers pooling around the car. "It's very different."

"It's quite a bit, eh?"

Felicity's *eh* was similar to a Canadians' *eh*, but more resigned and less of a question.

"What did you think of it?"

Erin faced Felicity. "I'm not sure. I'm digesting the experience. It's kind of a lot."

"I'm sure," Felicity said as they pulled away. "Tell me the best parts."

Felicity pointed out the route to the pool as Erin told her about Italian class. Felicity parked at the pool entrance as Erin poorly described the sport she'd seen at lunch.

"Sounds like rugby! You fancy a go?"

Erin closed her eyes and considered that. "They were mostly guys."

"They'd welcome you! Every girl has to play once or twice . . . to see whether she likes it."

"I'll think about it."

"Good as gold. I want to hear more after dinner, but you're nearly late. This is Jellie Pool. Suppose you could walk, but it's a haul to make it in time. You'll have to ask your teammates how they get around. I'll fetch you at half five, then?"

"That's just two hours," Erin said. "How about six thirty?"

"Tea's at half six."

"I used to practice four hours a day. I assume we'll have weight training afterward."

"Six on the dot, then. Have fun."

"Thank you." Swim practice was many things—grueling, challenging, taxing—but hadn't been fun for years.

———

After some confusion at Jellie Pool's front desk, Erin found the changing room and shifted gears from school to swimming. Or tried to shift gears. She was fried, and in desperate need of a nap.

Slowly, she followed signs to the pool and cringed when she stepped onto the pool deck. Erin hated short pools: flip turns broke her stroke twice as often, which seemed to prolong practices and races.

She checked in with the coach, who insisted she call him Percy and assigned her a warm-up lane with Summer and two other girls.

These girls were her new teammates, sure, but swimming was a very individual sport. Unlike softball or soccer, where everyone had to function together, in swimming she just did her best. On her own. And the fastest girl won, no matter what the rest of her team did. Except in relays, of course.

Erin liked being the fastest girl in the pool.

Damned Quigleys.

The girls in Erin's lane warmed up slowly, and Erin kept their pace. Working in the water was slice of normalcy.

Percy called a brief meeting, and Erin clung to the side of the pool with her new teammates. Her teammates had covered their tattoos during school, but the pool was a whole different story. Most swimmers had a little something—a clown fish, a graphic skull, a tiny rainbow—and many older swimmers had several. It was a literal sea of tattoos.

Erin couldn't fathom putting any image on her body forever. When the redhead next to her turned eighty, she'd be mortified at the name of the boy band scrawled between her shoulder blades.

Percy introduced Erin to the team. "She's from the States, and a fine swimmer."

After greetings all around, Percy recapped the season for Erin: most secondary schools had already qualified for New Zealand's national swim meet, but no one from Ilam was in yet.

"Erin?" Percy said *Erin* like an American.

She yanked off her goggles. "Yeah?"

"I thought we might sort out races and medleys for the rest of the season. Can you race a hundred-meter fly?"

"Sure." She climbed out of the pool as Percy directed Summer and another girl—Lily—onto the blocks.

Erin loved studying the water for that half second just before the gun. Or the clap, in this case.

Her ass was dragging; she waited on the block for a second before diving in. Trying to push the idea of sleep out of her head, Erin went through the motions in her lane.

Gracious, Percy had given Erin the center lane. The first 25 meters were easy; Summer and Lily were nowhere in her peripheral vision. Coming off the wall, she saw them both nearly a body length behind. And she was exhausted.

At the second turn, Erin flipped to find herself a full body length ahead. Adrenaline outpaced her jet lag and she continued to push; it felt amazing to be winning again. She was in her element, creaming the two behind her. Erin finished so hard that she was still panting two minutes after she hit the wall.

Percy bounced on the balls of his feet. "One-oh-four-oh-one! Eleven seconds off Summer's 100 fly."

Summer shook Erin's hand over the lane divider. "Relay's yours."

Erin's stomach twisted. Her performance had wrecked a relay team, which may not have been together three years like her own, but it had been together yesterday.

Next month, one of the Quigley sisters would compete on her Wheaton relay team. With her girls.

Erin was the Quigley now. Had she ruined these kiwi girls' lives? She definitely had wrecked something for somebody. Now she felt like a jerk.

She still had to survive on the team through the end of the season, though. When the Quigleys had usurped her position on the relay, she'd viewed them as pariahs. She didn't want her new teammates to see her that way.

"I am so sorry," she said to Summer.

Summer shrugged.

Percy posted the day's drills. Erin put her head in the water and worked. She kept pace with her lane during drills, but her anxiety persisted.

Percy focused on form for an hour. After warm down, he dismissed everyone. No lifting. No out-of-water conditioning.

No wonder they weren't winning.

They weren't winning, but Erin would. And, unlike cello, racing was something she truly loved.

As Erin climbed out of the pool, Percy repeated her time. "So you can race relay. Could you do the fifty-meter? The two hundred?"

"Two-hundred fly?" That was a long race.

Percy was giddy. "We have three fly races at championships. I'd love you to race them all. You can race whatever you want! We just have to submit your times by the middle of August. Imagine: we'll send you alone, and maybe take the relay team, too. No matter how we do at next week's meet, we'll have four swimmers competing. Welcome, Erin."

Erin was stunned that he had no directives, only excitement. "Thanks, Coach."

"Percy, please. See you on the morrow."

BEFORE SHE HAD HOMEROOM
BEFORE SHE HAD HOMEROOM

After ninety minutes of intense practice, Erin and her Wheaton teammates dripped on the pool deck while Coach Waterson gave (mostly) constructive criticism.

"Finally, I want you in top form for summer leagues: weights four times this week, no excuses. I don't care what else is going on. I don't care what happened at whose party—"

The guys in the back snickered.

"Be here on time and ready to work. We have a serious shot at some amazing races this year. Don't blow it. Showers."

Erin's teammates whispered about Claudia, Ruth, and Hillary Quigley. One of the freshmen asked for their autographs as the rest of the team disbursed into the locker rooms.

Jamie hammered on Erin's shoulder. "Surprised you went so deep today, Cerise."

She was attempting to parse that when Claudia Quigley said, "Hey, Erin?"

Silent, Erin crossed her arms.

Claudia bit her lip. "I just wanted to ask how you're feeling after Saturday. I tried to help, really, I did. You doing okay?"

Lalitha looped her arm through Erin's. "What's going on?"

Erin raised her chin. "I am fine. Perfect. Except for my swimming prospects and personal life, everything is perfect."

Arms linked, she and Lalitha headed toward the locker room.

EIGHTEEN

Half the team had disappeared while Erin was talking to Percy. The other half had adjourned to the hot tub.

If she were going to be an outcast here, too, she needed to know immediately. Into the fire.

"Mind if I join you?" Erin asked.

"Our pleasure! Welcome to the spa!" Lily slid to make room.

Summer said, "Did everyone meet Erin?"

Air-in. She was trying.

A chorus of hellos greeted her: Ruby, Nala, Marama, Gemma, Ryan, Indiana, Tavé.

"What was the relay team before I got here?"

Summer said, "I swam fly. Marama, free. Ruby, breast. Gemma, back."

What could she say to that? Erin didn't want to break up their party. Had Claudia Quigley felt any guilt when she replaced Erin on the relay team at Wheaton?

To Summer, she said, "I didn't think about how my being here would affect your season. I'm so sorry."

Summer was cheery. "Why? Because with you, the relay has a fighting chance at Nationals? Last year no one in our

90

Antipodes

school qualified, and this year we could qualify four? That's awesome."

Erin hadn't considered that. "I'm . . . happy to help."

"Sweet as."

"How are you finding New Zealand?" Marama asked.

"It's only my second full day. Still jet-lagged, so I haven't seen much."

"What kind of stuff do you like?"

Here it was again. For all her bragging about confidence and self-sufficiency, Erin had few ideas about her own passions. "I like variety."

Summer said, "Do you prefer the tourist route—bungee off a bridge and tour boats—or the native route?"

The word *bungee* struck terror in her heart. "Definitely the native route."

Marama laughed. "Correct choice." Her skin was a beautiful, flawless brown. Māori.

"Where to first, you think?" Summer asked.

A flurry of suggestions filled the hot tub: Hanmer, Castle Hill, Akaroa, Hokitika, Hell Pizza, Winnie Bagoes, Antarctic Center, Franz Glacier.

Marama said, "How about bouldering Saturday? It's rock climbing, but nearer the ground."

Erin stared at the water. She couldn't imagine spending an entire day hopping over rocks. "I probably can't Saturday. It's my host mother's birthday."

"Sunday, then," Marama said.

"I'm not sure."

Marama pointed a finger. "You owe me, after kicking my very best friend off my relay team!"

Erin's eyes widened, but Marama was grinning.

Erin grinned back. "Sounds great."

91

"I'm out," Summer said. "Family day."

"Same," Ruby and Ryan said.

"Minding my little brother." Nala rolled her eyes.

"Sunday. I'll find someone who's game," Marama said before changing the subject. "So, Nala. Out with it. You and Zane."

Nala's crimson cheeks told at least half the story. "He's sweet," she said.

"Looked more savory to me," Marama teased.

Erin relaxed against the hot tub for a half hour while conversation volleyed between old friends. One by one, swimmers left the spa until only Summer and Erin remained.

Erin said, "So, was this a typical practice?"

"Pretty much."

They hadn't gotten into the pool until 3:30, or half-three, and they'd adjourned to the hot tub shortly after 5:00.

Erin said, "Is there somewhere we can lift weights and do some extra training?"

On the dry concrete, Summer dribbled a floor plan and directed Erin toward the weight room. "And we can use it any time we want. I'm off now. See you tomorrow?"

"Same place, same time."

With forty minutes to kill, Erin headed to the weight room for conditioning.

NINETEEN

Felicity sang along to U2 as they sped home. The warm side of the house wasn't quite warm yet when they arrived, but it warmed slightly as Erin catnapped under piles of blankets. When the family of four sat for mince stew at 6:40, just ten minutes late, the dining room was toasty.

Before Erin was in the chair, Hamish asked, "How did you feel about your first day, Erin?"

Erin retreated to the same phrase she'd used on Felicity: "I'm still digesting."

Hamish prodded, "What courses have you chosen?"

Unsatisfied with a recap, Hamish asked Erin's opinion about everything: *Was she pleased with her courses? Was she excited about the relay team? How starkly did Ilam and Wheaton High contrast?*

Finished with the interrogation, Hamish handed Erin a credit card. "I finally got you a Metrocard today. It will refill automatically, so don't lose it."

Erin's brow furrowed. "What's that for?"

Hamish chuckled. "Felicity can't knock off work every day to drive you around! Metrostar will get you to school and back. I should have brought you a map."

She looked at Felicity. "I thought I'd be driving. On the 81, you said?"

"The 81 is a city bus. Metrostar, too," Pippa said. "I like to alternate."

"And Foreign Study Network prohibits driving in your host country," Hamish said.

Erin winced. "No."

"Yes," Felicity said. "It's in all their paperwork."

In May, Claire had handled all the paperwork and made Erin sign on six different lines.

She struggled to speak. After a full year with her own Fiat, Christchurch was relegating her to the bus? She had never taken a bus to high school. They were for freshmen who had no upperclassmen friends, enormously unpopular sophomores, and anyone else who had no sense of social order or survival.

Thanks to swim team, Erin had always ridden with upperclassmen. When she got her license—and the Fiat—on her sixteenth birthday, she helped the social order by driving others.

But here she was—seventeen—riding the bus. The city bus.

Pippa said, "I'll show you the way tomorrow. As long as we catch one of them before 7:24, we'll be on time."

Erin's head spun. She rubbed her chilly arms. She just wanted to crawl back to Pippa's room and put on all the clothes she'd brought with her. "So, when does it really start to feel like spring in Christchurch?"

Hamish said, "It's already starting to warm up a bit, I think."

Erin grabbed her mug with both hands. It was almost too hot, but she'd take what she could get.

Hamish said, "Put on a sweater."

She snapped, "I have on a sweater."

Hamish spoke through a mouthful of food. "Pu. on. Anuvah. Sweater."

"I am inside a house!"

The table fell silent. Pippa studied her plate. Hamish maintained a foul expression as he chewed. Erin held her breath. Felicity covered Hamish's hand with her own. "Hame?"

Hamish gritted his teeth and puckered his mouth. A moment later, he spoke. "Okay, Saturday is the big birthday celebration."

Erin exhaled slowly and tried to harness some civility and calm.

Hamish smiled. "We have a few things to finish up before then. You know what I mean, Pippa."

Their conspiratorial nod suggested they would be baking a birthday cake. Erin thought back to her last birthday celebration; whatever was in store for Felicity, it had to be better than that.

BEFORE SHE PRACTICED WITH THE QUIGLEYS

BEFORE SHE PRACTICED WITH THE QUIGLEYS

"Limo's here," Claire yelled up the stairs. She was still pissed but clearly was ecstatic about Erin's fun date night in a limo.

Erin descended in a Rent the Runway gown Ben had helped her choose. It was the precise shade of Erin's juniper eyes.

"You look amazing!" Claire said. "Where the hell is Ben? It's not like him to be late. Is he hungover, too?"

"We'll pick him up at his house," Erin lied. "He didn't need to drive over."

"Oh, good plan!" Claire spoke loudly and slowly to the limo driver: "She'll give you directions to another house before you drive in to Chicago. Can you do that?"

"Of course, ma'am," he said in perfect American English.

Erin slid into the black leather seat where she and Ben had planned to make out.

Her chauffeur rolled down the opaque divider. "Address, miss?"

Erin directed him to Lalitha's house and asked him to wait.

She rang Lalitha's doorbell for two full minutes before withdrawing the spare key from the turtle statue. She found her friend swathed in blankets on the basement sofa.

"Come on my birthday date with me," Erin said.

"Shhhhh," Lalitha said. "Hangover."

"Li, Claire is furious and I am grounded for months. My personal life of hell is all over the Internet. I'm off the swim team. Ben just dumped me. You are coming out with me. Take an Ibuprofen, and let's go."

"Restaurants are too loud. Concerts are way too loud."

Erin agreed. Anyway, the Chainsmokers were Ben's band, not hers. And her hangover stomach wanted grease, so she could skip her Topolabampo reservation, too.

Erin whispered, "I promise to be quiet. You don't even need to change your clothes."

Lalitha glanced from her pajamas to Erin's ensemble. "Sweet dress."

"You wouldn't want it to go to waste, would you? Come on. I promise you a night of tears and tissues, greasy pizza, and ice cream. Girls' night out . . . in a limousine."

Lalitha crawled off the sofa. Erin grabbed Ibuprofen from the kitchen and filled two water bottles. Five minutes later, Erin emerged from the house with Lalitha, who reeked of alcohol and still wore her pajamas.

Their chauffeur opened the door without batting an eye.

"What time are we supposed to be back tonight?"

"11:30, miss."

Seven hours. "Change of plans. Can we just drive around tonight?"

"I don't understand, miss."

"We're not going into the city. We're not going to dinner or a concert. My friend and I would like to pick up a greasy pizza and drive around. I'm buying. For you, too. You in?"

"You're the boss," he said, closing the door after her.

TWENTY

As Erin helped clean the table—together, naturally—Felicity touched her arm. "Do you think you'll be happy here, dear?"

"Sure!" Blatant, blatant lie.

Felicity ducked into Erin's gaze to look her in the eye. "You should let me know—let any of us know—if there's anything we can do to help. That's why we're here. We're family."

This was Erin's chance to pull the exit cord: tell Felicity the house was too tiny and too cold and New Zealand had cheap clothes and the stupid school wouldn't let her wear her grandmother's ring and makeup was out of the question. That her independence had been stolen from her. That she felt like a child. That eating together every night made her itchy.

But beating a hasty retreat to Wheaton wouldn't be unique. She must press on. "I'll let you know." Felicity handed Erin a plate of crusts and leftover mince stew. "Into the organics bin."

Erin eyed the silver container on the counter. "This one?"

"Indeed. All food scraps, bones, meats, by-products into there. Christchurch composts it all."

A half hour later, Erin and Pippa sat across from each other doing homework in front of the woodstove.

"What are you working on?" Pippa asked.

"Calculus."

"What's that?"

"Math."

Pippa's eyes gleamed. "I love maths. Mrs. Frisby taught us how to make hexaflexagons today. Want to see?" She pulled out a paper hexagon. "I folded this paper into a hexagon, see?" Pippa colored it red on one side, blue on the other.

"Nice." Erin returned to her book.

"No, no, no!" Pippa said. "Look." She flipped the paper inside out and had another folded hexagon, both sides white. "I'll color these purple and green. And do you think I'm done?"

"Yep. Sweet," Erin said.

"No! I'm not." Pippa turned the paper inside out a few times.

Felicity put her hand on Erin's shoulder. "Pippa, Erin wants to do her homework. Can she tell you when she's free?"

"Sure!" Pippa said, holding up another white hexagon. "But look! Still blank!" She colored that side orange before going back to her homework.

To Erin, Felicity said, "She will talk forever. When you need space, tell her you need space. It's kinder to everyone."

"Okay," Erin said.

Pippa worked for another thirty minutes, packed up, and left the table for the cold side of the house. Erin finished the last of her homework before accidentally walking in on Pippa brushing her teeth.

"You can come in," Pippa said.

"I can wait."

"I left the door open so you could come in when you were ready. That's what sisters do, right?"

Erin shrugged. It was a silly thing, brushing their teeth together. Pippa was very careful to get around all her crooked, gapped teeth.

While Erin was flossing, Pippa said, "So about Kapa Haka? My performance? It's traditional Māori dance. We have a performance fourth term. Maybe you'll come watch?"

Just in time, Felicity announced that she was ready to read to Pippa.

Not tired enough for sleep, Erin sat in the warm half of the house with her computer. She replied to her mother's email and reassured her everything was fine. She promised the cello was fine, too. Claire would be livid if she knew Erin wasn't back on schedule.

What she didn't know wouldn't hurt her.

Though it was the middle of the night in Wheaton, Erin texted Lalitha about Ilam and her new team. Regarding Ben, Erin decided what was happening was happening, whether she knew about it or not. She texted:

Erin: "I'm totally fine with hearing about Ben. Whatever's going on with him, let me have it."

"Off to bed, Erin?" Felicity asked.

"In a few minutes."

Felicity's smile froze. "It's important that you are well rested. Particularly as an athlete, you need a proper amount of sleep."

"I'm going." Erin scooped up her gear and bid Hamish good night. She didn't appreciate being treated like a child. Felicity already had a daughter, so shouldn't the whole child-management thing be out of her system? She still read stories to Pippa, who was ten. As soon as Erin could read, her au pair was off the hook for stories.

In under a year, she would be at college, telling herself when to go to bed, deciding what to eat and when. And not accepting to-do lists from her mother all the damned time, she hoped.

Erin was quick in the frigid bathroom before slipping into Pippa's dark, quiet bedroom, which smelled faintly of intestinal gas. Pippa breathed deeply as Erin tucked her computer into its case.

Erin dove into her bed to find three fuzzy hot pillows in her sheets: hot water bottles all in a row.

Ecstatic, she absorbed their heat until she was certain she wouldn't die of hypothermia.

She was warm. Really, truly warm. No hourlong grasshopper mating ritual required. She pushed one hot water bottle to her toes and slid the other two onto the floor.

Felicity was a saint. A somewhat bossy saint, but still.

TWENTY-ONE

Pippa wasn't in her bed Tuesday morning. Showered, dressed, and in the kitchen for breakfast, Erin asked Felicity where she was.

"She had a rough night," Felicity said. "She's still asleep in my bed."

Erin didn't want to press. She and Felicity performed a little pas de deux around the kitchen, packing lunches and foraging for breakfast.

Mounted on the dining room wall, a heater about a yard wide and a foot tall belched warmish air into the room. At that rate, Erin would be cold forever.

Felicity leaned around Erin to grab flatware. "Pippa! Breakfast!"

"Felicity?"

She looked Erin in the eye. "Yes?"

"Thanks for the warm bed last night. It was really . . . nice."

Felicity touched her arm. "I'm trying to help."

"You did, thanks."

A groggy Pippa joined them in the kitchen.

Felicity straightened the naked baby oil painting, which had been askew. "I'm a bit late today. It's hosing down out there. Fine on your own this morning, girls?"

Erin and Pippa assured her they were fine. A half hour later, they bundled up, pulled on their boots, and walked to the bus stop in the pouring rain.

"I like your wellies," Pippa said.

"They're Hunters."

"We call them wellies."

"I meant the brand," Erin said.

Pippa raised her bright rain boots decorated with emoji. "And this kind is called gumboots."

Pippa maintained a steady line of commentary as Erin grew more irritated by the bus requirement. After ten minutes, Erin said, "Pippa, I need a little space."

Pippa nodded and was quiet until the bus arrived and she blurted, "You've forgotten your cello!"

"I'm taking a break. And thank you for the space." Erin nodded to the bus. "You first."

Pippa climbed the steps and rubbed her purple metro card in a circular motion on a post. The beaming driver said, "G'morning!"

Pippa said, "Good morning, Ladanian!"

"G'morning!" he said to Erin.

Erin copied Pippa's movements with her card. "Hi."

"Have a seat!"

Pippa sat with Erin, but she talked across the aisle to Nadia, who wore an identical plaid Ilam Primary uniform. Other riders wore a veritable rainbow of uniforms. A sad rainbow: dark red, royal blue, blacks, whites, and one gaudy yellow.

Out of their neighborhood, over the bridge, and through the chaotic roundabout, Erin was the only rider in Ilam High blue.

"You're going to miss your stop," Pippa said, pressing a thin yellow strip next to her seat.

The driver stopped somewhat abruptly, just in front of Ilam High.

Erin walked toward the rear exit

"You have to cross at the Deborah!" Pippa yelled.

Erin furrowed her brow. "What?"

"You have to cross at the Deborah!" Pippa yelled again.

Erin could make no sense of that.

A small girl in black and yellow shouted, "The black and white stripes, just there? The zebra." She pointed to the crosswalk.

Deborah, zebra. Zebra stripes.

"Got it!" she yelled to Pippa, and she disembarked.

TWENTY-TWO

Erin's art teacher had been absent Monday, so Erin had doodled in a notebook as her classmates gossiped for the better part of an hour. Excited to begin creating, Erin was delighted to find Mrs. Campbell in class Tuesday morning.

As Erin was introducing herself, an air horn sounded and her classmates dove under tables. Curling into tight fetal positions, each student clung to a table leg and wrapped their other arm around their necks.

Erin froze.

"Erin?" Mrs. Campbell said. "Earthquake. Drop, cover, and hold!"

Erin crawled under a table and assumed the same position as her classmates. In the quiet that ensued, Erin decided earthquakes were uneventful. She'd expected them to feel more . . . quake-like.

Moments later, another air horn sounded, and a woman on an electronic megaphone said, "All clear."

Everyone crawled out from under their tables and took their seats as Mrs. Campbell apologized for missing Monday's class. "I was stuck in Oz for an extra day. Anyway, this term, we'll be working on watercolors." A true assignment would begin Thursday but, in the meantime, they'd experiment with watercolors, brushes, and different weights of paper.

Erin gathered supplies and painted a bold red line on her thinnest paper. She added more water to the red and created another line, then another, until she painted a faint pink line. The paper buckled under the wetness, and Erin switched to a thicker paper, repeating the experiment.

When Mrs. Campbell stopped at her desk, she said, "You're very methodical, aren't you?"

"You said to experiment."

"So I did. Now let's try to create a new image, and then re-create the same image on each piece of paper using what you've learned."

Erin didn't know how to paint much of anything. She imagined a boxy swimming block—a psychedelic swimming block, because that was more colorful—and started again with her thinnest paper. It was challenging.

Erin hadn't been allowed to take art since sixth grade because other electives were too important. And, of course, AP government looked better to Columbia than playing with paints. She had forgotten how easily she could lose herself in a project.

When Mrs. Campbell announced it was time to pack up, Erin was nowhere near done. And she found she couldn't wait for the next day's class.

―――

Alone at lunch, Erin cracked her Italian book to read ahead. The clouds had burned off during her art experiments, but everything remained damp. She juggled her Italian book and lunch until Jade called her name.

"In here!" Jade pulled Erin into the gymnasium.

They sat on the floor and Jade said, "How are you finding New Zealand?"

"Still jet-lagged," Erin said.

Jade held out a plastic container of brown and gray food. "True kiwi lunch here. Want some?"

"Every time someone mentions kiwi, I picture fuzzy green fruit," Erin said.

"Aye, we've got kiwi fruit, too. This is bangers and mash."

"Funny, isn't it? Last night, Felicity asked whether I liked—whether I *fancied*—kumara. An orange vegetable. Not a carrot. Soft in the middle when cooked, but not a squash. Then she served it and it was a sweet potato."

"Kumara are my favorite in winter."

"Yeah, my grampa used to make them with butter, brown sugar, and cinnamon. I love them, but it's a perfect example of how off-kilter I feel. Same cars, but yours are smaller. And slower. Everything is a little slower. We speak the same language, to an extent. But sometimes? I have no idea what people are saying. And sometimes, words have entirely different meanings. At home, biscuits are small, fluffy, buttery breakfast breads. What you call biscuits, we call cookies."

"Sounds delicious, either way," Jade said.

Outside, a circle of guys bunched up over the rugby ball, pushing hard but not moving in any particular direction.

"Aren't words funny?" Erin said as she watched them. "I once met a girl at a resort in North Carolina—that's actually in the southern part of America—and it took us a while to parse that when a Chicago native says she skis, she means skiing in snow. But we also go water-skiing. In the south, though, where it's warm, skiing means water. And they call the other kind snow skiing."

"Here, of course, the North Island is the warm part, and we get the cold down here," Jade said. "One of us is upside down."

"Yeah. It's definitely me."

"You're sweet, though. We'll keep you." Jade smiled.

"Thanks. I'm sticking around for the cute accents."

"Wait until summer. It's a dream."

One of the rugby players jogged into the gym, a ball under his arm. He spotted Erin and grinned. "Hey! I'm Richard."

"Erin."

"What's on for tomorrow, Erin?"

"Uh . . . school again?" she said.

"What say we pop round the dairy? Get us a cuppa or an ice block if it's warm?"

For translation, Erin looked to Jade, whose eyes were wide as she shook her head vehemently.

"No, sorry. Can't," Erin said.

"Erin is spoken for this week," Jade said.

"Gizza fighting chance!" Richard said.

"Sorry, mate," Jade said.

"Sorry. Mate," Erin repeated.

Defeated, Richard left them.

When he was out of earshot, Erin said, "What was that about?"

"That bloke doesn't take no for an answer. He is bad news."

Taken aback, Erin said, "What was he asking me to do? A date on a dairy farm?"

Jade giggled. "A dairy's a shop. He asked you to go for coffee or ice blocks, like sweet-flavored water frozen to a stick."

Erin squinted as she imagined that. "Oh, popsicles. We call them popsicles."

"Whatever you call them, don't get them with Richard."

"Thanks," Erin said. "I never would have guessed."

TWENTY-THREE

Swim team didn't practice on Fridays, so her first Friday in Christchurch, Erin met Pippa after school and diverted to Riccarton Mall. Erin had finally beaten jet lag and felt rejuvenated, but she would need Pippa's advice on a perfect gift for Felicity's birthday. For Claire, Erin would charge a pair of pumps or new bag, but Felicity wasn't really that kind of mom.

Pippa said, "She already chose her prezzie."

"Right, but I didn't."

"She says spending the day together is what she likes best."

Spoken like a person who was compensating for watching her wallet. Erin probably should buy Felicity an actual gift. Maybe on the AmEx this time. The bills came on different days, and if she was lucky, the leather pants and present could slip through undetected.

"Pippa, there must be something she really wants but can't have."

"Nope."

"Everyone has something they want but can't have. Something extravagant."

"She's not an extravagant kind of person."

No kidding.

Erin's hostess gift had included a box of consumables, so chocolates were out. Flowers were trite. "What is her favorite thing in the entire world?"

Pippa grinned. "Me."

Erin nodded. Felicity was kind of like her Grandma Tea, who had genuinely loved being with Erin, no matter what they were doing. Every Christmas, Grandma Tea just wanted to spend time in the same room, so that's what they did—reading or making music together or doing their own thing. She always said time was the most precious gift she could not give herself.

What could Felicity not give herself?

MAC. Erin could give her MAC.

"Do you know if there's a MAC here?" Erin asked.

"Like Mackeys? Golden arches?"

"No. M-A-C. Like makeup."

"Mum doesn't wear makeup except when she goes out."

Probably because it's too expensive. "Trust me, this will be a nice treat for her. It will make her feel great."

Pippa followed her to MAC, which they found next to Kmart.

No CND and no Banana Republic, but Christchurch had Kmart. America was exporting the wrong businesses.

An hour later, gift certificate in hand and experimental makeup on their faces, Erin and Pippa arrived home to find the FedEx box. Without space for anything more in her room, Erin stored it, sealed, in the garage.

She was ready for Felicity's birthday and whatever it brought.

BEFORE SHE ENTERED THE LIMO
BEFORE SHE ENTERED THE LIMO

On Erin's seventeenth birthday, she imagined she was living on Venus, where a day is longer than a year. She texted Ben an apology and told him her body was punishing her with a relentless headache.

It hurt from the hangover, from crying over her assured social implosion, from crying over Grandma Tea's ring, from crying over Grandma Tea and Grampa themselves, and from Ben's tardy reply.

She had no appetite but kept drinking water to rehydrate. *Some birthday.*

Two years ago, her last birthday celebration with Grandma Tea, she'd received a letter instead of a card.

Erin pulled files from her desk and quickly found the pistachio envelope, which had resealed since she first opened it. Gently, she pulled away the flap and reread her letter.

My Dearest Erin:

After the excitement of your birthday celebration subsides, once you've put away your new things and recycled your cards, I wanted to say once more how grateful I am to have you in my life.

Our summers together mark the best times of my life; your childhood was a second childhood for me, and for that I am truly grateful.

You have grown into a clever, fierce, stunning young woman, and I hope you find as much happiness in your life as I've found in mine.

I miss you always and am grateful you keep in close touch. As you prepare for big things, remember I am a mere phone call away.

I love you, Erin, and I'm beyond delighted you're my granddaughter.

XOXOXO,
Tea

Erin cried herself to sleep and woke to Ben's ping at last.

❤ ❤ **Ben**❤ ❤ :Stop texting! I am done with you.

She sat up in bed, her stomach in her throat again.

Erin: That's not funny.

Despite never before generating read receipts from Ben, Erin's phone indicated Ben had read her text. Panicked, she called him. It rang once and diverted her to voice mail. She hung up and called again. One ring and voice mail.

Expecting to vomit, she ran to the bathroom and stood over the toilet.

Nothing came up. She held the sides of the toilet seat and cried. First swimming. Then her social life. Her car. Now Ben.

How had she so angered the gods?

Erin called Lalitha. No answer.

Erin: Litha, I need to talk ASAP.

Lalitha must have been sleeping off her hangover, lucky girl.

Erin couldn't imagine eating alone at Topolobampo while other diners looked on. She couldn't imagine eating, period.

Her parents couldn't handle one more thing right now, so she'd have to fake it. Erin pulled up her hair, chose a tiny purse, and slipped into the dress meant for her birthday celebration.

TWENTY-FOUR

Most mornings, Erin's life in Wheaton felt light-years away. Lalitha was in school when Erin woke. When Wheaton let out, Erin was in class. Lalitha was never available during Erin's five seconds between school and swimming. And after Erin's swim practice, Lalitha was already in bed.

Texting across time zones was almost as painful as snail mail.

In Christchurch news, Erin learned Good-Time Girl had been at a beach bonfire the previous night. Erin must discover *that* Christchurch without becoming a creepy stalker.

She scanned her dad's daily How Are You/I Miss You/Sending My Love email, peppered with details of the weather, the Fiat, and Wheaton news.

Claire had demanded Erin text her as soon as she woke up. Erin drew a deep breath.

Erin: Hi, Mom. I'm up.
Claire: I have a client in five.
Erin: Okay.
Claire: Our plan isn't going to work if you don't keep in closer touch.

This plan was Claire's; Erin had not consented to such rules.

Erin: Okay.
Claire: I sent you the edits. She says you have to sell yourself in this essay. You're studying abroad, which is rare in high school. You're a great cellist. A great swimmer. Show them how amazing you are: you are relentless. They need to know you are ambitious and will stop at nothing to get what you want.

If that were true, Erin would destroy her phone to forestall more text conversations with her mother.

Erin: I'll send you a new draft soon.
Claire: Like tomorrow. We need to get this right.
Erin: Okay.
Claire: Are the classes rigorous enough? It will look bad if you are regressing academically.
Erin: They're fine.
Claire: How were orchestra auditions?
Erin: Everyone who wants to play gets to play.
Claire: What kind of cello is it?
Erin: It's fine.
Claire: Okay. Practicing every day? Keeping your schedule? Are you back in your routine?
Erin: Yeah.
Erin: Yes.
Claire: Okay. Keep working.
Erin: I am.
Claire: We'll get there. I promise.
Erin: I know.

Claire: Bye.
Erin: Bye.

Claire often texted to ensure she was on schedule, but this felt to Erin like micromanagement. To justify lying, she told herself she was mature enough to manage her own time. And what Claire didn't know wouldn't hurt her.

Or Erin.

TWENTY-FIVE

On Felicity's birthday, Erin sprinted to the warm side of the house as soon as the Wakefields started moving around, but she backpedaled to her room when she heard Hank, the guitar teacher, wishing Felicity happy birthday.

Her host family seeing her pajamas was one thing, but the tattooed dropout with amazing eyes was another. She shook her head awake. *What is he doing here?*

A half hour later, showered and dressed in her favorite clothes, Erin joined everyone at the table.

"Morning!" they chorused.

"Happy birthday!" Erin said.

"Thanks," Felicity said. "Coffee's on,"

The house looked just the same: no decorations, no tiara for Felicity, no fanfare.

"What's the birthday plan?" Erin asked.

"We got a late start today," Felicity said. "Once we're dressed and ready, I'll head out for a bit.

"Wait, no sunrise this year?" Hank said.

"Supposed to be cloudy all the way round." Felicity explained to Erin: "I like to watch the sunrise on my birthday. Another trip around the sun and all that."

Erin smiled. "That's how I think of birthdays, too! I always wish friends a great new trip around the sun. I don't get up for the sunrise, though."

"Too early for you, Erin?" Hank said.

"Actually, at home, I get up for swim practice well before the sunrise. I'm saying I wouldn't get up just for the sunrise."

The room froze. Felicity said, "You must not have seen many good sunrises."

Sifting through mental imagery, Erin couldn't recall a single sunrise. Not in Wheaton. Not on vacation. Not in the U.P. "I don't think I've seen one, ever."

Everyone turned their attention from Erin to their absolutely fascinating crumpets. Heat crawled up her cheeks.

Pippa said, "Erin plays the cello. Did you know, Hank?"

"I've heard."

Felicity said, "Erin, you know you're welcome to practice your cello in the living area, right? We'd love to hear you play. Your mother says you're quite good."

Erin shifted in her seat. "I was thinking we might return the cello. I haven't opened it since I arrived, and I'm enjoying the break."

"Okay," Felicity said. "Perhaps we could we hear you play it, just once?"

"It's her birthday," Hank said.

She rolled her eyes but could hardly say no to a woman receiving a single present from her family. Had Claire's birthday ever lacked fanfare, there would be hell to pay.

"Sure," she said. "I also bought you a little something."

Felicity opened the MAC gift certificate. "How extravagant!"

"I thought you might like it. It's something my mom likes . . . to do on special occasions." That was a flat-out lie, but Erin couldn't admit Claire enjoyed spa days monthly. She already felt guilty Felicity had spent hundreds of dollars on an unsightly uniform Erin had no desire to wear.

After breakfast, Erin tuned the cello, warmed up, and played the second movement of Debussy's sonata. Her phrasing felt cold, as if she were returning to an unwelcoming house. She pulled the bow over the strings—it was a fine instrument—and swayed a bit in her seat, but she felt nothing.

Cello really wasn't her thing. She loved listening—god, she loved listening! Claire had bought four Yo-Yo Ma albums to entice Erin to play, and she loved them; Yo-Yo Ma's music was gorgeous.

But Erin was not Yo-Yo Ma. Her heart didn't belong to the cello.

Cello hadn't come easily to her, but she did it, because— again, she needed to be a well-rounded person. At eleven, she'd swapped her guitar for intensive cello lessons to close in on her peers.

Her heart wasn't in the music today. It never had been. She couldn't compel herself to work hard at it anymore, either.

Erin finished her piece with a flourish and felt only relief.

"You found a well-crafted cello," she said to Felicity. "Thank you."

"Thank you, Erin."

As Erin packed up the cello, Hank regaled Hamish with a story about Mrs. Wellman, whose cracked foundation he'd finally fixed the previous day, and then everyone moved outside.

Hamish engaged the garage door to reveal Felicity's new bicycle and everyone yelled, "Happy birthday!"

Felicity hugged everyone before strapping on her helmet. "Maybe a wee spin."

The woman had no jacket . . . but away she went.

"Sweet as," Pippa said.

Hamish said, "I'd say she's happy"

"How did she used to get to work?" Erin asked.

"She biked. But this is the bike she wanted. It's a sweet bike. Light as a feather, carbon fiber. Twenty-two speeds. Took her ages to decide what she wanted. Been in the garage for a week, so she waited patiently!"

"Where's she headed?" Erin asked.

"Probably out to the wop wops and back." Hamish registered Erin's confusion. "How do I say it? Way out of the city. Middle of nowhere. Can't see one house from another. The wop wops."

"It's an affectionate term," Hank said.

Pippa giggled. "Hank lives in the wop wops."

"And you make an appearance for birthdays?" Erin said.

He shrugged. "I'm considering changing my surname to Wakefield. They're my second family, so I had to come 'round for birthday hugs."

His crooked grin forced something in Erin's chest to swell.

"What's the plan when she gets back?" Erin asked.

"Special pudding after tea tonight," Hamish said.

A bunch of kids on bikes came up the driveway. "Keen to play?" one asked Pippa.

"Yes!"

Hamish held out his arm. "Your uniform clean?"

"Yes," Pippa said.

"Bed made?"

"Yes."

"Room tidied?"

Pippa hesitated. "My things are tidied."

"Cleared for takeoff," Hamish said.

Pippa hopped onto her bike and sped down the driveway. "Birthday tea at half six!" Hamish yelled.

Erin wondered where they were going, how Pippa would eat lunch, and what the gang of young cyclists could do for nine hours.

Leaving Hank and Hamish in the driveway, she retreated to tidy her half of the bedroom and text her new friends that she was free today after all. Everyone was already out for the day, but every single one of them invited her to a party at Satellite Club that night.

Jade: Happy to give you a lift, if you need.
Erin: Yes, please!
Jade: I probably can't hang much once we get there.
Jade: I have a thing. Not really a date, but . . .
Erin: But WHAT?
Jade: A crush? A longing?
Jade: I am seriously grinning as I type that.
Jade: I don't want to say anything that might jinx it.
Erin: Been there, done that.
Jade: Pick you up at half eight?
Erin: Sounds good.

She had until 8:30. The idea of going to a party turned her stomach, but at least she knew Claire and Mitchell wouldn't be at her throat the morning after.

BEFORE SHE DRESSED FOR HER DATE
BEFORE SHE DRESSED FOR HER DATE

Late in the morning of her seventeenth birthday, Erin arrived home to hear her mother screaming in the kitchen, "Valentina is literally airing our dirty laundry for the whole world to see."

Living with two lawyers made for constant arguments.

"Claire," Mitchell said. "It is obviously clean laundry. And I don't know why you are so bent out of shape about this."

"It is embarrassing. It is rude. It looks like we live in the ghetto."

In the backyard, Erin spied four lines stretched from the deck to the back fence. Valentina was an artist in many ways, so the family's clothes hung in chromatic order, from Claire's white lacy thongs fluttering near the porch through a laundry ombre ending with Mitchell's black business socks near the edges of the yard.

Mitchell said, "Valentina told us to call the dryer repairman, and you didn't do it."

"You didn't do it either." Claire spied Erin sneaking in the back door. "We'll get to you in a minute."

"We discussed it, you put it in your calendar, and it didn't happen." Mitchell said to Erin: "And because Valentina is responsible to the nth degree—and has been for the last eight years—she washed all our laundry. She returned to her house for laundry line and clothespins and hung everything outside to dry."

"My panties are on the line out there," Claire said.

"So bring your panties in," Erin said.

Claire crossed her arms. "They're not dry yet."

Mitchell sat at the long kitchen table with his open briefcase and a plate of carnitas, one of Valentina's best dishes. As usual, he ate left-handed with his legal pad pushed far to the right to thwart drips of salsa otherwise destined for his casework.

He squeezed lime juice onto his carnitas. "Would you have preferred she not do the wash?"

"You are insufferable. Let's focus on the other mess." Claire turned to her daughter. "Why the hell are you half-naked all over the Internet this morning?"

Erin steeled herself. "I got drunk."

"That is obvious, to me and everyone else with a phone."

"Let me explain."

"This could jeopardize your whole future, Erin," Claire said. "Everything we have worked so hard for."

"No one tagged me in the video," Erin said.

"Yet."

"Well, let's lay it all on the line, Mom. I was drinking last night—"

"At a party, which was supposed to be a sleepover with one friend."

"Not my fault," Erin said.

"Lalitha just accidentally invited a few hundred friends to the sleepover? And just happened to have alcohol?"

Go big or go home. Erin blurted, "I'm off the swim team."

Mitchell said, "They can't kick you off without a formal hearing. We'll fix it. Public drunkenness isn't the only logical cause of this."

Erin bit her lip to stave off tears as she told them (nearly) everything.

"*The* Quigleys?" her dad asked.

"Yes. They moved here from L.A."

"They swim fly," Mitchell said.

"Yeah."

"At Nationals."

"Yeah."

"Oh, shit," Claire said. She walked fast circles around the island, her stare vacillating between ceiling and floor, repeating the phrase, "Shit, shit, shit." *Pace, pace.* "We'll get you into a second orchestra." *Pace, pace.* "I'll demand Principal Drouin add more college courses to your schedule next year. We will find something unique that will make Columbia want you."

"I know we will," Erin said. "Look, that's why I was drinking. That's why I was upset. You're having a shitty day. This is my third one in a row. With bonus birthday goodness. I would really, really feel better if I could have my present now."

Mitchell and Claire exchanged a glance.

Mitchell said, "The limo and restaurant are already booked. We have the concert tickets."

Claire pursed her lips. "Fine. You can go, but only because we already shelled out the money. And because Ben should not be punished for your bad decisions. When you get home tonight, you're grounded."

"I know," Erin said.

"Three months!" Claire said.

She didn't protest. Her grounding wouldn't last; it never did. In a few days, her parents would tire of hauling her around. She could wait it out.

"'Thank you for letting us go tonight, Mom,'" Claire said expectantly.

"Thanks," Erin said. She waited a beat. "Um, when I said present, I was talking about the other one. Grandma Tea's ring?"

Claire pursed her lips again.

"Mom?"

"We agreed the date in the city would be your present."

Erin tried to regulate her breathing. "Right, yes. But the ring was from Grandma Tea. And Grampa. For my seventeenth birthday. They promised it for years. Even after she died, that was the plan. Grampa promised me again last year."

Claire said, "When your Grampa died, the ring became mine."

"Are you kidding me with this?" Erin looked at Mitchell, who was suddenly very interested in his carnitas. "Dad, you can't let her do this."

He wiped his hands on his chinos. "Legally, the ring is your mother's."

Erin's voice quivered. "Don't lawyer me on this! I know I made a mistake. I told you why I was drinking."

"Erin, your father and I agreed after your Grampa died that I would be keeping the ring."

Grandma Tea had been Erin's favorite person and, for a time, her best friend. They understood each other in ways no one else did. When Tea died, it broke Erin's heart, but she'd held onto the knowledge that a tiny piece of Tea would come back to her when she turned seventeen. "You've known you weren't giving it to me for four months and didn't tell me?"

"There was never a good time."

Erin screamed, "I cannot believe you!"

"Don't do anything to jeopardize your actual present," Claire warned.

Erin was largely unsuccessful at stemming the flow of tears.

"It's not even your style," Erin said.

Claire crossed her arms. "It isn't, but I might wear it sometime, and people will like to hear I am sentimental about my late mother's jewelry."

"I would wear it every day. I miss Grandma Tea every. Single. Day." Anxiety bubbled in her stomach and tears filled her eyes. "I need to go see Lalitha."

"Grounded," Claire said. "Three months. Let's hope that's long enough to plug the new gap in your résumé."

TWENTY-SIX

True to his word, Hamish served a delicious dessert. Pavlova was a very light meringue cake with fresh fruit garnishing its crusted top. Felicity praised Hamish and Pippa's work before devouring a second slice.

Erin offered birthday wishes one last time before she climbed into Jade's car for the party.

Clad in her new white leather pants and a camisole under a black sweater, Erin listened to a nervous Jade talk about who would be there. Erin preferred to hang outside of parties and people watch; her wallflower routine would be even easier here, where almost no one knew her.

When they emerged from the car, Jade stood before Erin and smiled broadly. "Do I look carefree?"

"Having known you all of five days, I think you are carefree. I'm not sure you can project that with a smile, though."

They walked toward the club.

"Fair point," Jade said. "All right. This will be piss easy."

"Sounds good to me."

Inside the club, Jade disappeared into the mass of people talking loudly and dancing to clamorous music.

Erin grabbed a soda and had no luck finding Ruby, Marama, or Summer. Richard, the guy Jade had warned her about, found her, though.

"Erin, right?" he said.

She nodded.

"From America?" *Americur.* "And you're a swimmer?" *Swimma?*

"I do swim, yes. And you're Richard."

"I am Richard. What's on for tomorrow?"

"Some friends are taking me around."

"I'd be happy to take you around, show you our greatest stuff. Do you surf?"

"I don't."

He beamed. "I am an excellent teacher! Everyone needs to know how to surf. Let's you and me get out on the water this spring, eh? We'll get you a wet suit. Take a lunch with us and make a date of it."

His sparkling blue eyes were mesmerizing. Without Jade's warning, she would have agreed enthusiastically.

"Sorry," she said. "Not for me. I'm trying to settle in right now."

"Not *right now*, right now," he said. "Any time at all. I find America simply intriguing. Tell me, do you go to the prom?"

Junior prom had been one of her best—and last—dates with Ben, an evening she now preferred to forget. She breathed deeply. "I did go to prom, in a gorgeous silver gown."

"And will you go again, or is it a once-in-a-lifetime thing?"

Senior prom could be fun. She and Lalitha would either reenact her birthday date or maintain the swim team seniors' ritual of going as a pack. Even though she was no longer part of the pack.

"Whad'ya say? Will you go again?"

"Probably." At last, Erin spied Marama at the far side of the room and locked eyes with her.

"We could nick out and make a date right now, if you like."

She grinned at him. "I am so sorry, Richard, I see my friend. I should go."

"She'll wait. What say we try rugby? Or traditional New Zealand food? Or bungee? I'd love to introduce you to kiwi life, and you can tell me about America."

Marama steered through the crowd toward them.

"I should go," Erin said.

He wrapped his arm around her waist and pulled her closer. "So nice talking to you!" He kissed her roughly before giving her a little wave.

Erin loathed unwanted physical contact. Why did guys in every culture think that was okay?

"Please tell me you didn't agree to go out with him," Marama said. "He is bad news."

"Yes, I was forewarned."

"Thank god. Get you a beer?"

Erin hesitated. "Actually, Marama, I don't like beer. I've never found an alcohol I actually like."

"Me either, but I like the buzz." Gulping her beer, Marama assessed the room. "I wanted you to meet my climbing friends, but I haven't found anyone. My brother's already half in the bag, so you'll meet him tomorrow. Be nice and loud, would you?"

"Of course."

"Oh! There's someone!" Marama led Erin through the crowd by the hand and stopped so near the music that she had to shout. "This is Gloria. Gloria, Erin. Taking her to Castle Hill tomorrow."

Gloria was tall and athletic with a thick brown ponytail. She and Erin exchanged hellos as Jade arrived and handed Gloria a drink.

"Are you coming?" Erin asked.

Gloria blushed, wide-eyed.

"What's going on, now?" Jade asked.

"Marama is taking me to Castle Hill tomorrow. I asked whether Gloria was coming."

Gloria glanced from Jade to Marama. "I don't think so, no."

"No worries. Another time, maybe," Marama said. "Come on, Erin, let's dance."

The crowd moved casually to what Marama called house music. A tall guy trying to crowd surf from the sofa wound up on his back on the floor.

"And there is my idiot brother," Marama said.

"Charming!" Erin said.

She usually felt like a spectacle on the dance floor, but here everyone paid little attention to anyone not in their immediate vicinity. Erin swayed to the music and swung her arms. Without any liquid courage, it took a while to warm up to the evening, but within the hour, she was moving fast enough to remove her sweater and relax among her new classmates.

TWENTY-SEVEN

Sunday morning, the woodstove was cold, presumably because everyone was leaving for the day: Felicity to netball with friends, Hamish to rugby, and Pippa to a friend's house.

Sunday morning in New Zealand was Saturday afternoon in Wheaton, but she had no time to catch up with Lalitha before Marama picked her up.

Claire pinged Erin with new comments on her essay and demanded revisions before the end of the weekend. Erin promised to work on them after her outing with Marama.

Her phone rang. Claire.

"Hi, Mom."

"Erin, I see you were out last night, and that's okay. Make friends, great. But it feels like you're not taking this seriously. You're going out for the day today. Let's not lose sight of what's important and why you're there. I'm worried."

"Mom, I promise I'm on track. Swimming is going great. My coach thinks I'll do well at Nationals. I don't have any people here. I'm trying to connect."

"Just remember this is temporary. Med school is forever."

"I know. Mom, I have to go."

Erin ended the call to find Pippa staring at her.

"Do you not get along with your mother?"

Erin sighed. "I do. She just has a lot of advice for me, and right now I'm not very interested in taking it."

Instead, Erin was taking advice from Pippa: "Don't wear jandals."

"Don't wear what?" Erin asked.

"Your shoes. Jandals."

Erin regarded her Reef flip-flops. "I can hike in these just fine."

"Maybe in the States, but not here. Take tramping boots. Or something else."

Pippa was ten, but she was kiwi. And what the hell did Erin know about *tramping*? She laced her boots, which looked ridiculous with shorts, and threw her Reefs into her bag.

Felicity let Marama in and said to Erin, "You have a hat, yes?"

Erin didn't.

"Where are you headed today?" Felicity asked.

"Castle Hill," Marama said.

"I'll get mine." Felicity disappeared into the other side of the house and returned a minute later with a floppy red hat. "We'll buy you one next time we're out."

Erin said good-bye to her host family and followed Marama outside.

Marama opened her car door. "These are Roa and Hank."

Hank, again. "Hey," Erin said.

"Kia Ora!" Hank said.

"I called shotgun," Roa said.

"Because the git was totally pissed last night," Marama said.

Roa pulled his glasses over his eyes. "I fink I'm still pissed."

"Everyone buckled?" Marama asked. Cranking up the music, she pulled out of the driveway.

Hank sang along to music Erin hadn't heard before. His voice was surprisingly soulful.

"Can we turn it down a bit?" Roa asked.

"Hungover is no way to go through life," Marama said as she took a turn much faster than necessary.

"Careful," Roa said. "With involuntary vomit spews all your secrets."

Marama said, "Shut it."

A few kilometers from the house, Christchurch's flat edges gave way to brown hills, which Marama promised would be green soon enough. She drove like a demon, speeding between and around mountains as they gained elevation. Around bends, through switchbacks, and over bridges, the narrow road was a nauseating carnival ride over rivers.

Marama and Roa bickered about music, and Hank leaned between the front seats to interject his preferences before they settled on a playlist.

Erin pictured herself plummeting to hell between a gulch's trees. "Too close!" she shouted, leaning into the middle of the car when Marama was right at the edge of the road.

"Sorry, mate," Marama said. "Forgot you're not kiwi."

To her credit, Marama slowed a bit and moved closer to the middle of the road. "I've done this all my life."

Erin said, "I haven't."

"Are you scared of heights?"

"I'm not. It's the journey to the chasm below that terrifies me."

"I promise to be careful with you. I've done this heaps of times. If it were snowing, we might have an issue, but this is perfect driving weather."

Erin said, "Snow isn't that hard. You just have to become one with the car. Feel whether you have traction and you're fine."

Marama laughed. "Last month, the entire city shut down on account of two centimeters of snow."

"Skied Coronet over the hols," Roa said. "You been, mate?"

"That's the one where I went arse over tit on day one," Hank said. "Haven't been since."

"Next winter, you and me."

"And?" Marama said.

"Aye, come along," Hank said.

Erin tried to ignore the constant stream of conversation between these three. She pinched the skin between her thumb and forefinger, trying desperately to distract herself from the acid creeping up her throat.

Were kiwis immune to the rocking?

Another switchback, followed by a dip in the road, and she couldn't hold it in anymore. "I need to stop."

"Nowhere to stop," Hank said. From between his feet, he withdrew a Hokey Pokey container. "Use this if you need to spew."

Marama slowed a bit. A very little bit.

Hank rolled down his window. "Crack your window. Focus on the horizon. Stare at the thing furthest from us. It helps."

Had anything remained on the horizon more than seven seconds, his advice may have helped. Defeated, she opened the empty ice cream container and counted.

Marama drove on as Erin spewed toast, jam, and coffee. She'd liked it better going down.

Hank rubbed her shoulder before securing the lid of the

ice cream container. Without tearing his eyes from the horizon, he presented a second, empty ice cream container.

Marama said, "We keep empty punnets in the car for just such occasions. How you feeling, Hank?"

"Sweet as."

"How much longer?" Erin asked.

"Not long now," Marama said.

Erin focused on gray shrubbery in the distance. As they drew nearer, she shifted her gaze to a peak in the distance. When they passed the shrubbery, she realized it was actually hundreds and hundreds of sheep.

Five minutes after the sheep, she used a second ice cream punnet.

TWENTY-EIGHT

Marama turned into a pebbly parking lot across a green valley from a huge herd of cattle. They were surrounded by mountains when Marama stopped at last.

"There we go." Hank pointed toward a hill cluttered with rocks and pebbles. It looked as if a medieval castle was trapped inside the hill, desperately trying to emerge.

The hill was winning.

"They're limestone. Best playground we've got!" Hank said.

Erin recognized Castle Hill from Good-Time Girl's feed but couldn't remember when she'd posted it.

"Have a bit of water." Roa handed Erin a water bottle with the words ALL BLACKS on it.

She swished a mouthful and spat into the dirt beside their car. Erin threw out her punnets but the scent lingered. She dreaded another drive through the mountains.

"You protected?" Marama asked.

Erin wasn't sure.

"Slip, slop, slap, wrap?"

"I really have no idea what you're talking about," Erin said.

Marama tugged her shirt sleeve. "Slip on a shirt. Slop on some lotion." She handed Erin sunblock and tugged on her own hat. "Slap on a hat. Wrap your eyes with glasses. Basic sun safety."

Erin slopped on sunblock, pulled on Felicity's hat, and joined everyone else at the trunk.

Marama handed her two bags. "Provisions."

Hank said, "What are you, a 38? 39?"

Again, she had no idea.

"Your feet?"

"Oh. Sometimes 39. Sometimes 40."

Hank pulled out several pairs of tiny shoes. "My whole family climbs. We have just about any size you could need."

None of Hank's shoes looked remotely close to an eight and a half. He stuffed five pairs into a giant bag, slammed the trunk closed, and started walking. Marama and Hank each carried enormous sponge mats, folded in half and strapped onto their backs. Everyone but Erin stored their keys on metal rings attached to their belt loops. Hank also used one for his water bottle.

On their way up the well-trodden path, Hank pointed out recent climbing spots and Erin realized the pebbles she'd seen from the car were half her height. She compared the rocks near the path to others scattered around the hill. Some could be taller than she.

This could be fun.

Marama chose a steep path on the left and kept trekking. "You okay, Erin?"

"I'm fine." Erin said a silent thank-you to Pippa; hiking in flip-flops would have been murderous. Her thighs already ached.

Boulders, many of which were twice Erin's height, rose all around as they neared the middle of the "castle." Rock formations suggested a giant toddler had been playing with rocks when called away for lunch.

Marama stopped abruptly. "How's this?"

Erin dropped her bags and sat. "Looks great."

She turned back to see the valley rolling along, including a small pond around which cattle grazed. From here, the cattle looked like dots.

So much of New Zealand was about perspective, she realized.

Roa investigated nearby boulders and dropped his gear. "Yeah, this'll do."

———

Hank beckoned Erin to investigate the shoes. They smelled worse than Ben's basketball bag, but love is blind. And anosmic. Erin may have, on occasion, let her swimsuit and towel fester in a sealed plastic bag for an entire weekend. But that was her own gross nastiness.

Hank's rock-climbing shoe collection harbored some stranger's bacteria. In a sunny patch, Erin held each shoe up to her left foot, in turn.

"They're all too small."

At the base of the lumpiest boulder, Marama situated her sponge mat and forced on her own shoes. "Supposed to be small. They become one with your foot. See?" She thrust her shoed foot forward, and it was thirty percent smaller than her bare foot. It looked like a child's foot on the end of her leg.

Erin tried the bright orange shoes—the biggest ones—first and had trouble squeezing her foot into them. "It's a little snug."

Marama said, "Go for the next size down. They should hurt a little."

Erin believed shoes should fit comfortably unless they were quite fancy or red-soled. Climbing shoes were neither.

The second-largest pair was nearly painful when she stood up, and Marama couldn't coerce her into the third pair.

Erin walked like a bowlegged farmer eager to take a dump. "I gotta sit."

Marama ran her fingers over several rough patches of stone and dug her fingertips into a ridge. "See, you just want anywhere you can find a little purchase. See this?" She cupped the edge of the boulder and shifted her weight onto her right foot. Lifting her left leg near her hip, she dug her tiny shoe into one of the little ridges. "Up we go."

Up she went.

Marama scrambled across the enormous rock. Left and right, then up and down and up again, as if the rock had steps.

And Erin couldn't even stand.

"You ready?" Roa asked.

"Hardly."

Roa said, "Oh, sorry. Take off your shoes and check out the rock."

Barefoot, Erin ran her fingers over the flat rock. There was nothing to hold onto.

"May I?" Roa grabbed Erin's hand and guided her fingers over a ridge. "See that? You dig your fingers in for a good hold. This ridge near the bottom is perfect for your shoes."

"They're too small."

"You'll see. Look, just trust me. Just for today, trust me."

"You just admitted you're still drunk from last night. Why should I trust you?"

Hank jumped between them. "Because it's fun. Trust *me*."

"Or me," Marama said.

Erin squeezed back into the shoes and waddled to the rock. She fondled it but couldn't grab hold of anything. Hank scrambled up and down an adjacent face while Erin searched for something—anything—to hold onto. Defeated, she peeled off the shoes to placate her aching feet.

"It's okay. Have another go in a few minutes," Marama said.

Roa climbed until his feet were at Erin's eye level, stretched his arm out over the rock, and reached for something Erin couldn't see. He missed and landed on the mat.

"Crash mat."

Erin said, "I see that."

Hank scrambled up the rock, stood on top, and climbed down. He started on one side and scrambled across it, about two inches above the ground, all the way across—a good fifteen feet—without touching the ground.

"You're like Spiderman," Erin said.

He guffawed. All his laughs were guffaws. "That was my dearest wish as a boy. My mum sewed black ribbony stuff all over my favorite red shirt and I loved it. Wore it every day, even after I turned five. Most days I snuck it to school under my uniform."

"That's sweet."

Hank scrambled around the back of the rock and reappeared on top a minute later.

Erin crammed her feet into the orange shoes again, grabbed a few pieces of the boulder, and stuck her toe in a nook. Her right foot had nowhere to go.

Roa said, "Move your foot up and down until your shoe can grab onto something."

She jabbed her foot into what looked like another nook, shifted her weight, and fell off the rock. Seven times.

Marama said, "You know, Erin, this is advanced stuff. I know a better boulder for you."

"I can get it," Erin said before failing five more times.

Marama grabbed a crash mat. "Let's just take a look."

Leaving the guys and their gear, Marama led Erin through a narrow opening. They wended around enormous boulders until Marama stopped abruptly. "Whoops! Occupied."

Erin expected a couple making out but instead saw kids taking rock climbing instructions.

Marama trekked onward, as kids smaller than Pippa scrambled up the boulder even faster than Hank had. One kid actually crossed his arms and said, "Too easy."

Marama shouted, "Erin! Found one!"

Erin walked around the rock but Marama was nowhere to be found. She squeezed between two boulders and walked in circles, but still no Marama. Erin was a rat trapped in a maze. "Marama?"

Marama called again. Erin followed her voice until their bizarre game of Marco-Polo ended next to a rock that had been too manhandled by the mythical giant toddler: deep holes scarred its sides, and thick ridges ran around the base.

"This'll work for you."

Erin said, "We don't have to climb here. I'm sure I can handle more advanced stuff."

"Nah. It's fine. There are a couple rocks out here that will work for you."

Erin whispered, "I don't need to start on the kiddie rock."

"Erin, you have to start somewhere. It's like driving. Do you think a fifteen-year-old is an idiot because he doesn't know the wipers from the signals? Start in your tramping boots."

Too easily, Erin grabbed nubs of rock and stuck her feet into enormous holes. She was on top of the rock in no time. "It's cheating. It's practically a ladder."

Marama shouted, "You can't have it both ways. You climbed it! Well done. Now come back down."

Erin took approximately the same route and stood next to her friend. "It's easier in boots."

"This time, use whatever holds you want for your feet, but don't use anything bigger than a golf ball for your hands."

That left almost nothing.

Marama said, "You can do it. Just think about it. Anything concave is fair game for hands."

Three feet above the ground, Erin couldn't find anything concave for her hands. She fondled the rock again with her right hand.

Marama said, "Other way."

"I'm halfway up already."

"I mean, try with your left hand, to the left."

Erin reached straight left and found nothing but flat. Well, a really good nubbin, that was almost baseball sized, but nothing to stick her fingers into. "There's nothing there."

"Breathe. Now, reach all the way up as high as you can."

"There's nothing there, Marama."

"Right. Without bending your arm, walk your fingers down the rock to your knee."

Feeling ridiculous, Erin did it.

"That's your arc, right there. Instead of reaching straight out, test everything inside that semicircle."

Just above her head, slightly to the left, Erin found a divot big enough for three fingers.

"There ya go. Now, I want you to pull left. If you're pulling left, where should your weight be?"

Going up with her left leg, her weight should start on her right. She braced between the right leg and left arm. Briefly.

She pulled her body away from the rock so she could look below her. In a split second, Erin was on the ground, Marama's hand on her lower back.

"You okay?"

"Did you try to catch me?"

"I was spotting you. Are you all right?"

"Fine, thanks."

"Whenever your feet are above waist level, I'm spotting you. We have to watch out for each other, you know?"

Erin nodded, though watching out for her friends back home had never been so literal. She nodded again. "Will you show me how so I can return the favor?"

TWENTY-NINE

Erin studied the rock again. Her next foot hold was left of where she'd been. She climbed back up to where she'd been, used the hold, and five moves later, she was on top of the boulder again.

"Nice. Have another go?"

Erin climbed down more quickly. "Okay, what's the new rule?"

Marama smiled. "Nothing smaller than a golf ball for your hands, and no hole bigger than a two-dollar piece for your feet."

Holy crap. Erin stared at the boulder, studying its texture. The pockmarks were more nuanced than they had seemed at first glance. She climbed three-quarters of the way up and stalled.

"Look at your feet."

If she looked down, she'd flatten Marama. She hugged the rock and felt around with her feet. Nothing. Her boots were too big.

She climbed down, stuffed her feet into the orange shoes, and headed back to the rock. Her feet whimpered, but the shoes were a miracle; she had one giant toe that found lots of little ledges on the way up.

On top of the boulder, she towered over Marama, and drank in the view. Hundreds of boulders stood around them, waiting to be discovered. All alone out here—up here—Erin wanted to climb them all. Maybe Claire was right: when Erin really wanted something, she was relentless.

————

Two hours and five boulders later, Marama and Erin met up with the guys.

"Show us what you got," Roa said.

Erin slowly made her way up the boulder in front of her.

Hank would not shut up about hand holds and footholds and shifting her weight. Erin made a mental note to puke on him in the car. Seriously. Who was Hank, a high school dropout, to give her advice on rock climbing, life, or anything else?

"Right on," Hank said when she was back on the ground.

"Training her up!" Marama said. "Lunch break first."

"We ate an hour ago," Roa said before gripping the boulder.

"Could've waited for us."

"Had no idea when you were coming back, did we?" Roa said.

Marama pawed through the few remaining sandwiches. "Tangaroa. You ate all my chicken salad?"

"It was great, mate," Hank said.

"Of course it was." Marama yelled at her brother, who was climbing briskly, "Yo! Pig! Down here!"

Roa jumped down. "What do you want me to say?"

"Mum made that chicken salad for me. This morning, when we talked about lunch, I said I wanted chicken salad. You wanted BLTs. I want my chicken salad sandwich."

"I don't give two-thirds of five-eighths of fuck all." Roa started climbing again. "I packed it. I ate it."

Hank raised his hands to spot Roa. "Sorry, Marama. I didn't know."

"Yeah." She took the lunch bag several yards away and sat. "Erin? Ham and cheese, vegetarian, or BLT?"

"Ham and cheese."

They sat facing the guys. Marama pulled out three beverages, containers of vegetables, and hummus with pita before devouring her sandwich and lying in the grass with an ALL BLACKS hat over her face.

"Marama?"

"Aye?"

"What's the All Blacks thing?"

She lifted her hat and looked around. "What thing?"

"The words. They're all around. Your All Blacks hat. Your brother's water bottle. There are signs everywhere. What is it?"

Marama returned the hat to her face. "Ah. National rugby team."

"The team is called All Blacks?"

"Aye. Rugby's our national sport."

"I was freaking out. I thought it was some kind of racist thing."

"Oh, country's racist, don't get me wrong. But mostly, kiwis are against the Chinese."

Erin talked to Marama's hat face. "Why against the Chinese?"

"They're 'taking over.' For every one Chinese we let in, we also have to let in his partner, their parents, and their kids. So, you let in one, and you get at least five more. Some people think they'll control most of our government soon enough. There are as many of them as there are of us. Māori, I mean."

Hank's accent was decidedly kiwi, but Erin wondered how long he'd lived in New Zealand. And who in this country resented him for being Chinese.

She dipped carrots in the hummus, which struck the perfect balance between creamy and coarse.

Hank climbed between two boulders, and Erin realized he'd forged those muscles on a rock face. His climbing was deliberate, like a cat stalking its prey. Grasping a tiny button of rock, he pulled himself toward the top. Hank's climbing was artful. Careful. Sexy. She imagined him without those tattoos.

When Hank slipped off the rock, Erin realized she had been staring, slack-jawed. She was relieved Marama hadn't caught her. Lifting his T-shirt to wipe his brow, Hank revealed a rock-hard stomach.

To shake free of those thoughts, Erin studied the azure sky and ate hummus. She wanted to run her fingers over Hank's arms. And his six-pack. Or eight-pack, she couldn't be sure.

Vowing to swear off guys and the inevitable pain of relationships, Erin focused on the moment. She was glad she'd come. Plopped in the middle of boulders, the afternoon was quiet.

A bird overhead cut the silence and Erin realized she'd finished the hummus.

"Good, eh?" Marama said, sitting up.

"Yeah. Thanks."

"Mum's chicken salad is really the best."

"My lunch was great, I promise."

"Roa is a complete ass. Do you have brothers?"

"Nope. I'm an only."

"That sucks," Marama said.

Hank jogged toward them.

"I think being an only is kind of cool," Erin said.

"I guess. We're five, so I don't have a clue how it is to be just one."

Hank grabbed an apple. "Can I have this?"

Erin caught a whiff of onion and flinched.

"What?"

"I just—wow. Did you eat a raw onion?"

"He had Mum's chicken salad," Marama said.

"Potent," Erin said.

Hank cocked his head to the side. "Really sorry about your sandwich, Marama."

"Yeah." Marama pointed at Hank with her thumb. "Thanks to this fuckwit, I almost lost one of my brothers."

Hank's face fell. "Could we skip this?"

"Yeah, no," Marama said. "Once, soon after Roa had gotten over mono, Hank convinced him that a hundred-kilometer race was within his grasp. Tangaroa had to be medevac'd off of Arthur's Pass."

Erin said, "You did not."

"Roa loves cycling. And, in my defense, I knew he would regret missing the race," Hank said. "I want everyone to have the maximally enjoyable experience."

"Bite your bum. You dared him," Marama said.

"And I've been apologizing every day since. I will never forgive myself," Hank said before returning to his boulder.

Once Hank was out of earshot, Marama said, "We give him hell for it, but most everyone was pissed at Roa. Hank's a

149

work-hard-play-harder type of bloke. He said he believed in Roa. And when Hank says he believes in you, there's something about it that makes you want to make it happen, you know?"

Erin's cheeks flushed. "I wouldn't really know. I just met him." She packed what was left of the food. Thinking about the return trip made her regret scarfing down the hummus. She needed her lunch to settle before reliving those hairpin turns. "More climbing?"

"Really? You're into it?"

"I am. I could stay here all day."

THIRTY

Erin slid into her dining room seat at precisely 6:30. Famished, she buttered a slice of warm bread and dug into Felicity's shepherd's pie.

"Squeaky cheese, too!" Pippa said, her mouth full of food.

Felicity pointed to a browned slab of cheese. "Halloumi. Squeeze a bit of lemon on and try it."

Dubious but polite, Erin pierced a slice and added lemon. The warm cheese squeaked as she chewed it. Soft and mild, it had a fibrous texture. She took a second bite.

"How was your day, then?" Felicity asked.

Effusive, Erin shared her impressions of Castle Hill and bouldering.

"Did you crawl into the tiny space under the tilted boulder?" Pippa asked.

"I did not crawl under anything."

"Dad always dares me, but I wouldn't want to get stuck under in an earthquake."

"No kidding," Erin said. "I also saw Marama's brother, Roa, do some amazing stuff. He and Hank are like spiders; they can cling to anything."

"Hank was there?" Felicity feigned disinterest, but her tone suggested Hank's presence was of paramount interest.

"He was. He's really good."

"Explains why he canceled my lesson today," Pippa said.

"Oh, Pippa, I'm sorry," Erin said.

Felicity said, "It's not you. That is a boy who chases his heart."

"One of the best blokes I know," Hamish said.

Erin couldn't deny her attraction to him, but he had quit school, which was unconscionable. Hank should apply his passion for rock climbing to something important. He needed to grow up.

Erin would have Columbia. She hoped to have Columbia. And she'd be a doctor. She was going places; Hank seemed satisfied staying put.

"Nothing to say, Erin?" Hamish asked. "You don't care for Hank?"

"We don't have much in common. I don't typically care for high school dropouts and I especially don't care for people who try to tell me what to do."

Hamish set his jaw. "Hank isn't a dropout. And neither am I. Don't confuse being overeducated with being smart or kind. Don't imagine a medical degree will make you a good person. I'd choose a good person over a brilliant overeducated arsehole any day."

"Hamish?" Felicity said.

"Excuse me!" He threw his napkin on the table and walked out the front door.

"That's not what I meant," Erin said, though her words had meant little else. "You know that's not what I meant, right, Felicity?"

Pippa's eyes were as big as quarters as Felicity drew and released several deep breaths.

"Here, Erin, school is compulsory only through age sixteen. Hamish and Hank, and our neighbor Dean, and Jade's parents, and my brother Nick? They're not dropouts. And they're some of the best people we know. Our best mates.

"Staying through year thirteen or going on to university provides nothing but more schooling, which is fine if you need it. Medicine is your calling, so of course you'll go to university and medical school. But look at the big picture: our country—any country—needs bus drivers and grocers. I find pleasure in doing good work and coming home. I don't need a big fancy job and a big paycheck, but I need a grocer who ensures my produce is fresh. Pippa needs a bus driver who takes her to school safely. We couldn't function without construction workers. Imagine Christchurch without rubbish collectors."

Erin hadn't thought of that. Everyone she knew in America—everyone!—was trying to get into the best possible college. She'd never considered working straight out of high school. She'd worn Columbia and Harvard onesies before she could walk. College was a given, and she'd always assumed people lacking a degree—cashiers, garbage collectors, bus drivers—had failed at attaining one.

While that assumption may be flawed, she couldn't fathom choosing an unambitious or small life. In fifteen years, she would have the things—her own house, car, medical degree, and respect—that would make her life great.

Great medical school, great job, great life. And great friends, to boot.

BEFORE SHE FACED CLAIRE

BEFORE SHE FACED CLAIRE

The morning of Erin's seventeenth birthday, she found her best friend passed out in a tangerine shirtdress that complemented her deep brown skin and black hair. Reeking of alcohol, Lalitha snored loudly as Erin borrowed clothes from her closet.

Erin showered quickly, taking care to remove the crusty pink vomit adhering to her hair.

When she'd dressed, Erin sat on Lalitha's bed and attempted to wake her gently. Failing that, she shook Lalitha's shoulders.

"You're gonna make me puke again."

Erin sniffled as tears bubbled in her eyes. "I need you to be awake for a second."

Lalitha sobered. "What happened?"

"Claire knows. About the party, about the puke, about me passing out—all of it."

"How?"

"Does it really matter?" Erin shouted.

Lalitha covered her ears.

Erin gently pried one of Lalitha's hands off her ear. "I'm

grounded, and I have to go home right now. I just wanted you to know."

"Bit of advice?" Lalitha asked.

"Do yourself a favor: drink lots of water and take two Ibuprofen."

"No." Lalitha looked Erin in the eye. "Advice for you: tell them today about the Quigleys and swimming. And any other bad news you've got. They'll never be more pissed than they are right now, so go big or go home."

"Thanks. When are your parents home?"

"Tuesday. You go. I'll handle the mess once I can stand up straight. Thank god it's Sunday. I should not get into a pool right now."

THIRTY-ONE

With only two swim meets before Nationals, Percy was eager to pit Erin against other teams.

Her first kiwi swim meet involved no pep talks, no all-hands-in for a cheer, and no rituals. Unlike crowds in Wheaton, where parents screamed instructions from the bleachers, the riotous kiwi crowd quieted during races.

During Erin's first-ever swim meet, she'd heard Claire shouting every time she came up for breath. Today, she anticipated utter decorum from the Wakefields. Felicity, Hamish, and Pippa missed her first race, but Pippa gave two thumbs up when Erin climbed onto the blocks for her second.

Staring at her toes, she was in her element. At the gun, she dove into the water and pushed.

Dolphin, dolphin, dolphin, dolphin, breathe, breathe, breathe, breathe. Flip.

Breathe, breathe, breathe, breathe, breathe, done.

Percy had been right: she won all three races easily.

Erin's teammates congratulated her briefly before turning their collective attention to plans for the weekend.

Erin fielded several invitations—for surfing, for Castle Hill, for the beach—and chose mountain biking with Jade. A minute before the relay began, Erin's teammates offered trail advice and debated the best views in Christchurch.

For a few minutes, Erin and her three relay partners focused intently on the race, in which they set a record, but relaxed completely afterward. The ebb and flow was a stark contrast to the hours-long adrenaline-filled meets of Erin's past.

The crowd seeped from the bleachers and Pippa ran to Erin, wrapping her in a hug. Pippa's T-shirt was soaked when she let go. "That looked like fun! Can you teach me how to do the butterfly?"

"I'm sure I can," Erin said.

Pippa flipped open her steno pad. Upside down, Erin read her scrawl: *Swim with Erin. Learn the butterfly.*

"I don't think we'll forget, Pip," Erin said.

"We haven't got 'round to black holes again. I want to be sure we do eventually."

Felicity said, "That was amazing."

"You must be stuffed after all that," Hamish said.

Erin's brow furrowed.

"Knackered? Buggered? Exhausted?"

"Oh! I'm feeling okay, actually."

Felicity said, "Go and have a quick change, and we'll head home for tea."

Most of Erin's friends were in the spa, but tea sounded like just the thing.

THIRTY-TWO

Three weeks into her study abroad, Erin accidentally told Claire she was taking art. She woke the next morning to a barrage of texts.

> **Claire:** I've been thinking about your elective art class.
> **Claire:** We both know you're not an artist.
> **Claire:** Would that school let you use the art period on something more important? I think you could compose music for cello to counterbalance the lesser symphony experience.
> **Claire:** An immersive project like music composition would look really good: shows initiative, skills, and perseverance.
> **Claire:** Let me know if I need to lean on the administration to make this happen.

That morning in art class, Erin's landscape looked like child's play, literally. She was working from a gorgeous photograph of an ocean storm, but hers looked like blue blobs beneath a wet, gray mess. No nuance. Five years without art had rendered her embarrassingly inexperienced.

Erin maneuvered herself between her painting and Mrs. Campbell, who was critiquing the class.

"I'd like to see your work, Erin."

She blushed. "It's just that . . . it's very bad. I'm sorry."

Mrs. Campbell studied it closely. "For a first year, I'd say it's pretty good. Use the watercolor pencils to draw in the fine details, then flood it with water to get a delicate watercolor look."

"Thanks. And I'm sorry."

"You are *learning*."

Erin nodded. With blue and white pencils, she differentiated her painted sea before adding water.

The ocean moved. That changed everything.

She kept working.

BEFORE SHE WOKE LALITHA

BEFORE SHE WOKE LALITHA

On her seventeenth birthday, Erin awoke on Lalitha's bath-room floor, smelling of vomit and feeling as if she'd swal-lowed a cat.

Still dizzy, she leaned against Lalitha's bathtub and turned her phone back on. She ignored her mother's voice mails but read her texts.

> **Claire:** I WOKE UP TO A CALL FROM THE PTA PRESIDENT TELLING ME YOU PASSED OUT DRUNK LAST NIGHT.
>
> **Claire:** THEN I SAW A VIDEO OF YOU RUNNING AROUND HALF NAKED.
>
> **Claire:** WHAT THE HELL?
>
> **Claire:** WERE YOU EVEN AT LALITHA'S HOUSE?
>
> **Claire:** GET YOUR ASS HOME IMMEDIATELY.
>
> **Claire:** WHERE THE HELL ARE YOU?

Still disoriented, Erin sent a single text.

> **Erin:** I am fine and will head straight home.
>
> **Claire:** ENJOY YOUR DRIVE IN THE FIAT. IT'S YOUR LAST ONE.

THIRTY-THREE

Saturday morning, Jade arrived in a vintage Honda. As promised, she'd borrowed her cousin's bike and loaded it next to her own on the back rack.

"Hop in!"

Erin said, "I thought we were biking."

"We're driving to the Port Hills first."

Erin hadn't brought a Hokey Pokey container. "You said no windy roads."

"Relax. We're going partway up. No mountains. No real switchbacks."

To a girl from the flat Midwest, the Port Hills were mountains. And while they paled in comparison to the Southern Alps, they were plenty big enough to nauseate her during the drive.

"Under the seat," Jade said.

Erin withdrew a punnet—cookies n' cream—and held it in her lap. "Well, I'm ready."

"Sweet as."

"You're always saying that. I get what it means, but where did it come from? Sweet as what? Sweet as pie? Sweet as a peach? There has to be something there."

Jade considered that as they drove into hills that were actually mountains. The relatively flat city stretched below them, from the foot of the hills clear out to the ocean. Beyond the ocean were more mountains, where New Zealand curved in on itself. From a distance, Christchurch was picturesque. Gorgeous.

Near the top of the hill, Jade said, "I think we mean 'sweet as can be.' Or 'big as can be.' 'Clever as can be.'"

"See? Now that makes sense."

Jade parked on a residential street. "Here we go."

Erin shifted her weight awkwardly while Jade unloaded the bikes and strapped on a huge backpack.

"Was I supposed to bring something? I didn't bring anything."

"Nope. I've got you covered."

"Okay." *Sweet as can be.*

Jade adjusted the bike seat and threw Erin a helmet from the back seat of the car. On foot, she led Erin across brown grass that probably belonged to someone's farm, transferred the bikes over a gate, and double-checked their gear.

Jade said, "The Port Hills live between Christchurch and Lyttelton, a port city. The view from the top is spectacular. You want to lead?"

"I hardly know where we're going."

"There's a path."

"I might be slow."

"All right then. Holler if you want me to stop." Jade threw her leg over the bike and clipped her shoes into its pedals. Erin cringed. If Jade crashed, her bike would stay attached all the way down the hill.

Jade was off, and Erin tried to keep up. Halfway up—or what she believed was halfway up—Erin panted, standing on the pedals so her body weight kept her going. Jade zoomed ahead.

Holy crap.

Jade crested the hill and disappeared. There was water over there, but how far down? *She probably stopped just on the other side of the crest, right?*

Erin hoped she'd stopped. This was real work. Way harder than a couple miles in a pool. Harder than swimming in the ocean. Erin felt out of shape, and she was in great shape. Then again, she had never biked in the mountains before, let alone up and down them. Swimming and biking must be two different shapes.

Her thighs screamed as she crested a mini-hill—where Jade hadn't stopped. Erin couldn't even coast to follow her. The trail dipped briefly before climbing again.

Erin stopped long enough to rip off her windbreaker and fleece, then followed for another twenty minutes, catching a glimpse of Jade each time she crested a hill. Eventually, she fell so far behind that she caught only a glance of Jade's helmet cresting a peak in the distance.

She didn't think she'd make it, but when she crested that peak Jade was sitting comfortably on the ground, digging through her backpack.

"Hi! Have a sit." Jade was breathing normally.

Erin lay in the grass near Jade to catch her breath. She was beat. New Zealand was winning. Erin stared at the cloudless blue sky, which went on forever. Maybe because the houses were short, or maybe because she was on a mountain top, the sky felt different. Bigger.

"We can't bike down the other side. No way I'd make it back up here."

"Bit dramatic, aren't you?" Jade said. "You're the fastest girl in the pool!"

Erin closed her eyes. "I was utterly unprepared for this. You are a beast! Give me a week or two and I'll be able to keep up."

"Right on." Jade produced three sandwiches and handfuls of chocolates. "Tried pineapple lumps?"

Erin shook her head.

"They aren't really pineapple. It's like a chocolate fish, but pineapple-y."

Erin hadn't tasted chocolate fish either, but any chocolate sounded appetizing. She bit a pineapple lump in half, but the chocolate coating was waxy, and the filling was . . . not pineapple.

Jade noticed her expression. "I'll have it." She popped the other half into her mouth and it was gone. "So, this is what I wanted to show you: Lyttelton and its port."

Erin had been so preoccupied with catching her breath that she hadn't soaked in the view. Christchurch and the ocean lay behind them, but before them several mountains harbored a small bay and a busy shipping port.

"Wow."

"So glad you like it. It's not even one of the most beautiful places on the South Island. You'll see. Before Christmas, go to Hokitika. There aren't any shops in Christchurch like it anymore. Find some kiwi stuff to take home."

"And Hokitika is beautiful?"

"Not so you'd notice. It's an artist town on the Tasman Sea. The beautiful part is Hokitika Gorge."

"I dunno, Jade. This is pretty amazing."

"It is. But you'll find better spots. Beaches and mountains, lakes and springs. We've got loads of great stuff. You'll find the places that are for you."

They sat in silence for a long while. A container ship entered the port and Erin recalibrated her brain several times: each brightly colored block was the size of a railcar. Or a semitruck's haul.

"What do you think is in those containers?" Erin asked.

"Everything," Jade said.

"Everything?"

"Everything not made in New Zealand. Those containers are the reason we have bell peppers, tomatoes, and other produce that doesn't grow in winter. So food, for one. And we don't make a lot of stuff here. So we import a lot: materials, technology, books. Everything."

"There's nowhere like this in Chicago," Erin said. "I mean, there's a lake. Lake Michigan is a Great Lake, so it kind of looks like ocean, but it's surrounded by city. And the beaches are tiny. And fake. And, you know, it's not actually ocean."

"And no port, of course, if it's in the middle of the country."

"Yeah. I hadn't really thought about ports. I know we have them on the coasts, but that's all sort of invisible to me."

Jade nodded.

Cranes unloaded shipping containers from another vessel.

"So, is this what you do for fun?" Erin said.

"I find a bit of fun doing whatever, with whoever else likes doing it."

It sounded simple, but with college deadlines looming, Erin couldn't afford to waste time. After applications were in, during those excruciating months of waiting, she'd do whatever she wanted with whoever else liked doing it. Until then, there was too much on the line.

Erin's unambitious pal said, "Down to Lyttelton, then?"

"Jade, I really don't think I can make it back up."

"Tell you what, we'll ride down to the car and drive to Lyttelton. You lead."

————

Leading downhill was easier but colder. At the car, she bundled up while Jade loaded the bike rack.

"Actually, Jade, I've kind of seen Lyttelton now."

"Yeah, but my mum requested chocolates, so we have to go."

Jade drove over the Port Hills and into a roundabout at sea level. Here was Lyttelton up close.

A working port from a distance was one thing. Up close, the cranes lifted tons of full containers as if they were toys.

And the containers were filthy.

Looking up from the port, rows of colorful old houses lined Lyttelton's streets. But driving up into town from the port, Erin noticed half the Lyttelton streets were vacant. Enormous craters separated buildings. Children—probably children—had decorated a chain-link fence with paper cups, streamers, and plastic cartons pressed into every hole within arm's reach. The fence encircled a vacant lot a half-block long.

Up close, Lyttelton was a little ghetto.

Jade parked outside a small store standing between two vacant lots filled with construction debris. Or demolition debris? Erin didn't know.

Sufficiently creeped out, Erin locked the car doors while Jade ran in for chocolate.

When she returned, Jade threw a white bag into the backseat and handed Erin a small salted truffle. "All set, then?"

THIRTY-FOUR

Headed back toward the harbor, Jade said, "Oh, SeaGlass is open! Can't miss that. It's the greatest café."

The "café" was in a metal shipping container, and it wasn't alone. The shop next door was in a shipping container painted red. Across the road a restaurant filled a double-wide shipping container. Erin had never seen anything like it.

They walked through an improvised container/plastic door and Jade bellowed, "You're open!"

An exuberant bearded guy ran around the counter to hug her. "Just three weeks now."

"Mum will be thrilled. We haven't been over in a month. She probably just missed you."

"Stewart's & Brown is opening in a fortnight. High-Life in October in time for holiday shopping. Tourism is picking up."

Erin couldn't imagine Lyttelton as a tourist destination.

"Can I have a flat white?" Jade asked.

"And your friend?"

"This is Erin. Erin? Alistair. Erin's doing her O.E. from the States."

"Sweet as! Where 'bout?"

"Chicago. Well, twenty-six miles west of Chicago. Wheaton. It's quiet and safe. And I'd like a hot chocolate, please."

Erin stared out the window as Jade and Alistair chatted about their families. If the Wakefields' neighborhood was bad, Lyttelton was horrid. Worse than Parma. This was squalor. A beautiful Victorian house stood adjacent to an empty pit.

The gorgeous scene—gazing down a hill toward blue water and towering green mountains—was lovely, but upon further examination, it was all a façade.

Alistair left to greet other customers.

"Gorgeous view, innit?"

Sometimes it was as if Jade could read her mind.

"It is." Erin sipped her hot chocolate. "But what's up with the shipping containers?"

"It's a port."

"Right, I get it." Erin lowered her voice. "But we are sitting in a shipping container."

Jade didn't lower her voice. "Actually, we're sitting in a café. Alistair!"

He abandoned other customers when Jade beckoned.

"Alistair, tell Erin about SeaGlass. The original one."

He transformed into a bright-eyed child on Christmas morning.

"Two floors, and the second was floor-to-ceiling windows. Well, almost. We had two spiral staircases—one for guests, one for staff—and the view was astounding. Three-sixty degrees of our beautiful little town. They used to call Lyttelton the Port of Christchurch, did you know?" His face fell. "I suppose they still do, but it's not the same. Most of the shops, gone. Half the houses, gone. So many of our best people, gone. Not dead, mostly, but friends and neighbors left and won't ever come back."

Erin had spent most of June staring in the mirror, and Alistair looked worse than she ever had. He was mourning.

Alistair and Jade stared at the ground, shaking their heads.

Alistair looked out the door's plastic window, giving no indication of how he'd gone from a 360-degree view to one tiny plastic window in an artificial door.

Erin imagined The Nothing sweeping through *The Neverending Story*. "But what happened?"

"When SeaGlass came down, we waited years to build a new café. We started small," Alistair said.

"But what happened?"

They glared at her. A trio of shoppers entered, but Erin desperately needed an answer from Alistair before he left.

"What happened to your cafe and the houses and the shops?"

Jade stood up. "I'll show her. You go help them."

One last gulp of hot chocolate and Erin was out in the chilly air with Jade. Across the street and a block away, they stopped on a corner in front of yet another crater. The building next to the pit was missing half its staircase.

Jade jiggled a fence that was clearly marked NO TRESPASSING. Erin suspected she soon would learn New Zealand's secrets. Jade was a covert wizard. Perhaps only vampires could see the buildings. Or aliens had attacked.

Erin remained at the crater's rim as Jade walked downstairs to rock bottom.

"It was right here. You can sort of imagine the view, if you were two stories up, right? Look up the hills. There were houses for days. Well, not days, but straight up the hill— yellows and reds and blues and whites. Old houses that had been here for generations. And look down."

Erin saw the bay, though most of the ships were obscured.

"It was the best of both worlds. Right here. And just the nicest people in the world serving up whatever you wanted for tea."

Erin whispered: "Jade, what happened?"

"You're joking, right? The earthquakes? The two quakes that destroyed everything?" Jade climbed out of the pit and led Erin back toward the car. "In September of 2010 and February of 2011, two huge earthquakes shook Christchurch to its core. Half of downtown Lyttelton fell. Thousands of people were rendered homeless. Huge buildings toppled in Christchurch's CBD, including the cathedral, which was just . . . . It was our best thing."

It sounded like science fiction.

Jade enumerated the buildings destroyed by those quakes. "There are quakes all the time. That's why we had a drill first week of term. You get used to quakes, but those two were different. Art museum, gone. Medical center, gone. Cafés and churches and houses, gone, gone, gone."

Each new thing was a punch to the gut, and matter-of-fact Jade quieted. She started the car. "A hundred and eighty-five people died."

In earthquakes. Right here.

Five minutes after Jade's admission that two earthquakes had destroyed half of Christchurch, two minutes after she'd said Erin would get used to it, Jade drove into a tunnel.

Heavy, unstable mountains in the Ring of Fire, prone to earthquakes. Erin was not particularly interested in getting used to earthquakes yet.

She could have died right there.

"Faster? Faster, Jade?"

Erin wanted to hold her breath but her body had other ideas. By the time they emerged from the tunnel, completely unscathed, Erin was practically hyperventilating.

"All right, Erin?"

"Fine," she lied.

She was desperate for answers. How was Christchurch rebuilding? How was everyone who didn't die? What was destroyed? And, most importantly, why the hell hadn't kiwis moved out of the Ring of Fire?

THIRTY-FIVE

Back at the house, Erin pulled out her phone to discover several missed calls from Claire and a single voice mail:

> Erin, it feels like you're avoiding me. I've just read through our recent texts, and it seems like an awful lot of hanging out and not much work finding your unique factor. Sweetie, I love you. I need you to focus. We're in the final stretches here. We are so close. Don't lose sight of our goal.

After promising Claire via email she was focused intently and her next essay would be amazing, Erin spent hours plummeting into the earthquake rabbit hole. Wikipedia said the September 2010 quake had been powerful and damaging enough to topple hundreds of Christchurch's buildings.

A second massively destructive quake in February 2011 was so substantial, seismologists considered the September quake a mere foreshock.

Every year, New Zealand experienced 15,000 earthquakes, 100 to 150 of which were large enough to be felt.

That's one every three days.

Japan felt 2,000 quakes a year. The United States had maybe 40, mostly on the west coast.

Turned out New Zealand was nearly the exact size and contained a population comparable to Colorado. Four and a half million people opted to live in the Ring of Fire.

Erin filtered New Zealand's quakes by magnitude and absorbed the data: kiwis had felt five earthquakes in Christchurch since Erin's July arrival.

She hadn't felt a thing, including one her first Tuesday in New Zealand.

She'd traveled to a wrecked Christchurch knowing nothing about its history. Yes, 185 people died, but more than 6,600 others were treated for injuries at hospitals. Immediately after the quakes, kiwis were anxious and scared, but now those emotions had given way to anger. Thousands of downtown buildings must be demolished for safety reasons. People complained about insurance. People begged for retrofitting. Kiwis were irate about inefficiency.

Why wasn't the family discussing this every night?

The big quakes had been years ago. Why had Lyttelton— and Christchurch's business district—not yet risen from the ashes?

Hamish worked in construction; why wasn't he laser focused on rebuilding his city? Erin reserved her questions for dinner, when the whole family would be around the table.

THIRTY-SIX

After Pippa's guitar lesson, Hank stayed for dinner.

The previous hours had done little to douse Erin's anger, so she charged ahead anyway. "I want to talk about the big earthquakes."

Felicity reached for Pippa, who had frozen with her fork halfway to her mouth. "You okay, Pippa?"

Pippa ate her peas. "I'm okay, Mum."

Felicity said, "Some days we don't talk about it."

"It's okay, Mum."

Felicity straightened her flatware and leaned back. "They were devastating. It's going to take us decades to rebuild, but it will never be the same. Half of the Central Business District is still closed."

Pippa pushed food around her plate but didn't take another bite.

"What about your business, Hamish?" Erin asked. "What if, instead of building houses, you started rebuilding the city?"

"We're trying."

"Right, but could you start working on the downtown? Everyone uses it. It's the district that made Christchurch *Christchurch*. I saw photos of cute shopping districts. Could you rebuild the cathedral? Everyone is bummed about the cathedral."

Hamish dug into his dinner.

Felicity laid her hand over Erin's. "He's working, Erin. Every day. There's too much work to be done. They can't rebuild the city yet. We have to break it down before we can really rebuild."

Hamish said, "To start with, houses are easier to repair. Neighborhood infrastructure wasn't destroyed completely. Houses are further apart. Houses can be repaired. It's easy to raze a house, haul away the debris, and start over. It's a lot harder when you're dealing with a whole city. I'm working all the time. Everyone is working all the time. Bringing people here from overseas to get the construction and infrastructure underway. But it takes time. A lot of time."

"In Wheaton, they built our new middle school—a huge school. Brick. In exactly one summer. You could work harder and make it happen."

"I don't expect you to understand," Hamish said.

Erin raised her voice slightly. "It seems like everyone is complaining about what needs to be done, but no one is actually doing the work. I've read about this all afternoon. Everyone is sort of mellow and slow. Why aren't you rebuilding today?"

"We are," Hank said. "That is literally what we do every day."

"You're fixing cracks in houses," Erin said. "That is such a small thing. Many things are more important than cracks."

No one moved until Hamish crossed his arms. "Tell me about this middle school built in a single summer."

Erin knew nothing about construction, but when her dad was on the school board, she heard how the school was planned and how it went up and how it worked. They had LEED silver certification, which meant the school was a leader in energy and environmental design. It was a big deal. "It's one of the greenest schools in America."

Hamish said, "Yes. And where did they build it?"

"On a huge plot two miles from downtown Wheaton."

"And did a firm design it?"

"Yes. The best architects."

"That must have taken a long time to plan before they started building."

She hesitated. "Maybe."

"And then they had to procure the materials, which took some time."

"Probably."

"Imagine this." Hamish leaned in. "First, you have to raze a building. Excavate it."

"The water and sewage and utilities are crap," Hank said, "so you have to wait until every other building tied into its infrastructure is razed."

Hamish tagged back in. "You have to go to the central business district and fix the main stuff first, so when you build something it has water and electricity and whatnot."

He had a point.

"And you have the plans for the building that used to stand there, but you can't just build it again because you already know it can't withstand a strong quake. So you have to wait for someone to design something that will. And then wait for the government to approve it. And then, because you live on a small island in the Pacific, you have to import building materials from other countries that have resources and facilities to manufacture brick and steel."

Hank said, "And then we build!"

Oh.

"And you're talking about one building. Hundreds of buildings need to be rebuilt. We have to lift buildings that survived in order to pour new foundations." Hank shook his head. "CBD—our Central Business District—is a mess."

Erin stared at her plate. She was an ass.

"So I know you think we wouldn't know shit from clay. And America is bigger and better and faster and stronger. But this traumatic thing happened to our country. We are working together to build it back up again. To make our children feel safe. To stay strong."

Erin stared at her hands as Hamish resumed his meal.

Felicity said, "It's not your fault, Erin."

Pippa said, "Yeah. You can't move tectonic plates!"

Felicity put one hand over Pippa's and her other over Erin's. "What I meant, Pippa, was that Erin couldn't have known. She was trying to help."

Hamish was quiet. "We're all trying to help. You're making plans, fine. I'm working on houses. Fourteen thousand homes destroyed or condemned. The people trying to rebuild the city need roofs over their heads. I'm doing what I can. Don't get me started on insurance companies standing in our way."

Erin whispered, "Sorry."

"You don't know is all," Hank said.

There was more she didn't know. Erin stayed up late reading about Christchurch, old and new. Economists estimated it would take fifty to a hundred years for the economy to recover. After the big quakes, New Zealand suffered a mass exodus. Some left because they had no power. Many homes were condemned, so families couldn't return. The resulting housing shortage caused prices to soar, so many families couldn't afford to return.

Erin clicked back through Good-Time Girl's history. She'd been too young to post during the earthquakes, but two years ago, she'd returned to Christchurch after years away. She posted photos of her old, now-demolished house in Sumner Beach and expressed gratitude for family friends who'd housed her family.

Obviously, those weren't good times.

One summery day, earthquakes had rattled generations of kiwis, and they'd never be the same.

Erin's own problems seemed a bit smaller.

She wanted to tell Good-Time Girl she was sorry about her city, but that definitely seemed like stalking. Instead, she read through Marama's and Jade's recent posts, liking and responding where appropriate.

This tiny city was resilient. This community was resilient. This *family* was resilient. She wanted to wrap them all up in love.

THIRTY-SEVEN

Wednesday morning, Erin called Claire ten minutes before she left for Nationals. Claire raved about the revised iteration of Erin's essay.

"It's fabulous, Mom. It just doesn't sound like me."

Claire huffed. "It sounds like a Columbia student. This woman has a great track record of Ivy League acceptances. Did you look at her website?"

"I did," she lied.

"Well, I think the essay is a winner. Tweak it if you want, but then I need to see it again. And if everything goes well this weekend, we can make that the focus."

Felicity knocked on Erin's door. "Percy's here."

"Thanks, Felicity," Erin said.

"How's everything in that tiny house?" Claire asked. "Still sharing a room?"

Erin wished she'd never mentioned that. "I am. And it's not that bad. We're all together a lot. We eat dinner together every night. They call it tea. Some nights we all do our own thing together—homework or reading for Pippa and me, a project for Felicity, or cards for her and Hamish."

"If I had the luxury of an easy job, I would have a lot

more leisure time, too. It's a trade-off, Erin. They have a slow, small life. You'll notice none of them are eyeing a champion-ship medal."

"The family is pretty great, actually, even without med-als." Smiling, she nodded to herself.

"Do not start talking that way. Only people who can't get medals are blasé without them. You're better than that. You can win. Go out and do it."

"I need to go, Mom. My coach is here."

"Call me as soon as you know anything, okay?"

"Okay, Mom. Say hi to Dad for me."

"Okay. Swim fast."

The line went dead. *Swim fast.* As if she'd swim any other way.

Erin took her bags to the kitchen, which was warming quickly in spring's morning sun. "Christchurch is thawing out."

"Yes," Felicity said. "Winter is tough, but she'll be right here soon." She confirmed the time and location of Erin's first race in Queenstown.

"You're really coming?" Erin said.

"Of course I am. Swimming is important to you."

"But it's in Queenstown. Hours and hours away for a few short races."

"I'm well aware of where Queenstown is. I already have a flight. I am happy to come."

Lucky Felicity was flying to Queenstown. Erin had to endure an eight-hour road trip. Percy had rented a people mover, the kiwi word for minivan, to drive the four girls and Marama's mom to the south end of the South Island. Erin scored the middle row, which she hoped would spare her the back seat's added nausea.

On the road, Percy and Marama's mom talked about rugby for an entire hour. Ruby and Gemma traded music in the backseat, and Marama snoozed next to Erin, whose earbuds courted a headache.

New Zealand was waking up to spring. Lush flora and fauna grew everywhere: splashes of purple and pink spotted green hills, as mountains loomed in the distance. Erin turned off her music and focused on whichever mountain was furthest away.

The highway was a two-lane road with a higher speed limit, and Erin appreciated signs limiting drivers to 100 kilometers per hour. Driving 100 felt cool, even if it was only 60 miles per hour.

About an hour and a half in, they circumvented an enormous, calm lake surrounded by mountains. A few inches above the water, a layer of fog suggested mystery and intrigue.

This was what Mrs. Carey had meant when she taught Erin the word *sublime* in sixth grade. Mrs. Carey claimed a sublime scene would make Erin feel something.

She felt compelled. Calm.

Michigan wasn't sublime, but Erin's annual retreat into the U.P. had felt like this. Every summer, she left everything behind—her friends, her classes, her expectations—for ten glorious weeks.

This time, she'd brought her expectations with her.

A half hour later, they passed a fogless lake with no evidence of humans. No houses, just nature, hanging out, being gorgeous.

Erin wished they could pause here, but Percy plugged southward to Queenstown, driving through one sublime scene, and rounding a mountain to spy another. New Zealand must be the most densely sublime country in the world.

And, determined to travel without vomiting, Erin kept her focus wholly outside the minivan. She saw it all.

Four hours in, traffic came to an abrupt halt. Percy cracked the windows and cut the engine.

"Why are we stopped?" Erin asked.

"No idea," Percy said. "People'll clear out, I'm sure."

No one else seemed remotely concerned. Traffic resumed ten minutes later but remained slow and deliberate until they passed a herd of cattle. On the road. Being herded by two dogs.

A hundred cattle had halted highway traffic, and no one batted an eye. Herd in the road was a totally normal thing.

Erin started laughing and couldn't stop.

"All right there, Erin?" Ruby shouted.

Marama's mom turned to stare as Percy studied Erin in the rearview mirror.

Erin tried to stifle herself but chortled loudly. "Cows in the road!"

"Herds change pastures so they don't run out of grass," Percy said.

"I'm sure, it's just . . ."

Erin had seen people in movies so high they couldn't control their laughter; this felt exactly like that. It took her several minutes to breathe normally.

"You all right?" Percy said.

She giggled a little. "It's just absurd. We sat in traffic—no one blaring their horns or swearing or anything—and then resumed as though we hadn't just wasted fifteen minutes while a herd of cattle walked down the road."

"What's fifteen minutes?" Percy said. "No rush."

"That's the thing. No one is in any rush. You're all so polite."

Marama's mom said, "Does no good to rush. Cattle take as long as they take. Sounding the horn would just make everyone angry."

Erin stared, blankly. "But they're wasting your time."

"Sometimes we wait on their cows. Sometimes they wait on ours."

Marama's mom was almost prophetic.

Erin was going 100 in a people mover with five people she'd met a few weeks prior, driving south through mountains and around lakes in an island country in the middle of nowhere on her way to a swim meet.

A herd of cattle had detained their drive southward, toward colder weather. And it was spring in September. Everything was backward and upside-down. Call it a break or a fermata or a holiday or a sabbatical, but she was definitely out of Wheaton.

And while she'd been living in Chicago's flat western suburbs, while she'd been killing herself in the pool and racking up contiguous days of cello practice and engaging in intensive study in everything under the sun, this gorgeous country was literally under the sun.

And she'd been missing it.

THIRTY-EIGHT

Erin congratulated herself for making it to lunch without vomiting. She took a few nibbles at the picnic table on the side of the road—next to a lake, naturally—before returning to the van.

Four hours later, they rounded a mountain to find another great lake.

"Hello, Wakatipu!" Marama's mom said.

Lake Wakatipu didn't rival Lake Michigan's size, but nestled among ragged mountains, it was awesome, in the truest sense of the word. Slanted rows of houses, each with a birds-eye view of the lake, covered the mountains.

Queenstown was a quaint mountain village on an almost-great lake. Erin's heart was full to bursting.

Just as the sun was setting, Percy steered away from Lake Wakatipu. Off the major thoroughfare, they began a steep ascent to Summer's aunt's house. Summer's aunt had refused to rent out the house during national championships for three years, just in case Summer needed it.

This year, Summer wasn't with them, but her aunt's offer stood, of course.

Percy missed the turnoff by a few meters and reversed

down the hill to try again. After the turnoff, they faced a steep descent and three switchbacks, one of which required a five-point turn. Erin thought they were lost until, two minutes later, Percy stopped in front of a plain wooden house.

In the fresh air at last, Erin walked around the house to investigate. Motorboats zipped through the water and around a lush green park jutting into the lake. Shops and restaurants lined much of the shore, beckoning visitors.

The house was propped up on stilts. Erin gazed uphill to see the entire neighborhood was perched on similar four-by-fours.

Only a few wooden posts prevented them from sliding down the side of this rather substantial mountain.

Holy cow.

North Carolina propped houses to keep them safer in hurricanes, but North Carolina wasn't in the Ring of Fire. In the last two weeks, Erin had watched too many YouTube videos and seen too many photos of houses sliding into the sea.

Everyone else piled into the house.

From the door, Marama said, "All right then, Erin?"

"Are you sure it's safe?"

"I promise you it's safe." Marama reached for Erin's hand.

Reluctant, Erin took it and tiptoed through the front door.

Inside, she could almost forget they were on stilts. The entire western wall was floor-to-ceiling windows, featuring a dazzling scene of water and boats and houses all turning on their lights. The sun had disappeared beyond the mountains, leaving a soft pink sky with streaks of blues and purples and whites.

There's a reason they're called picture windows, Erin realized.

"Check out the fittings!" Ruby flung herself on the smaller of two white leather sofas.

The furniture and upscale decor put this house on a different level than anything Erin had seen in Christchurch.

"What say we stay in for the weekend?" Ruby's outstretched arms claimed the sofa and she propped her feet on the table. "Order in some fish and chippies. Live the life!"

Jade sat on the adjacent sofa. "Can you imagine? Some people live like this all the time."

Erin said nothing about her own furniture, nor her mother's decorator.

"My uncle lives in Auckland," Gemma said. "His husband claims it's twice the price, half the view."

"Where's Auckland?" Erin asked.

"North part of the North Island. It's quite crowded: maybe a million and a half people."

Erin nodded, but Chicago dwarfed Auckland. Since researching the quakes, she was keenly interested in size and population comparisons. "My town is tiny, but we're close to Chicago—almost three million people. The whole Chicago metro area—suburbs and all—is nearly ten million."

"Is that more than New Zealand?" Ruby asked.

"New Zealand is nearly five million," Erin said. "I only know that because I looked it up a few weeks ago."

"Ten million people? Don't you feel suffocated?"

Erin had felt slightly suffocated in downtown Chicago; her lungs seemed to expand every Saturday afternoon when she returned to the suburbs after symphony rehearsal. "My suburb, Wheaton, is pretty small. It never feels crowded except during festivals. Or at the ice cream shop on summer Saturdays."

Ruby shot up. "Do you think there's ice cream?"

Erin's teammates mobbed the tiny kitchen, pulling out snacks and bowls as if this were a slumber party. Summer's aunt had stocked the house, as promised.

Marama said, "Oooooh, chocolate fishies."

Ruby scooped out chocolate ice cream and threw jelly beans on top.

Gemma reached over her for pineapple lumps and returned to the sofa. "How long are you staying?"

"December."

Gemma rolled her eyes. "You're going to miss the best part. Summer hols are the best of New Zealand."

"I have to go back for second semester," Erin said.

"Why?"

Good question. Erin had already missed several weeks of her senior year: swim team pep rally, football games, lockdown drills. Honestly, she was glad to skip football season. In January, she'd undertake more college courses to comp out of gen ed classes at Columbia. Or wherever. She couldn't swim varsity. She couldn't audition for symphony midyear. She'd barely heard from anyone but Lalitha since landing in New Zealand.

She could just as well study abroad again—perhaps somewhere warm. Like Fiji.

"Erin? Why?"

"You know, Gemma, that was the plan, but now I'm not sure. I could just spend the semester somewhere else instead."

"That's lucky. If I could go anywhere, I'd travel to Italy. The food. The wine!"

Jade munched potato crisps. "Choose France instead, and you'd have food, wine, and cheese."

The girls romanticized trips abroad until the sky was black.

Downstairs, all four bedrooms had views of the lake. Erin had one all to herself because Felicity would be sharing with her the next night.

Erin sent snaps to Lalitha, hoping the gorgeous scenery would finally elicit a response. They hadn't texted for two days.

Erin: In Queenstown for Nationals.
Erin: It's the most gorgeous place in the world.

There was no reply.

Gemma knocked on her door. "You coming up, then?"

"In a minute." Erin pulled out her suit for the morning, double-checked her bag, and laid out her school-sanctioned gym attire. She enjoyed this mental space, when practice was done and her body was in the best shape it could be. Mostly. If she were training in Wheaton, she might be stronger.

Still, she was ready. Percy had her tags and paperwork, but everything else was ready.

Upstairs, Ruby said, "Percy ordered fish and chips, since no one is keen to cook."

Erin's mouth hung open. Filled with junk food and destined for a late night, they would be too slow tomorrow. Before meets, especially big ones, Erin always ate a carb-heavy dinner, slept as much as possible, and prepared a healthy protein-heavy breakfast. That's how she took first at States two years in a row. That's probably how the Quigleys would win States this year.

Marama's mom studied a Queenstown directory and circled a few restaurant options for the next night.

Ruby tucked up on the sofa with a bowl of crisps and a remote control.

Erin was the only one taking this seriously. "You guys. Do you think we'll win on fish and chips and junk food?"

"We're on holiday!" Gemma said. "Sport is supposed to be fun."

Erin knocked around the kitchen until she found pasta and a pot. "I'm eating carbs for dinner. Anyone joining me?"

No one.

"Your American is showing," Ruby said.

"Ruby!" Jade said.

"What? It's true. All work and no play? Sport is supposed to be fun, like Gemma said."

"Winning is fun," Erin said.

"Winning doesn't last," Ruby said.

"Neither will your sugar high," Erin said. She clanged around the kitchen, boiled an entire box of pasta per the instructions on the box, and ate alone at the table. Halfway through a movie, Percy arrived with dinner and Erin's teammates swarmed the table.

After Erin wished everyone good night, she heard someone say, "Someone's quite the tall poppy."

She crawled into bed early after one final text to her best friend.

Erin: More than anything, I wish you were here, Li. ❤

THIRTY-NINE

The morning races were eerily quiet. Like meets in Christchurch, there were occasional shouts, but most people cheered as swimmers mounted the blocks or once the race ended.

Only one woman coached from the sidelines. It was like having Claire right there. *Lift!* and *Faster!* and *You're trailing!* as if her daughter (Erin was guessing daughter) could hear her underwater.

Felicity arrived an hour before the relay race and sat alone with her jacket in her lap. When Erin caught her eye, Felicity smiled and gave a thumb's up.

Soon enough, Gemma was in the pool, mounted and ready for the gun. Marama, Ruby, and Erin wished her luck, and she was off. Erin couldn't watch the race. Peripherally, she could see that other girls would make it back before Gemma, but she focused only on Gemma's cap.

When she returned, Ruby dove in and gained a little on the other teams.

As Erin climbed onto the blocks, Marama slapped her on the shoulder.

Some swimmers focus on form in the water, but that

had never worked for Erin during a real race. The second she stood on the blocks, her adrenaline amped up, muscle memory took over, and her mind went blank.

Ruby hit the wall and Erin was in the water without thinking.

Dolphin, dolphin, dolphin, dolphin, breathe, breathe, breathe, breathe. Flip.

She pushed it. She wanted it. Breathing every single stroke, she put everything into the race.

Breathe, breathe, breathe, breathe, breathe, done.

Erin popped out of the water to watch the finish. They were going to qualify, no question. It was down to Marama, who killed it.

Everyone hugged one another and dried off.

Between races, Erin found Felicity in the stands. "Well done, Erin! I love watching you swim."

"Thanks."

"You've worked very hard for this. How are you feeling?"

Erin kept her eyes on the qualifying races for backstroke. "Great."

"But how do you feel about the culmination of years of training?"

"Great."

"Erin?" Felicity waited for Erin to look at her. "Are you happy? Does this feel as you wanted it to feel?"

Happy wasn't the right word. "I'm proud of what I've accomplished."

Felicity nodded, and Erin focused again on the pool.

That afternoon, her relay team qualified to quarterfinals, but not semis. Alone, Erin qualified to semis in three races, all of which were Saturday morning.

She texted Claire.

Erin: Relay team DNQ. I Qd in 50M, 100M, and 200M fly.

Percy said, "Great job, ladies. While you're changing, decide what you fancy for tea."

Decide what you fancy for tea. No coaching. No commentary. No judgment. The no-judgment aspect was a relief. No one was recording her race as a coaching device. Her team's loss wouldn't be posted on social media.

It was heavenly.

BEFORE SHE WOKE ON HER BIRTHDAY
BEFORE SHE WOKE ON HER BIRTHDAY

She threw open the door, colliding with the intermittent knocker. Tiny phone cameras focused on her as she ran, half-naked, from the observatory toward the bathroom. She vomited on the spiral staircase, in the hall, and across the ankles of Lalitha and one of the Quigleys, who were animatedly discussing the team's swimsuit options.

Her stomach empty, Erin dry-heaved over the toilet. Minutes later, she lay on the cool stone floor, focusing on caulk at the tub's base to keep the room from spinning. Retching convulsed her body every few minutes for an hour.

Lalitha brought a hair band and forced Erin to finish a glass of water. When Erin refused to move to the guest room, Lalitha brought her a blanket and travel pillow.

Finally, the room slowed enough that she could close her eyes without feeling nauseated.

Erin pretended to sleep when Claudia Quigley peed on the toilet next to her.

Shortly after midnight on her seventeenth birthday, Erin passed out.

FORTY

At the house that night, Erin kept her head in the game. While her teammates crammed onto a sofa for another movie, Erin slipped out for a walk. She hiked up steep switchbacks to the mountain road and headed uphill.

She couldn't shake memories of meets past. She missed Lalitha and their pre-meet routines. Erin hoped to win one of her races tomorrow and capture her unique factor. But she still felt off-kilter, upside down, and for that there was no end in sight.

Near the end of the road, a chill brushed past her. She should be warming her muscles and tending to her body right now, doing her own private race prep.

She turned back toward the house and accidentally spied the moon, the thing she'd been avoiding for months. She had loved the moon so much that she'd told Ben everything about it. He never could remember which crescent was waning and which was waxing, and Erin's little mnemonic device, *Now you C me, now you don't,* helped him get the shapes right, if not the concept of waning.

And here it was, the waning moon, peeking through thin clouds.

Erin shuddered.

She had no more tears for Ben, only a gaping sense of loss. And now, probably for the rest of her life, that stupid moon—waning or waxing—would remind her of the stupid boy for whom waning was an impossible concept.

Staring into the heavens made her feel part of something much, much larger. She—and trillions of other small somethings—were part of something big. Mars, Earth, luminous balls of hydrogen and helium, the moon, and Erin. Everything single thing sprang from the same stuff.

She drank in the moon. Crescent, half-full, full, new, she loved it all. But the full moon held a special place in her heart. And it would be full in five days.

Erin squinted. Five days? But it was waning. Erin knew dates for all the full moons, and the moon had been new nine days ago.

She felt upside-down again.

Of course! That was the problem: she was upside-down. A Southern Hemisphere's waxing moon was a c. A waning moon was a backward c.

Erin's cheek muscles pulled into a huge smile. And she cried. Everything was backward and upside-down, including the moon . . . and she was probably the only person on Earth thinking about it. And even if Ben was looking at the moon at this very instant, this view of it was hers.

Finally, the moon was hers again.

FORTY-ONE

Erin advanced to finals for all three butterfly races: 50M, 100M, and 200M.

Waiting for the judge's signal to mount the block for the 50M final, Erin tried to focus.

If she didn't compete at college, this was her last day of competitive swimming. Ever. Her heart leapt to her throat. She almost couldn't breathe, and breathing was the number-one most important thing for swimmers.

The race would last under a minute, and they were nearly ready to start. *Hold it together for one minute. Think later.*

The judge called them to the blocks.

Erin grabbed the platform and waited.

And she was in the pool. For the first length, Erin stayed under for every second stroke, but on the return, she breathed on every stroke. Her lungs screamed. She was a single muscle, flexing herself through the water, pulling, pulling, pulling.

She touched the wall, and it was over.

She hung onto the rope for a second, her forehead against the wall.

Part elated, part terrified, she rested her head until her teammates swarmed.

Jade said, "Well done, WELL DONE!" and Percy beamed.

Erin checked the clock.

Her mind was racing.

Next to her time was NR.

Percy grabbed her hand, pulled her from the water, and wrapped her in an enormous hug, pool water seeping from her suit to his sweater.

Erin couldn't find Felicity among the throngs of people, most of whom were on their feet.

They hadn't stood for the other finals.

Percy said, "National champion. National record. You know what Americans say: go big or go home!"

Lalitha.

The crowd was on its feet for her.

Her time was good enough for States at home. She never would have won U.S. Nationals, but here she was a national champion. Amazing. Unique. She had done it. Claire would be overjoyed.

She waved to the crowd and wrapped herself in a towel before calling Claire.

"I did it!" Erin said. "I won. And I set a national record in the 50-meter fly."

"Great," Claire said. "Can you win the other two?"

Staring at her feet, Erin swallowed hard. "I don't know. Probably?"

"I'll bet you can. Do you feel strong?"

"I do. I'm on."

"But how's your endurance? Can you hold out the rest of the day? You need to win them all. New Zealand is pretty small. Here, you're competing in a country of 320 million. New Zealand is what? Four?"

"Almost five. And I am the national champion. I just set a national record."

"Okay," Claire said. "You know national champion will impress, but if you hold three championships, no one can turn you down. No one, Erin."

"You're right," Erin said. "I can do it. I know I can."

"We're having a phones off date tonight—Bien Trucha—so if you miss me, leave a message to let me know you've done it. I'll tell Dad when we're done."

Erin's voice was quiet. "Okay. I'll call when I'm done then."

"You'll get there, Erin. Close the deal. You're almost there."

Aren't I there already? "I will."

"Go win!" Claire said.

"Bye, Mom."

Tears stinging her eyes, Erin dressed in her warm-ups and returned to the pool area.

FORTY-TWO

New Zealand does a medal ceremony for their national championships. Erin stood on a podium while the announcer read her name and time. She'd broken a nine-year record, set more than half her life ago. Erin's name would appear in the aquatic center lobby, which was kind of like Wheaton's athletic hall of fame, where Elena Basignani set all the cross-country records in the 1990s.

How long would her name remain in the kiwi hall of fame?

Erin stepped down from the podium and hugged her teammates. The girl who had won third said, "I thought you looked familiar. You're the pink puke girl."

Erin's eyes widened as silence descended.

"What's that?" Marama asked.

"The online girl who ran around naked throwing up pink everywhere. I have a GIF of it in my phone." She reached into her bag.

Jade and Marama wrapped their arms around Erin's shoulders and guided her to a private corner. They shooed people away as Erin cried, "Oh God, oh God, oh God."

Jade knelt in front of Erin. "Tell us what's going on."

Erin's tears gushed. "I had just lost my swim captainship. It was the night before my seventeenth birthday. And it was a Saturday. Date night with Ben." She drew a deep breath, ready to release her shame into the wild again.

BEFORE SHE PASSED OUT

BEFORE SHE PASSED OUT

Erin had nursed her beverage long enough that her head was cloudy and feet were fuzzy.

Ben grabbed her hand and grinned.

Lalitha got close to Erin's face. "You all right, sweetie?"

Erin grinned and added an exaggerated nod for good measure. She was perfectly fine.

Ben led her upstairs, away from their friends and the vibrating speakers. Two unidentifiable girls sat, lip-locked, on the hall window seat, all arms and legs and hair and slurping.

Bed led Erin up the spiral staircase to the locked observatory door. Eager, she kissed his neck while he fumbled for the key in his pocket.

Ben snaked his arms around her. "I really like this version of Erin. Hairy Buffalo makes you a little aggressive."

Erin hiccupped and giggled. "What are we really doing in there, Ben?"

"We're looking at Jupiter. Lalitha said I could give you Jupiter for your birthday."

"It's cloudy tonight," Erin said as her brain continued clouding over. "And opposition was over a week ago."

He kissed her again. "I know that." Another kiss. "You know that." A longer kiss. "They don't know that."

She leaned into him, half wishing Jupiter were an option and half grateful they would finally be alone together. Alone with Ben was Erin's favorite pastime; she loved their private jokes and knowing he had chosen her over every other girl in Wheaton.

"Get a room, you two," someone said from the hall.

Ben unlocked the door to their room—a genuine observatory—and Erin stumbled into the darkness. The telescope sat atop a rotating pedestal that spun to focus on different segments of the sky.

Lalitha's mom, a professional amateur astronomer, traveled a lot, so Erin had used this telescope only twice. Erin wanted to make a whole life for herself in this room. The top five feet of the walls were window, and the ceiling, too. Windows on the universe. A vast void. The good kind.

Ben sprawled on the cushy white sofa. "This is kick-ass."

Erin ran her fingers up the enormous, smooth telescope. It was old, so the tube was long, but she knew the brand, Meade, and they didn't make cheap telescopes. Erin's grampa's best telescope had been a Celestron, but he'd longed for a professional Meade.

Ben extended his arms on the back of the sofa. "I'll bet, with clear skies, you could get a really good look at the Big Dipper, huh?"

Erin preferred planets, asteroids, and meteors to connect-the-dots constellations, but Ben liked the light side of astronomy: constellations' shapes and stories. Erin thought constellations reflected silly human efforts to make sense of the night sky, but she was afraid he would dump her if she mentioned that.

She peered through the eyepiece. "I want to see the crack in the moon. Or butterscotch Mars." Erin's grandfather had suggested Mars was more butterscotch than red. He had known everything about the universe. Together, they had written songs about living in Jupiter's hurricane for a hundred and fifty years and imagined gravity on the moon.

"Erin? We have the room to ourselves. Lalitha promised not to interrupt our stargazing."

"You said Jupiter."

"Jupiter-gazing, fine. Whatever," Ben said. "Can you just relax a minute?"

She tripped on her way to the cushy sofa and fell into Ben's arms.

He laughed. "Happy birthday, my beautiful birthday girl."

Erin tried to ignore the distinct taste of beer as Ben's tongue darted into her mouth.

"You're so warm," he said, reaching up the back of her shirt.

Erin grabbed a cup—Ben's, hers, she wasn't sure—and spat into it. She had too much saliva in her mouth. She spat again. *Better.*

Ben stroked her back and unfastened her bra. Their routine now on autopilot, she kissed him. Who cared about the Quigleys when she had Ben? He loved her.

Ben pulled her shirt over her head.

Trying hard to focus as he tugged on her shorts, Erin said, "I need to slow down a little."

Ben fanned a handful of condoms onto the table and reached for her again. His hands ran over her back, up her neck, and into her mass of tangled hair. His kisses elicited a flip-flop in Erin's belly, but the flop didn't feel quite right.

Ben maneuvered Erin into a supine position and lay on top of her.

Despite Erin's enthusiasm, Ben felt too heavy on her stomach. She pushed him over and crawled on top of him.

He groaned. "Yeah, I like that!"

Erin kissed his belly and bit his T-shirt as she had the first time he'd said he loved her.

"This is like the perfect day," he said.

"Yeah?"

"Yeah. Happy early birthday."

"Thanks."

Someone knocked on the door.

"We're looking at the moon." Ben grabbed Erin's butt and she giggled.

He put his hand down the back of her underpants, squeezing her right butt cheek. Quickly, she sat up to make the room stop spinning. *Too fast.*

Ben pumped his hips upward, and it reminded Erin of dressage lessons long ago.

"Could you stop a minute?" she said. "Little dizzy."

Ben propped up on his elbows. "Sure, yeah."

They ignored more knocking.

"I need to stay upright, I think." Erin coughed and spit in the cup again. "I think I'm okay."

"If we're not going to, you know, maybe I could sit in the chair and you could . . . play?"

She should have said no.

Sitting in the armless chair, Ben pulled her hips toward him. Her stomach flipped over again in a way that had nothing to do with Ben.

Kneeling on the floor, she felt queasy. "I'm feeling a little not right."

She spat in the cup again and felt better. *Just too much saliva in my mouth.*

"I like it when you unzip me," Ben said.

A zipper would have been easy, but his button fly was another matter altogether. Even her most intense focus could not force her hands to do the work.

She focused on speaking clearly. "Got to be you."

Ben grabbed her hands and laughed. "Sweetie, how many drinks did you have?"

"Maybe two? And a half. An then jus fruit."

Ben unbuttoned his pants.

More knocking.

"Give us a minute. Or ten. We'll come out when we're done." Ben cringed. "Can you lick your hands or something?"

Erin licked her hands, but they dried in an instant. "Vaseline?"

Ben glanced from one end of the spinning observatory to the other. "Like, from where?"

The look on his face suggested they were both thinking the same thing, but Erin knew she shouldn't put anything near her mouth.

Erin opened her mouth to apologize—and spewed pink vomit everywhere.

"The hell?" Ben shot from the chair, wiping the pink from his jeans and crotch.

Erin fumbled to the door. More pink stuff was on its way up.

FORTY-THREE

Jade and Marama stared at Erin.

"I was drunk. Like, fast drunk. Hairy Buffalo tasted like red Kool-Aid. Do you even have Kool-Aid? It was super sweet, so I couldn't really taste the alcohol. And it had tons of fruit floating on top, and I just kept eating it, but Lalitha's brother had soaked the fruit in vodka overnight, so it was super alcoholic.

"I ran into the hall and vomited everywhere. Everyone saw me, and everyone saw him. And everyone had video. I vomited until I passed out on Lalitha's bathroom floor. Because my vomit was all over his, you know, general area, people assumed my mouth had been right there. And they started calling me Gag Reflex."

"That is revolting."

"Thanks, Marama."

"No," Marama said. "I mean, yes, it was probably nasty to have vomit everywhere. But why didn't Ben do something? If you were close to vomiting, you were too drunk to consent to whatever it was you two were doing. Why didn't he stop when he knew you weren't right?"

Erin hadn't thought of that.

"And the way people reacted is disgusting," Marama said. "Why didn't you say something? Just tell the truth?"

Erin said, "The thing is, if you say 'No, no, no, I don't have a gag reflex, I was just drunk,' then you're someone who can't hold her liquor. It's just another thing they're going to talk about."

Jade said, "Who is this Ben wanker, anyway?"

"My very ex-boyfriend."

"What happened to him?"

"He ghosted and got a new girlfriend."

Marama's eyes narrowed. "You know what you should have said? You should have said his penis wasn't long enough to trigger your gag reflex."

Erin felt the left side of her mouth curl up. "That would make me no better than him."

"Yeah, but at least it would make him look just as bad as you."

"Thanks."

"Fuckwad," Jade said, and Erin smiled.

Marama said, "Ignore that girl and her phone. If she comes by again, I will spew on her."

Erin's friends surrounded her for the rest of the meet. She lost the 200M, won the 100M, but considered Marama and Jade her true winnings.

FORTY-FOUR

Erin texted Lalitha on the way to drop off Felicity at the airport.

> **Litha:** Is that good enough? Can you come home? I MISS
>   YOU.
> **Erin:** Miss you, too. Still have to stay through December.
> **Erin:** Plus, what would I do there? Can't swim. Can't start
>   classes mid-semester.
> **Litha:** Won't you be starting mid-semester in Jan?
> **Erin:** Maybe I will take a vacation until second semester starts.
> **Litha:** Maybe we BOTH can take a vacation!
> **Litha:** NYC, we're coming back!
> **Erin:** Or Fiji
> **Litha:** Hawaii!
> **Erin:** Keep dreaming. I have to say good-bye to Felicity.
> **Litha:** ❤
> **Erin::** One more thing.
> **Erin:** Please send Claudia's contact information.
> **Litha:** What now?
> **Erin:** She never called me, and I want to talk to her.
> **Litha:** Wait, why?

Erin: Long story. All good.
Erin: Talk soon.
Erin: ❤

At the airport, Erin hugged Felicity good-bye. She wished she could fly instead of enduring another eight hours on the road with ice cream punnets.

Felicity said, "I'm so proud of you."

"Thanks."

Felicity touched Erin's arm lightly. "Erin, this is a major accomplishment. You aren't just the fastest in the meet, you set two national records. Among all racers. Ever."

"Yeah. It's great."

Felicity frowned. "You don't seem remotely excited."

Erin shrugged.

"What's the matter, love?"

Erin stared at the ground. "I'm New Zealand great, not American great."

Felicity set her jaw.

"That didn't come out like I meant it to. I just meant it's not the same here as in America."

Felicity took stock of her luggage. "I'll see you at home, then."

"Felicity?" How could Erin remove the foot from her mouth? "Here's the thing."

"No, here's the thing, Erin."

Ear-in. She wanted to plug one ear to prevent any ear-out.

"That is the weird dichotomy of America: kids get awards for participating. Everyone gets a trophy! Everyone gets a medal! Have a ribbon, even if you're the very worst player ever."

Erin agreed. Only winners should receive trophies.

"Everyone gets a prize, so your prizes mean absolutely nothing. Except the big prize. National champion. Olympic champion. World champion. Well, there's only one of each, Erin. Everyone wants to be the very best, and anything less is not enough. Why can't you feel proud of your accomplishment today? Acknowledge how hard you've worked and for how long, and be proud of that work? No matter what it means to anyone else."

Erin couldn't look at her.

"I think you're setting yourself up for a long and unhappy life. If you feel proud only when you're the very best, you never will be proud. If you're happy only when you've beaten everyone else, you will never find happiness."

Felicity gently turned Erin's chin and stared into her glassy eyes until Erin looked away. "I'll see you at home."

Erin watched Felicity walk into the airport and straight to the terminals without any security whatsoever.

Erin told herself Felicity didn't know how it felt to lose something she really, really wanted. Or to be upstaged in her own pool.

Erin could claim national champion on her Columbia application, but being champion of a tiny country wouldn't change her life.

She joined Percy in the car. "Are you sure it's safe for Felicity to fly? There was no security or anything. Couldn't a terrorist hijack the plane or something?"

"Not likely in New Zealand," Percy said. "If you were going to hijack a plane, you'd better do it somewhere closer to wherever you wanted to be."

Erin wasn't sure where she wanted to be. She didn't want to return to Wheaton. She mostly didn't want to be in the tiny house in Christchurch. She wanted to be settled in her great life, fifteen years from now.

"The general rule here is: if your plane is big enough to reach Australia, go through security. Otherwise, hop aboard."

Of course. Because kiwis were all so happy. Most hijackings were for or about the United States, and what hijacker is patient enough for a flight that long?

Percy zoomed back toward the house on stilts. "You all right?"

"I'm fine."

"Seem pretty blasé after such a huge accomplishment. Something else going on with you?"

New Zealand good, not American good.

Erin reached for the next truth in line. "I'm not sure winning the championship will make any difference to colleges, is all."

"Can't help you there. Hey, want to get pizza for our crew? We'll have a proper celebration tonight."

Hairy Buffalo and Ben were still too front of mind for Erin to consider any sort of celebration.

BEFORE SHE ABSCONDED TO THE OBSERVATORY
BEFORE SHE ABSCONDED TO THE OBSERVATORY

Tears welled in Erin's eyes as she stepped inside Lalitha's house. They had been swimming together since elementary school; surely their friendship could withstand Erin's fall from grace.

"Erin?" Lalitha's tiny sandals slapped the hardwood floor as she rushed to embrace her friend. "What is it?"

"Everything is ruined," Erin said.

Lalitha held her at an arm's distance. "Is this about those damned Quigleys barging into our pool? Their timing is shit. That is a truly lame pre-birthday surprise."

"You think so, then? I'm off the team?"

"Maybe? Probably. I'm so pissed I could spit."

"Spit, Li? Really?"

"I'm so pissed I could drink."

Erin squared her shoulders. "Right. Where's the alcohol?"

"Atta girl." Lalitha taped a sign to the door—COME ON IN!—and led Erin to the kitchen where a mountain of junk food covered the double island. Five towers of blue plastic cups flanked a pyramid of soda cases.

Lalitha raised three fingers in mock salute. "I solemnly swear I will not swim relay with any of the damned Quigleys."

"Don't martyr yourself for my sake."

212

Erin had reacquainted herself with the Quigleys' times, so she knew any Quigley would guarantee her relay team a berth at States.

"I'm speaking on principle, Erin. How do we know they won't throw a race to spite us?"

"You're flirting with conspiracy theories, Li. They're not trying to ruin our record."

"Damned Quigleys."

Erin whispered, "You're not helping."

"Ah, but I do have something that will help!" Lalitha withdrew a vat of pink liquid from the fridge. "This is special for you! I couldn't buy wine coolers or ciders because I sort of exhausted my brother's patience with the beer. But this is something special that Anil drinks at U of I. It has some vodka in it. And strawberry stuff, so it tastes good. Three pounds of fresh fruit, too, so it's kind of healthy? I guess? He calls it Hairy Buffalo, which I find hilarious." Lalitha filled a plastic cup and garnished it with extra fruit.

Any alcohol was a fine alternative to beer, so Erin poked a pale-pink pineapple chunk floating on the surface and took a swig. "Li, you'll still love me if I'm off the team, right?"

"Are you kidding? For life. And tonight, you are going to drink that, party with friends, and feel all better. Tomorrow we can work up a plan to send those damned Quigleys back where they belong."

"Still? We're still talking about this?" Ben wrapped his arms around Erin's waist from behind.

She faced him and forced a smile. "Hi."

Lalitha said, "You two are too cute. Birthday pic! Gimme your phone!" She snapped photo-booth pics of them, cheek to cheek, forehead to forehead, lip to lip.

Ben looked beyond Erin to Lalitha. "Did you tell her yet?"

"It's your surprise, Loverboy." Lalitha pulled something small from her pocket and passed it to Ben, who palmed it.

A dozen guys swarmed into the kitchen, offering Lalitha and Erin cursory hugs before pawing through the snack mountain.

"Keg is tapped on the back porch," Lalitha said, handing each of them a plastic cup as they filed toward the back door.

Erin glanced between her best friend and boyfriend. "Tell me!"

Ben and Lalitha shared a conspiratorial look.

Ben wrapped his arms around Erin again. "For your birthday, I convinced—"

"We convinced!"

"Right," Ben said. "Lalitha's mom is letting us—you and I—use the observatory tonight."

Erin's heart leapt. Studying the night sky had been a nightly affair at her grandparents' lake house; it took the universe to a whole new level of intimacy. And Lalitha's mom rarely shared her observatory, let alone allowed an unsupervised visit during a party.

Lalitha's mom was very protective of her ten-thousand-dollar telescope, so Erin was dubious. "Did she really say it was okay?"

Lalitha shrugged. "I'm not saying she did. And I'm not saying she didn't. Suffice it to say the room is yours for the night. Wipe down any parts you touch. And don't touch anything but the telescope. And not the lens or the eyepiece. She is very particular, okay?" Her piercing stare darted between Ben and Erin until their eager nodding convinced her they would behave.

"Good. When you're done, lock the door, come find me, and put the key back in my hand. Got it?"

"Got it," they echoed.

Ben shouted, "Happy birthday!" and voices echoed all around. He rested his hand on Erin's hip. "What are you drinking tonight?"

"Hairy Buffalo. Really, really sweet, but light-years better than beer." Erin sipped the sickeningly sweet Pepto-colored beverage.

"Maybe we finally found a drink for you!" Ben whispered, "And at midnight, we can really celebrate your birthday. Nothing stands between you and me and the best night of our lives."

Erin sucked in a wisp of air as Ben's fingers ran along her upper thigh. She'd rather skip the socializing and head upstairs immediately.

FORTY-FIVE

After swimming year-round for half a decade, the end of swim season left Erin with a gaping hole in her schedule. Felicity asked her to meet Pippa after school most days, so that killed an hour.

At Ilam Primary, parents chatted on benches circling the playgrounds. Erin untied Grandma Tea's ring from inside her bag and slid it onto her left middle finger as young siblings wrestled on playground equipment until school was out. Erin eavesdropped on moms' conversations as kids climbed up a row of posts and leapt into a sandpit.

Pippa burst from room 12, bounded toward Erin, and greeted her with an enormous hug. Erin tried to hold Pippa at arm's length. Hanging off a big sister could make Pippa look clingy and ruin her reputation for years.

She refused to hold Pippa's hand as they walked toward the bus stop, where several dozen other Ilam Primary kids lounged in the grass in uniform.

On the Metrostar, they squeezed into adjacent seats and Pippa's attention turned to Erin.

"Do you have a story of your life for me today?"

One afternoon, Erin had talked about singing with her grandparents, and now Pippa wanted a story every day: about summers in Michigan or her old friends or life in Wheaton.

Pippa's rose-colored glasses were almost charming. She reminded Erin of herself at ten. Pippa would have loved summers in the U.P.

Erin held up her left hand. "Today I want to tell you about my ring."

Pippa wanted to hold Grandma Tea's ring. Erin held her breath as if the ring would magically transfer ownership when Pippa slid it down her finger.

"Why aren't there any stones underneath?"

Erin had no idea why the channel setting only went three quarters of the way around. "That is a very good question. My grampa gave that ring to my grandmother for her seventeenth birthday. He would have been twenty at the time. I don't imagine he could afford stones going all the way around."

Pippa had a million questions—*Was it an engagement ring? Did she always wear it? What did she do when he gave her a real engagement ring? How did Grandma Tea feel about the stones not going all the way around?*

Erin knew her grandmother had admired a different ring in a shop window, and this one was similar, but she didn't know whether the original one—the one Erin's grampa presumably couldn't afford—had stones going all the way around it. But knowing Tea, she probably was just happy to have the ring.

And to have him. They were always sappy in love.

Grandma Tea claimed the spark had never left them. Grampa definitely would have stood by Tea if she'd accidentally barfed in his lap.

Erin couldn't imagine her grandparents in Lalitha's observatory. *Ew.* Not an image she wanted in her head.

Finally, on the way home, they covered black holes and dying stars.

After Pippa and Erin shared afternoon tea, Pippa retreated to the trampoline and Erin sat on the sofa with her homework. Between feeling mad at Ben and feeling sorry for herself and worrying about what kind of social scene awaited her in Wheaton, Erin was a complete wreck.

She was unwilling to relive the Hairy Buffalo incident over and over, but she couldn't help it. She wished the whole world already knew, so she would never need to rehash the story again. Then, perhaps, she could leave it behind her.

Pippa retired from the trampoline and joined her in the living room. "You're staring into space, you know?"

"Sorry," Erin said and opened her computer. Hitting rock bottom, she pored over hundreds of photos of Ben she'd tucked into a folder on her hard drive. Ben playing basketball. Ben snuggled up to her on her sofa. Ben driving her Fiat. Ben doing a keg stand. Her arm wrapped around him, holding their twin plastic cups at Lalitha's party. That was the last one of them together.

Screw him.

Before she could change her mind, she pulled up Claudia's contact information and fired off a few texts.

Erin: Claudia, this is Erin Cerise.
Erin: First, thanks for your kindness when I was drunk.
Erin: Second, steer clear of Ben.
Erin: What happened between us in that observatory wasn't what it seemed.

Erin: But I was super drunk, and he didn't treat me the way a
good guy would treat his girlfriend.

Erin: It is clear to me (both from that night and from Lalitha)
you deserve a good guy.

Erin: Actually, all of us deserve good guys.

"Please reply," Erin said. As if in reponse, someone pounded
on the front door.

FORTY-SIX

Through the bay window, Erin spied a grinning Hank bearing a cardboard box.

Pippa yelled, "Hank!" and let him in without consulting anyone.

"Hey, Pip!"

"Can you stay for dinner? Mum is making shepherd's pie!"

"We can talk about that. Is Erin here?"

Erin wished Hank had either heard nothing about Hairy Buffalo, or heard everything and was already past it.

Pippa led him by the hand to the living room.

Hank bit his lip. "Hi."

Erin did not roll her eyes, shake her head, or use a dismissive voice, as she knew she'd done in his presence in the past. She played it straight. "Hi."

"You're home early," he said.

"Swim is over."

"I know. I mean." Blushing, he thrust the box in her general direction. "I heard." Hank looked at Pippa, then back to Erin. "I heard you'd had a rough couple of days. I also, uh, heard that you came to New Zealand because of, um, stuff at home."

Flames burned from her chin to her forehead. Now Hank knew all her secrets. All of New Zealand knew about the pink puke. And Ben. And the Quigleys.

Damned Quigleys.

Erin squared her shoulders. She could stand up for herself.

Hank stared at the carpet and fiddled with the metal rings hanging off his pants. "So, uh, this is to sort of cheer you up. And, uh, I thought I might continue with your tourism efforts and show you a little about Christchurch and the CBD."

He held the box toward her again, and Erin accepted it with straight arms, as if it might be a bomb.

"I'm getting around just fine."

He bit his lip again. "Right. I just. I go rock climbing at The Roxx a couple days a week. It might be a good way for you to meet people now that you have more time for fun."

"I've met plenty of people, thanks. Swimming is over, but we still hang out."

"Right. Well. I wrote the address inside the box, so if you change your mind. It's 4:15 Mondays and Thursdays. Come any time. Tell Felicity I'll have you home for tea. Only if you want."

Pippa said, "Stay for tea today. Mum would love to have you. She'll be home any moment."

Erin said, "Pippa, enough. Let the guy go."

"What is it with you? Don't you like boys?"

If only Pippa knew. "I think I'll finish my work in my room."

"Want to jam?" Pip asked Hank.

"Sure, I can stick a minute."

Erin slammed her bedroom door and threw the box on her bed. She didn't feel like homework.

Hank's box was full of junk food: Arnott's Caramel Crowns, a bar of Cadbury's milk chocolate, Hokey Pokey Squiggles, gummy bears *(SCORE!)*, mini Crunchie bars, pineapple lumps, and chocolate fish.

She texted Lalitha.

Erin: You will never believe who just stopped by the house.
Erin: Hank.
Erin: He knows the whole story.
Erin: Lalitha?

It was Friday evening in Wheaton, like the one time a week when Lalitha could reliably text.

Erin: HELLO OUT THERE
Erin: He brought me a box of candy.
Litha: I am on a DATE, Erin. Talk tomorrow?

Well, fuck.

Erin read Hank's note about climbing and found more written on the back. *Dear Erin: We don't have Dove chocolate, Twix, Oreos, or Butterfinger. And we have nothing anywhere close to fudge stripe cookies. But we do have Haribo gummy bears, agreed far and wide to be the very best. (I tossed in some pineapple lumps and chocolate fish, which are my favorites.) I hope this cheers you. Sorry about your bad week.*

She flipped over the package of Caramel Crowns to find a note scrawled in Sharpie: *Twix?* Caramel Crowns had caramel inside, not entirely unlike Twix. The Squiggles had a note, too: *Oreos?* The huge Cadbury bar: *Not Dove, but our best.* At the bottom of the box, a small white box held a rectangular piece of chocolate cake: *I doubt you've found your favorite café slice yet. Based on everything else I know you like, I chose chocolate caramel for you.*

Lucky guess. And how had he known about everything else? She reread his notes. She couldn't remember mentioning any of this to him.

This box of sweets was the most thoughtful gift she'd ever received. And it was from *Hank*.

She picked up the box and found him and Pippa playing guitars at the dining room table. Felicity was home and prepping dinner.

Felicity said, "Hank, what are your plans for the holidays?"

"Rock climbing with the crew. We're heading up to Wharepapa for ten days."

Erin said, "You take off work for the school break?"

"Most of New Zealand just stops for two weeks. People don't want you working in their house when they're home with their kids, or when they're away at the batch for a week."

Erin said, "Are we going to the beach for a week?"

"A bach—B-A-C-H—is like a summer place or holiday house," Felicity said. "We're thinking about the North Island. If we don't head up there, we might hit Tata and Pohara on Golden Bay."

Tata and Wharepapa were so New Zealand.

Hank said, "I should go."

"Thanks for the box."

He studied his shoes. "No worries. And the rock climbing offer still stands."

This guy had searched all over Christchurch for something approaching a comforting care package for her. She couldn't very well say no. "Sure. I'll try next week."

Hank hugged Pippa good-bye. "Lesson on Sunday?"

She gave him a thumb's up and saw him out.

Erin asked Felicity, "So, what's Golden Bay?"

"Huge crescent beach on the north end of the South Island. It stretches forever. On fair days, you can see from one tip to the other. We don't have a bach, because we like to explore. What did Hank bring you?"

"A box of sweets."

"That was a pretty big box for sweets."

"Yeah," Erin said, opening the Caramel Crowns. "He did a good job."

Hank had searched for ways to comfort her and had been so attentive he somehow knew exactly what she needed.

BEFORE SHE PARTIED WITH LALITHA

BEFORE SHE PARTIED WITH LALITHA

Erin needed to see Ben.

She drove up the long driveway to find him perched on the front porch in jeans and a striped sweater. Ben pulled Erin from the Fiat and into his arms; he was an instant balm to her panic.

Bushy firs shielded them from the street, but not from Ben's next-door neighbor, who weeded his garden between surreptitious glances in their direction.

When Ben pressed Erin up against his house and kissed her, she didn't care who could see. Who needed a swimming captainship when she had Ben?

He slipped his hands to her backside and shifted Erin into their most comfortable vertical position: limbs encircling each other to maximize contact.

When their frantic, hungry kissing relaxed into sated pecks, Ben toyed with Erin's ringlets. "Symphony practice good this morning?"

Erin nodded before voicing the fear growing within her. "I told you about those new girls—the Quigleys—do you think Waterson will kick me off the team because of them?"

"I think—" Ben's hands swept across her belly, searching

225

for the right words. "I think a lot can happen in a few months. Look at us! Last May I didn't even know you, and by July we were—well, you know."

Their relationship had taken root quickly, growing from unknown to full force. Within two months, Ben had become her present and her future.

She searched his face for answers. "But what if it's over for me?"

"So what? You gotta find that silver lining. You can make more of my basketball games. And you'll have more time for moon gazing, right next to me instead of over the phone."

The moon's constant presence comforted and fascinated her. Nothing outside of Wheaton fascinated Ben, but witnessing Erin's awe during a penumbral lunar eclipse had inspired him to indulge her. They often stared at the moon during their brief nightly phone calls; it was the one daily moment that was irrevocably theirs.

Erin had also believed swimming, speed, and competitiveness defined her and was irrevocable. Before she could explain that, Ben was kissing her again.

Swimming, cello prowess, and great (but not amazing) grades formed what Erin's guidance counselor had dubbed "the tripod of her Columbia candidacy," and a third of that tripod was teetering.

Time with Ben might diminish the pain of leaving swimming, but Ben had no pull at Columbia; she couldn't put him on her résumé. An Ivy League education—complete with solid connections and lucrative opportunities—would propel Erin into a great medical school, a great job, a great life. Erin's mom attested that breaking into the Ivy League after undergrad was a steep, uphill battle, so she needed to get in now.

Erin needed to be exceptional.

Ben kissed up her neck and held her so close that his features blurred in her vision. "Hey, I get that you're worried, but it will all work out. This won't change us. I love you, and that won't change. We're solid, Erin."

Here their opinions diverged. Ben had already committed to play basketball for Stony Brook, where he could keep his car and visit her in New York City on weekends. Rejection from Columbia would be fatal: she and Ben would have an expiration date.

Ben kissed Erin, but she struggled to lose herself in him again. This was the same helpless feeling she'd had the night before when Ruth Quigley had pulled ahead of her during time trials. The wall of the pool had seemed to retreat into the distance, virtually unreachable.

Without Columbia, her entire future would fall apart.

Ben palmed Erin's glutes, pulling her closer. She turned her head away as he kissed her ear.

"If I can't captain the team, that leaves a huge void in my college applications. I can't swim JV as a senior." She searched his face for a glimmer of understanding.

"Why not? Your times are the same either way. And I don't care if you're JV or V." He breathed heavily in her ear and tugged at the waist of her shorts. "Well, I care about your 'v.' I care about your 'v' a whole lot."

"Ben!" She whipped around to find Ben's neighbor leaning on his rake, staring.

Ben maneuvered himself between the neighbor and Erin, her Fiat blocking them from the waist down. Erin's core pulsed as Ben slipped his hands up her shorts, brushing her upper thigh. She loved that Ben made her body hum.

"I cannot wait for our long limo ride tomorrow night," he said.

"We don't have to wait that long, do we?"

"Nope. I have an amazing surprise for you tonight." Ben kissed her between words.

"What is it?"

"Can't ruin the surprise! Call it an early birthday present."

She loved surprises. "How about a hint?"

A cobalt sedan reversed into the driveway and Ben retracted his hand to wave. Erin readjusted her outfit.

"I'll show you tonight. Gotta go to Jamie's." Ben and his best friends had plastered their cars with bumper stickers for radio stations, music shops, and cringeworthy phrases like MAYBE THE HOKEY POKEY IS WHAT IT'S ALL ABOUT. When they drank too much, they often crooned "The Hokey Pokey," sometimes removing articles of clothing instead of the usual motions.

Ben pecked Erin's cheek. "Sorry to get you all hot and bothered."

"I'm sure you are. Text me when you're on your way to Lalitha's."

Ben walked backward toward the car, his eyes still on Erin. "I'm sure we'll have things to say before that."

Erin arrived home to an empty house and a note from her parents. *Sailing with Heather and Paul! One hour of cello, one draft of admissions essay in my inbox, and all homework done or you can't sleep over at Lalitha's.*

Privately, Erin added *Spend the rest of the day on intensive worry about your college prospects* before making a snack and heading to her room in silence.

FORTY-SEVEN

Felicity was going to Wellington for three days to meet her brand-new niece. As Hamish loaded her luggage into the Nissan, Erin said, "May I try out your bike while you're gone?"

"It's not a mountain bike," Felicity said.

"I'd like to try biking to school so I don't have to stick to the bus schedule."

Felicity pulled her helmet off the wall and handed it to Erin. "Think you can suss this out?"

"I'm sure I can."

"Careful on the roundabout. There are signs for bikers. Use the footpath on the bridge, then take care when crossing roundabout exits. Drivers will watch out for you, but it's tricky. Do *not* try to use the roundabout as a car might."

"Got it," Erin said. "Thanks."

"You're welcome."

Erin was stunned by the straightforward transaction. She often had to convince Claire she'd already agreed to something to get her to agree to it. If Erin claimed to have received a green light while Claire was at work, on the phone, working out, or otherwise occupied, Claire never refuted it. She knew she was always distracted, and Erin took full advantage.

Yes, she was a bit of a manipulator back home, but she needn't be one here. Here, more importantly, she would become a biker.

With each gust of wind, Erin's skirt flew up. For several minutes, she held the hem to keep her underwear private. At the bridge, she gave up. Underwear was practically a swimsuit, and half the world had seen her dressed down to that. She rolled up the waist of her skirt and biked away. It was freezing. *Christchurch mornings.*

Getting to school was easier than she'd expected, and the roundabout signage was no trouble.

At Ilam, Erin surveyed the treasure trove of bicycles to the left of the administration building. Swathes of students chatted as they unbuckled their helmets and parked for the day. No bikes were locked.

They were either trusting or stupid, and she couldn't afford to be either with Felicity's new bike. She locked it to the huge, metal structure.

Good decision. No bus ride. Not using her bus card meant she didn't have to find time to refill it, either. She hadn't been sardined into the back of the bus. And she could bike to The Roxx far more easily than transferring buses.

"Waited for you at the bus stop this morning," Marama said at lunch.

"I biked today."

"No kidding. Mind if I borrow it to run to Bush Inn? I bused today and I'm dying for sushi."

What could go wrong?

"Sure. No worries."

Erin walked Marama to the bike rack and unlocked the bike. "It's 0-9-1-9. You have to lock it up at Bush Inn, okay?"

Marama agreed and was off.

Being the one with the bike was cool.

Ruby's guitar trio fumbled through "Under the Bridge" as Erin settled back into her corner. It had taken her ages to learn that riff; she should offer to help them.

Giving up, they switched to original music. Words were never Erin's forte, but these musicians were rhyming *a capella* with *stellar*. Stella! Pure brilliance.

Marama wasn't back with the bike when the bell rang for fourth period. Erin rushed to class, the bike on her mind.

She texted Marama and didn't hear back.

Bush Inn wasn't that far away. Maybe Marama had an accident. Or totaled the bike.

Shit, shit, shit.

Erin stood outside her classroom door until the very last second. Still no sign of Marama.

Erin didn't see her between classes, and she was absent from literature.

By last period, Erin was in full-on panic mode. She may have enabled the sweetest girl in school to break her neck or worse. And Felicity would kill her for wrecking her perfect brand-new bike.

———

Marama stood against the admin building as usual after school. She smiled as Erin approached.

"Thanks again, Erin," she said. "My salmon sushi was yum."

No mention of any accidents or lost bicycle. Erin feigned composure. "Sure thing. Any time."

"It's a nice ride."

"Thanks. It's Felicity's. Did you lock it up?"

"It was tricky, but I think I did it right."

"Awesome."

Relieved, Erin circled back around the admin building to the bike rack. She congratulated herself for being cool. New Zealand cool, which was different from being cool in Wheaton. Cool in Wheaton was more about what she owned, how she dressed, and how she managed adults. Here, it was about being laid back. Ironically, she had to work pretty hard at that.

Felicity's bike was nowhere to be found. Erin perused the length of the bike rack five times before dropping her books and running back to Marama, who also was nowhere to be found.

This wasn't happening. Hamish and Felicity would be pissed. Any equity Erin had built up after her Not American Good comment would disappear. What could she do?

"Erin?" Jade called out. "Something wrong?"

"I lost Felicity's bike. It's not on the rack."

Jade grabbed Erin's upper arm. "Look at me. Relax. We'll look together."

Jade followed Erin around the admin building, where only three bikes remained. Everyone else had cleared off after school.

"Well, I guess it isn't lost among the throngs," Jade said. "You're sure this is where you left it?"

"Does it matter? I don't see a bike lying out in the open, either."

"Touchy."

"Sorry. It's just—she kind of thinks I'm spoiled and irresponsible. This is going to seal the deal for her."

Jade's face softened. "It will turn up. Are you sure you locked it here?

"I lent it to Marama at lunch because she wanted sushi." She wanted to say Marama was flighty.

While Erin explained, some huge guy picked up one of the remaining bikes. Two girls casually collected the last two. Erin wasn't expecting Felicity's bike to magically materialize when all the other bikes were taken, but still, the empty bike rack pained her.

What have I done?

"I'm sorry, Erin. I have to catch the next bus or Mum will be furious. You going to be okay here?"

Erin nodded, though she was decidedly not okay. She was screwed.

Jade turned back two times on her way off campus. The second time, she gave a thumb's up, as if everything would be just fine.

Erin walked to the middle of campus. No bike. Between buildings and around the canteen. No bike. The racks were still empty when she passed by on her way to—yes, the bus.

Erin felt like an asshole for losing Felicity's bike. Her birthday present. A thousand-dollar bike! A thousand dollars was undoubtedly a lot of money for Hamish. Without a bike, Felicity had no transportation to work until she could shell out a thousand dollars for another bike.

And she'd believe Erin was irresponsible.

If you can fix it for under a thousand dollars, it's not a problem.

Erin probably could fix this problem for around a thousand dollars. Did that count? The only consequence of buying a thousand-dollar bike was a very angry dad, and he'd get over it.

A thousand dollars wouldn't affect her parents' bottom

line. And Felicity would have a bike and wouldn't be out the money.

And—if Erin was really good—Felicity and Hamish would never know she'd lost it.

Erin needed empathy.

And help.

And wheels.

She called Hank.

FORTY-EIGHT

A half hour later, Erin and Hank entered Spokes, Hank's best guess for the shop where Hamish had bought Felicity's bike.

After much deliberation, they agreed on a make and model. When they explained the dilemma to the guy working the shop, he checked his books and proved that Erin and Hank had no clue what they were talking about. Felicity's had been a limited-edition women's Diamondback, and Spokes had only one left in stock.

Another woman in the shop was keen to hear about this particular model.

Erin dialed Marama to be sure there was no other way out of this situation. Unfortunately, Erin was unable to play cool. Instead, she left a breathless message asking for Marama's assurance that she'd locked up the bike.

"Can we think about it for a minute?" Erin asked the shopkeeper, who immediately started touting the bike's features to the other customer.

Really? Today? She couldn't have come looking tomorrow?

"What do you think?" Hank said.

"If Marama didn't lock it, there is a small possibility someone accidentally took it home."

"Were there any bikes left on the rack?"

"Empty."

"So, where did the accidental bike borrower leave their own bike?"

Damn. "Maybe someone took it for a joyride?"

"Doubtful." Hank's fake, hopeful smile didn't help.

She scowled. "You look like a helpful person, but you're not all that helpful."

"Anything that sounds helpful would be a lie. I'm not going to lie to you."

"What would you do?"

"I wouldn't lend a friend my mother's sweet ride, that's for sure."

Hank wasn't sure how to react when sobs heaved out of Erin. He wrapped his arms around her but was tentative about actually touching her with his hands.

It was fake comfort.

He whispered, "Call Felicity. Tell her what happened and ask her what she'd like you to do."

"No chance."

The shopkeeper adjusted a helmet onto the head of the other woman and let her take a test ride on the street.

"We can look for it tonight. And tomorrow."

That sounded like the sanest option, but Erin felt certain that by tomorrow she wouldn't be able to buy a replacement. Spokes wouldn't have another one for two months.

Marama called. "I promise you that I locked it. I locked it up at Bush Inn and at Ilam the same way you had it locked: through the frame and the wheel. I don't know what else to tell you."

She could say she was joking. She could say she'd split the cost of a new bike.

No. This was on Erin. Felicity would be back in two days. Erin had to fix this. "Thanks, Marama. I'll see you tomorrow."

If Marama was sure she'd locked it, someone had cut the lock deliberately and stolen it. It was gone.

Under guise of dusting his inventory, the shopkeeper eavesdropped on their conversation.

Erin was done pretending. "If I buy the bike and my bike turns up within the week, could I return it?"

The shop owner smiled. "We take returns for malfunctions only, not change of mind."

Of course not. Of COURSE NOT, New Zealand.

Hank jumped in. "What if she didn't ride it? I could drive the bike home and store it in her garage for a week until we've done a thorough search."

"I'm sorry. I have a customer who seems keen to buy it today so that is a poor value proposition for me."

Erin cursed flighty Marama. Something rumbled a second before the floor started shaking. Bikes hanging from the ceiling swayed and Hank and the bike guy held the counter tightly. Erin's first genuine earthquake. She held her breath until the room settled a few seconds later.

"Well, if that's not a sign, I don't know what is," Erin joked.

No one answered. She turned to find Hank pale and wide-eyed.

"Are you okay?"

Hank nodded quickly, his expression unchanged. He and the shop owner exchanged looks.

"Never gets easier, does it?" the shopkeeper said.

"Never," Hank said. "I can't get away from it. Never had trouble until 2011. Now? Every single time."

Erin asked, "What happened to you during that quake?"

Hank stared at the ground. "Can we skip it?"

"Of course."

The other customer returned, flustered. "Not today."

"No worries," the shop owner said. "Are you all right?"

"It never gets easier," she said before leaving.

Relieved, Erin pulled out her dad's Visa. "I'll take it."

Erin fought back tears as Hank parked in her driveway later. Her dad was going to kill her.

Hank said, "I can't believe you just spent a grand on a bike!"

"Yeah. My dad says if you can fix it for under a thousand dollars, it's not a problem."

Hank went silent. He managed the complex unbuckling of Felicity's new bike from his bike rack.

"Guess you're in luck. Twelve hundred is under a grand when you convert, innit?"

That was something.

He said, "I hope the bike turns up."

"I don't. If it shows up now, what will I do with it? What's lost is lost."

"Should have gotten that lady's number. Could have made a deal."

They parked the bike in its spot and Erin cursed. "The helmet. I can't replace Felicity's helmet." That would prove another issue entirely, because Felicity's helmet was old. As in no one was making orange helmets with racing stripes anymore.

Not to mention the fucking stickers.

"That's less than fifty bucks," Hank said.

"But then she'll know."

"I'm telling you. Being honest would be a lot easier."

Erin would have to fess up eventually, but at least she had fixed her own mistake. Or her dad's Visa had fixed her mistake.

Lucky for Erin, it was nearly her dad's birthday, when Claire forbid Mitchell to check credit card statements for fear he would ascertain his own birthday presents and ruin any surprises she'd planned. Christmas followed close behind, so at the very earliest, Erin could expect a lecture in January.

FORTY-NINE

At school the next day, Jade spotted Erin and broke away from her group of friends. "Sorry to leave you buggered last night," she said. "Did you work out the bike?"

"Sort of."

Jade cocked her head sideways.

"The bike was stolen. I bought a new one. It's identical."

Jade's jaw fell open. "Just like that, you bought a new one? How did you even find one? How did you pay for it?"

"It was Felicity's birthday present. Brand new a few months ago, so I went to the shop and dropped twelve hundred dollars on a bike."

"That's quite a dear mistake."

Erin frowned.

"Cost a lot of money, I meant. Amazing."

It was kind of amazing. Erin had taken the problem into her own hands and handled it. So what if Felicity would know anyway because of the helmet? Erin had owned her problem and fixed it, to her own detriment. "It is kind of amazing, isn't it?"

"Felicity might be impressed, actually."

"Yeah." Erin hoped.

"I was thinking," Jade said slowly. "Marama lives in Cashmere, right?"

Erin stared at her blankly. Who the hell cared where Marama lived?

"I'm asking because if she usually comes from the south, she's probably used to parking at the back entrance."

Two months in, Erin became aware of Ilam High's back entrance. With a bike rack. Where Marama, her totally responsible friend, had locked up Felicity's inordinately expensive bike.

And had tucked a tiny chocolate truffle into the helmet as thanks.

For the first time since she was ten, Erin now had her very own bike.

FIFTY

Thursday afternoon, Erin biked halfway across the city and parked at Hank's rock-climbing gym, The Roxx. Too late, she realized she'd forgotten climbing clothes.

"Hey!" she said when he arrived.

"Erin. Hi!" He opened the door for her.

Erin had seen a climbing wall or two online, and there once was a rock-climbing tower at the annual Cream of Wheaton festival, but Hank's gym was unreal. Some climbers bouldered close to the ground as she had at Castle Hill, but most were attached to ropes, climbing several stories overhead.

Erin turned to find Hank laughing with Marama's friend.

"Erin, this is Gloria, one of my best climbing partners. Gloria, Erin."

"Hi again," Gloria said.

"Hi!" Erin said, her cheeks growing hot at the idea of Hank climbing with Gloria.

"You went out with Marama, right?" Gloria asked as she pulled out her climbing shoes.

"Castle Hill, yes. And I was planning to climb today, but forgot a change of clothes."

A second later, Gloria withdrew clothes from her bag. "You can wear my emergency clothes if you want."

"Emergency clothes?"

"You know, if I'm up on a rock and *someone* spills his beverage from on high—"

"Once," Hank said. "It happened once."

"When it happened, we were a hundred kilometers away. All the ropes were set for the day. I spent the rest of the day green and sticky."

Erin grimaced. She hadn't heard about any climbing trips a hundred kilometers away. And who the hell was Gloria, anyway?

Gloria said, "Come on, Erin. Clothes are clean. Change up and have a go."

"Okay. I have to be home for dinner at 6:30, and I'm on a bike."

Without divulging any embarrassing details about the bike, Hank said, "I'll drive you back, if you like. Home by 6:30. I promise."

Out of excuses, Erin changed into shorts that were a little too tight and a shirt that was a little too loose in the bust. Gloria was the perfect shape, apparently.

When Erin emerged, Gloria was waiting. "You're all checked in! Just sign this."

Because Erin had surprised Hank, he hadn't brought his sisters' shoes. Erin rented a pair from the front desk and tried not to think about the masses who'd worn them before. She pinched them between her fingers and scrunched up her nose.

"Better or worse than foul breath?" Hank asked.

"What?"

"You and bad breath. Stinky shoes. Does every bad smell bother you?"

"I was trying to convince myself the gym washes them after every wearing."

Hank handed her a tangled bunch of straps. "Not bloody likely. Here: see whether this fits."

See if it fits what? She held it in front of her while Hank pulled bright ropes and a hundred tiny metal trapezoids from his bag. Gloria had her own thing-that-might-fit.

"Need help with your harness?" Hank asked. "Threw you in at the deep end, didn't I?"

"Deep ends aren't a problem for me. I just don't know what this thing is."

"You swim. Which stroke?"

"Butterfly."

"Make you a deal. I'll get you climbing, and you can teach me butterfly. Fair trade?"

"Fair trade," she said.

Hank twisted the harness around a few times until the shape made more sense. Two loops were burnt orange. He squatted and held one toward her right foot. "This leg in here. Other leg in here."

When her legs were in the right holes, she pulled the belt up near her hips, tugging the leg holes around the tops of her thighs.

"Those are too loose," Hank kneeled before her and slipped his hands through her legs. The titillating moment made her blush. Hank tightened the straps until they were snug around her thighs. It felt like a diaper.

She was well out of her comfort zone, clothes-wise. But then, Gloria and Hank were wearing the same gear. No one cared.

Rocks and holds in an array of colors cluttered the walls. People had decorated with patterned duct tape.

Hank said, "One of us will belay you. We'll hold the end of your rope taut so you can climb safely." He looped the rope through Erin's harness and tied an elaborate knot in the end.

He taught her simple belay commands. "And if you need to take a break on the wall, just yell 'take' and wait for me to say 'got.' Then you can rest and I'll hold you."

I'll hold you. Despite that not being remotely romantic, Erin blushed and her belly flipped over.

She stood at the bottom of the rock face. "On belay?"

"Belay on," Hank said.

"Climbing?"

"Climb on."

And she did.

FIFTY-ONE

Her first time up the rock face, Hank said almost nothing. While she was on the wall, Marama arrived and roped in with Gloria. The two of them had a whole conversation about good holds and stemming out and slopers.

Climbing had a foreign lexicon Erin knew nothing about.

Hank didn't use any of it. He left her to find her own holds. She ran her fingers over the rock above her head until she'd found something big enough to hold onto. She looked down to find something for her opposite foot, and when she found it, she pushed up and pulled up simultaneously.

Repeat.

Halfway up the rock, she stalled, her feet throbbing in the torturous shoes. She rested her forehead against the rock.

"Need a wee break?" Hank asked.

"No. I'm fine."

"Take!" Marama yelled.

"Got!" Gloria yelled back.

Marama scrambled back and forth like a pendulum until she was two feet from Erin. "You okay?"

Erin said, "Just trying to find something to hang onto."

"Yell 'take.' And have a rest."

"I don't need a rest."

"Trust me."

It was almost a whisper. "Take."

The rope yanked her up an inch or two. "Got!" Hank yelled. He held her entire weight.

Erin pulled up on tiptoe and still couldn't find a sufficient hold. What's more, Hank had hoisted her up two inches, which must be cheating.

Marama said, "He's really got you. You can sit and have a break if you want."

Erin's harness made a reasonable seat, and her thighs were grateful for the rest. From her perch, she spotted three reasonable handholds.

"Climbing," she shouted before scurrying up the wall in no time.

She held onto the top, dangling her legs in the air. "Falling!"

Hank called, "Fall on," and lowered her to the mat.

Gloria untied Erin's rope and tethered it to her own harness. Marama had gone bouldering in the other room.

"What did you think?" Gloria said.

"I loved it. Indoors is a lot easier than outside. Just hang onto anything and go."

"Yep. This is a great place to practice, but the real challenge is outdoors." Gloria turned to Hank. "I'm going for the 30."

She didn't climb straight up the rock face. Her moves were slow and calculated.

"What is she doing?" Erin asked.

Hank said, "The 30. Route's marked in red."

The patterned duct tape made sense as Gloria climbed what seemed like a strenuous and tricky route. Gloria shifted from full-on spread eagle to a tiny crouched position in a matter of seconds, then reached for a marked hold slightly out of reach.

She fell five feet.

"Missed it by a hair," Hank said as Gloria set up in her tiny crouched position and tried again.

She tried seven times, with longer and longer breaks between attempts. "I'm done," she hollered, and Hank lowered her.

Gloria untied the rope. "I'll have another go after I've warmed up."

While Gloria belayed Hank, Erin said, "Well that was a damn sight harder than just scrambling up the wall."

"What's that?" Gloria kept her focus on Hank, who was climbing a blue route.

"I said you were doing something really hard. I thought I was doing okay, scrambling right up the wall. But you were doing something amazing."

She nodded, her eyes on Hank. "You got it, baby!"

Each time Hank moved up a couple of feet, Gloria pulled taut the rope between herself and the thing at the top of the wall. A loop? A pulley? Erin couldn't tell from the floor and hadn't looked while she was climbing. With Hank's every shift, Gloria went through three motions: pull down with left, grab, pull down with right. Pull, grab, pull.

Belaying wasn't complicated.

Gloria grinned as Hank returned to the mat. "Took long enough," she said.

Erin said, "I thought that was pretty fast."

"I've has been trying that 27 for two weeks," Hank said. "In my defense, it was set by a tiny contortionist woman who does not design routes for human climbers."

Gloria unhooked her belay device. "I didn't have a problem with it."

"I didn't say superhuman."

Erin said, "Can I try?"

Hank and Gloria wore matched expressions of surprise.

"Maybe we should try you on something a little easier," Gloria said. "There's a really nice 14 over there."

So Gloria was a 30, Marama and Hank were 27s, and she was a 14? *No way.*

"I'm pretty strong. A month ago, I was the best swimmer in New Zealand." She couldn't believe she'd brought that up.

"Sure, go for it," Gloria said.

And, of course, they were right. Erin couldn't even stabilize herself on the starting holds. The barrette-shaped handhold was barely a nubbin sticking out of the wall. And that was the better handhold. The other one was reachable only after opening stance was established, and she couldn't even do that.

Hank kept the rope taut, but he and Gloria were quiet as Erin worked. Her face sweat as she moved her fingers around that stupid little nubbin, trying to find purchase where there was no friction. She chalked up her hands like Hank had taught her. She chalked the hold. She chalked the wall.

It wasn't happening.

At eye level, Erin read the route key. Erin's stripe-y route was rated a 27. She also could try Gloria's 30, another 27, a 19, or a 13.

The starting holds for the 19 felt reasonable. Without looking at them, Erin said, "I'll try the 19. Climbing."

"Climb on," Hank said.

She followed Gloria's instructions: two whole seconds on the starting holds before climbing. And, finally, she could move upward. She made quick work of the first four feet but wasn't even out of bouldering range before she was stumped.

Gloria called, "You have a right foot inside your right knee."

What the hell?

"If you feel around near your right knee, you'll find a foothold for your right foot."

She felt around and found it.

"Not that one. Up a little."

Her shoes were starting to hurt again. She tapped another with her right toe.

"That's it. Turn your right knee in and lean back."

Erin reached up with her right hand, but the hold was out of reach.

Gloria would not shut up. "Look up and to your left."

Erin found it. They continued this way—Erin trying holds just out of reach and Gloria helping her work up the wall—until she reached the top.

"Falling," she said.

Gloria said, "I got some pics of you up there. Nice work."

"Not as nice as that 30," Erin said.

"Been climbing since I could walk. Did you have fun?"

Had she? Climbing was a puzzle. A physical puzzle. And it was a lot different than managing her air and maximizing her strokes. "It was fun. And a damn sight harder than bouldering."

"View's not as good, either: We're heading up to Payne's Ford over the summer holidays," Gloria said. "Limestone, with climbing for all sorts of abilities. You should come."

Even weak-ass people like Erin could climb there. "Maybe.

I am supposed to go back to the States when term 4 ends. That's in December."

"I am keenly aware of when I graduate!" Gloria said.

"You're in school?"

"Christchurch Girls. That's how I met Hank. His sister, Meg, was in year 13 when I was in year 9."

"She taught you to climb?"

"I taught her, more like."

Hank smiled. "In our age bracket, Gloria is the seventeenth best climber in the world."

Gloria rolled her eyes. "It's not about the title. Competing gives you access to the most challenging and gorgeous terrain on Earth. I do it for the views."

Erin had only ever competed to win.

BEFORE SHE DROVE TO BEN

BEFORE SHE DROVE TO BEN

Quigleys.

Erin heard the whispers before she saw them. Three lean swimmers, walking in file, approached her swim team.

Erin's summer team coach, Waterson, pushed out of the crowd, falling over himself to present them, though introductions weren't required. Claudia, Ruth, and Hillary Quigley were three of the best swimmers in the nation; everyone anticipated an Olympic berth for the whole family. The littlest sister—the sophomore—had won the 100-yard fly at Nationals, but all of them had raced in finals.

Something funky was going on in their gene pool, for sure: one was blonde with brown eyes, one brunette with blue eyes, and the third brown on brown with olive skin. The oldest Quigley, Ruth, was shorter by an inch, but with extra years of muscle.

Waterson asked everyone to give their names and strokes.

Lalitha grinned so hard she had dimples, but Erin could hardly smile. "Erin Cerise. Hundred-yard-fly and relay."

Claudia Quigley said, "We swim fly, too."

No fucking kidding.

Losing her relay team for the summer season wasn't dire. And, if she trained with the Quigleys all summer, Erin might learn a few things.

Her future was still bright.

Waterson, grinning in full veneers, said "Erin, Lalitha, Sam, Jamie—these ladies are transferring to Wheaton, so they'll join your team next autumn. Be sure to show them around."

And just like that, Erin's future slipped through her fingers.

FIFTY-TWO

At ten past six, Hank hugged Gloria and Marama good-bye and loaded Felicity's bike onto his rack.

He closed his door and turned to Erin. "That's an amazing facsimile of Felicity's helmet."

After hearing the whole story, Hank said, "I assumed you'd scoped all the bike racks."

"Next time, I will."

"So you're up shit creek in leaky gumboots."

"Oh, I like that one!"

"Good, eh?"

"Really, Hank, I can't thank you enough for your help. And thanks for the delicious care package."

"So, I have a confession, too," Hank said.

"You stole the bike in an effort to spend more time with me?"

He laughed. "That would be a brilliant ploy. Next time, I will. I was going to say Marama was partly responsible for your care package. She gave me the idea. I just dug around your posts to find specifics."

Erin imagined how that could have happened. "Well, thanks. It did help. Thank you."

"Any time. Swinging by the sweetshop for caramel slices was no problem. Caramel is my favorite."

"Well, it was really thoughtful."

"My pleasure. I like seeing you happy."

"Have you seen me happy before?"

"Not much. But then, I don't think you subscribe to my life philosophy."

"And what might that be?"

Erin considered her own life philosophy while Hank focused on the double roundabout. If pressed, she might say *great medical school, great job, great life.* That sounded good.

As Hank zoomed into traffic, Erin caught his musky scent. Essence-of-Hank wasn't fresh, nor was it gross. She drew another breath. His scent was almost intoxicating.

After the roundabout, Hank said, "My philosophy is 'always ask for what you want, and always do what makes you happy.'"

That suited him. Quietly, hopefully, Erin asked, "So, what is it you want?"

He smiled. "My greatest skill in life has been to want but little."

Erin gaped at him.

"I didn't say that. That's Henry David Thoreau. It's from *Walden.*"

Erin knew it was Thoreau, but how did Hank know it was Thoreau? "I don't understand you at all."

"Howzat?" He turned into the driveway and their attention turned to Felicity, who stood in the garage with the new bike.

Hank unloaded the old bike, and Felicity said, "I'm so confused."

She looked between the twin bikes and back at Erin.

Hank said, "Erin bought a bike, but forgot to buy a helmet."

Grateful, Erin smiled at him. *Quick on his feet, this one.*

Felicity walked them into the garage and ran her fingers over her new bike seat, now Erin's new bike seat.

"I suppose you enjoyed biking to school?"

"I did."

"I guess it's going to be an everyday thing with you, then?"

Crap.

Erin said, "Yeah, and this one is actually yours. We'll need to find a way to tell them apart."

"I've got it!" Hank jogged back to his car and emerged with a sticker from The Roxx, which he plastered onto Erin's new top bar. "She's a rock climber now."

Felicity raised her eyebrows in disbelief.

"I am a convert," Erin said.

Felicity said, "I want to hear all about it."

FIFTY-THREE

Spring break in New Zealand was two full weeks. Same with autumn break and winter break. Two weeks, three times a year, and one six-week summer break at Christmas.

And every single time schools were on break, the Wakefield family traveled.

"I thought we'd bop around Golden Bay this year," Felicity said.

Pippa leapt at the news. Literally.

"Golden Bay it is."

Pippa was bouncing. "Can we stay at the caravan park?"

God, no. No.

"Maybe, Pip. Most people have been booked in for weeks. We'll see what we can do."

Pippa left, and Erin said, "So where will we stay, actually?"

"I do think the caravan parks will be full. But we can park the caravan almost anywhere. Not on the beach, of course, but we can get close."

Either option forced Erin to camp for days on end.

She said, "Do you think I could just stay here? I'm very responsible and have been alone overnight loads of times."

Felicity said, "This isn't an issue of trust. Of course, I trust you, but we'd miss you. And you'd miss out. It's a family holiday, and while you're here, you're family."

That afternoon, Erin muscled her FedEx box into her room, sliced it open, and could not fathom why she'd packed so much stuff.

She'd sorted most of her summer wardrobe when Felicity knocked.

"Erin, mobile service is lousy at Golden Bay. Maybe your holiday would be better if you brought a friend?"

"Probably, yes."

"Bring anyone you like, then. I really like that Marama."

"I do, too." Erin whipped out her phone and texted her.

"Erin?"

"Yes?"

"I'm sorry, I wasn't thinking before. I don't have much practice parenting teens."

Gobsmacked, Erin paused. "I think you're doing a pretty good job, actually."

Felicity bit her lower lip and smiled before leaving Erin to her phone.

Marama was sport climbing with Gloria, Hank, and other advanced climbers. Jade was heading to Dunedin. Gemma was seeing relatives on the North Island. Ruby was visiting her grandparents in Perth.

She had to go alone.

In her room, Erin spun in the chair and the room flashed before her eyes: bed, window, bed, stuffed closet, door, bed, window, bed, stuffed closet . . .

She stopped spinning and texted her mother.

Erin: On "holiday" with no cell service for the next two weeks.

Erin: Email instead and I'll reply when I'm back.

Claire didn't respond right away, but Erin knew she wouldn't text if she thought Erin wouldn't respond immediately. Two weeks of peace.

She still resented a two-week break without anyone her age. Even the best vacations dragged when Erin was away from her people.

BEFORE SHE GAVE HER HEART TO BEN

BEFORE SHE GAVE HER HEART TO BEN

The summer Erin was sixteen, she drove her new Fiat to the U.P. as soon as school was out. Six hours was a long time to dissect five small words.

I'm interested in your brain. The new guy, Ben, had said that to her. Twice. What did that even mean?

She debated until she crossed the bridge into the U.P., and Ben texted her. She pulled over at her first opportunity.

Ben Grey: When do you come back?
Erin: Ten days.
Ben Grey: June 16th?
Erin: At the latest. And I leave again on the 17th.
Ben Grey: Where to?
Erin: Summer study in Massachusetts.
Ben Grey: So are you free the evening of the 16th?
Erin: I am.
Ben Grey: May I take you out on a date?
Erin: You may!
Ben Grey: Do you get a signal up there?
Erin: I do.

Ben Grey: Let's keep in touch.
Erin: Will do. I'm nearly there. Talk later.

A date, a date, a date, a date! Erin didn't know people had dates anymore. So formal. And so cute. What did Ben have in mind?

He'd only been around two weeks, and already half the population of Wheaton had their eyes on him.

And he wanted to go on a date. With Erin. And her brain.

Grinning, Erin turned onto her grandparents' long, leafy driveway. Spotting Tea's birdhouses nestled among the ivy, she felt at home. Wooden wind chimes hung over the open porch where Grandma Tea sipped from a mug. She ran to Erin, and enveloped her in a hug.

"You're a sight for sore eyes."

"I'm happy to be here at last. Where's Grampa?"

"He'll be around," Tea said. "I just talked to your mother. She says you have to practice cello the instant you get here. Where's George?"

"In the car. I'll get him in a minute."

"You could probably take a day off," Tea said.

"Not a chance. I'm closing in on two thousand days."

Tea put her arm on Erin's shoulder as they walked into the cottage. Projects and artwork filled the rooms. The cottage always had secrets to explore or invent; it was magical.

"I'm in my suit, you?" Tea asked.

"Not yet. Give me a sec."

Erin slipped into her room and scanned more texts from Ben.

A few minutes later, Erin's Grampa rapped on the door.

"Getting slow in your old age, Fish?"

"Nearly ready!" Erin dropped her phone on the bed and slipped into her swimsuit. She opened her door and wrapped her grampa in a hug.

"Back to Harvard this summer, I hear. Astrophysics!"

"I am beyond excited! I have to study human anatomy at College of DuPage the rest of the summer. Prep for med school, you know."

Her grandparents exchanged a look.

Tea passed Erin a towel, and they walked to the dock barefoot.

"You do the honors!" Tea said.

Erin hooked her toes over the edge of the dock as if she were about to race. She dove into the crisp water.

Summer at last.

Ten days after that dive, she had her first date with Ben.

Eleven days after that dive, she left for Harvard.

A month after that dive, Grandma Tea died of a massive stroke.

Seven months after that dive, Erin's Grampa died in his sleep.

FIFTY-FOUR

Driving to the north end of the South Island was a six-hour trek in the RV, and a two-punnet journey for Erin. She'd been completely fine until Takaka Ridge, where switchbacks and steep declines forced her to vomit twice in the span of fifteen minutes.

Cresting a peak, Erin spotted Golden Bay, stretching on forever. After spying the crescent beach, Erin scanned the horizon for ocean at every turn and didn't need another punnet.

Though the caravan park had, indeed, been booked, Hamish inquired about walk-up options. While Pippa and Felicity used the toilet, Erin studied dozens of RVs parked in rows, half-dressed children roaming in packs, and lines of laundry billowing in the wind.

No longer was she offended by laundry lines because everyone in New Zealand hung their laundry out to dry; it saved heaps of energy, and—like uniforms—if everyone aired their underpants outside, there was no shame in it. Hamish had taught Erin to use a washing machine, and schooled her in the fine art of hanging laundry in the sun.

Hamish got the last spot—furthest from the water and adjacent to a fence. Felicity negotiated the caravan park's narrow paths past adults in camp chairs, a small playground, a rugby scrum, and people barbecuing.

Felicity backed into their spot, and Pippa was off and running, leaving Felicity, Erin, and Hamish to set up camp.

The sun warmed Erin's skin as she rinsed her punnets at the spigot and returned them to the caravan for the trip home.

Last spring break, six months ago now, Erin's family had spent ten days in Cancun, where Erin admired the glistening ocean from her balcony but had little time to swim. She'd had ten days to complete her AP government project, two research papers, a stack of calculus problems, and two thick ACT prep books.

This spring break, Ilam's teachers had bid Erin farewell with zero homework.

"Do you guys mind if I check out the beach?"

"Sweet as," Hamish said.

"Super low tide today," Felicity said. "Be back in time for tea."

Erin responded to her fellow campers' happy greetings with quiet hellos. By the time she reached the edge of the caravan park, she was smiling.

Between the caravans and the beach, a squat building housed laundry, kitchens, a small convenience store, toilets, and showers. On the other side of the building, Erin walked between large rocks to sandy Pohara Beach.

As promised, Golden Bay stretched on forever. It boasted no cabanas or ocean-side pool. No eager waiters served lunch on the sand. It was a long, flat beach. Full stop.

As a child Erin had considered tides only when they

made for dangerous snorkeling in Hawaii. But when she'd studied the moon—really studied it—she'd learned about proxigean tides. Her classmate from Japan had been thrilled to learn why some tides are extremely high.

Learning not all tides were created equal fascinated Erin, and here she saw its effects. Tide was very low, so Erin walked a long way out through wet sand and tide pools. Near the gentle surf, she removed her shoes and walked in the shallows. Three months into her journey, she finally dipped her toes in the ocean. She walked along the water's edge, gazing from the ocean to the beach to the mountains beyond. Pippa and her new pack climbed among the rocks that separated the beach from greenery.

Inhaling crisp New Zealand air, Erin enjoyed her vacation—a true vacation, from her life.

She pulled out her phone to see who was online. Marama and Jade hadn't posted all day. Erin checked on Good-Time Girl and, to her utter chagrin, recognized her own ass in the last snap from a few days earlier. She'd captioned it *Everyone is doing it, so why don't you?*

Gloria was Good-Time Girl.

Erin scrolled back and caught glimpses of Gloria's life orbiting her own: pics from Castle Hill last February and a shot from Satellite Club several weeks ago. Gloria's July skiing trip had been to Queenstown; Erin now recognized the scenery.

All the pieces fell into place, and Erin understood why she and Jade and Marama were friends and why Hank climbed with her—was climbing with her this very instant. How could Erin ever compete with that?

For these hours, she needed only to breathe. She inhaled the scenery until teatime.

FIFTY-FIVE

After tea, Felicity and Pippa pulled out their books. Without a television, Hamish also resorted to reading. Life on holiday looked a lot like life in Christchurch.

Erin pulled out her phone. "Felicity, I've been meaning to play something for you. It's one of my favorite recordings of Jacqueline du Pré." Erin flicked through her music to find the song she wanted. "I am truly happy not to be playing cello, but I could never live without listening. Here you go. Chopin's 'Sonata in A.'"

Felicity closed her eyes when the piano gave way to du Pré's dulcet timbre. She held her breath through sections of the second movement, and Erin understood that Felicity understood Chopin's anguish. She heard music the way Erin heard music.

When it ended, Felicity was quiet for several minutes.

"Thank you for sharing that, Erin."

"Thank you. For letting me quit cello. I really love listening, but I'd become a slave to it. I feel . . . free, somehow."

Felicity grasped Erin's hands briefly. "I'm glad you're free."

Getting there, at least.

When the darkening landscape prohibited entertainment, with no candles and no lights and no television and no electronics, the foursome gathered around a fire pit.

Felicity, Hamish, and Pippa shared stories of their previous trips here and elsewhere. Their current plan was to stay at Golden Bay until it got crowded or they got bored.

Pippa asked, "Where is the Southern Cross, Daddy?"

Everyone looked up.

Hamish spun in a circle to get his bearings, lit on the crux, and pointed Pippa toward the Southern Cross. Erin followed Hamish's right arm toward his fingertips and out into space.

There it was, her night sky.

"Oh!" Erin couldn't help herself. The sky was replete with stars, more than she'd ever seen. She'd found true darkness. A thin sliver of moon lent no threat to the dark of night, and the stars went on forever.

Erin's astrophysics professor had lectured at length about light pollution, but Erin could always see constellations just fine. Now she understood: the night sky wasn't spotted with stars; it was lousy with them. The universe had texture.

Thank you, New Zealand.

The whole messy spring and painful adjustment to life in Christchurch had brought her here, to a night sky full of stars. She could have lived her whole life—captaining the swim team, fifth chair cello, working her ass off day and night—and never, ever experienced this.

Hamish said, "Southern Cross isn't that miraculous. Smallest constellation there is, actually."

Erin knew that. "I've always loved the night sky. I studied astrophysics last summer, but I've never seen the universe like this."

"From the underside, you mean?

Sort of. "It's truly dark here. So many stars. It's hard to wrap my head around them as suns, with planets orbiting, and moons orbiting the planets. It's . . . it's a lot."

Erin spun in a circle, gazing at the night sky. Finally, she felt grounded. Here was her place in the world, staring outward at everything that was possible.

"Are you okay?" Pippa whispered, and Erin laughed.

"Pippa, I haven't felt this okay in years. Maybe ever." Outside. Surrounded by stars. With nothing to do and nowhere to go. "I'm sure we can see Saturn tonight."

Pippa said, "Or constellations."

"Maybe. I never studied the ones down under."

"We could make some of our own. They're not real, you know."

Pippa got it. Constellations weren't real, just as relationships weren't real. Ben was real, but he and Erin were just a passing fancy. He never actually belonged to her. Maybe the only real Erin was the one without him, the Erin who belonged to herself.

The family lay on a blanket to stargaze. Hamish had some guesses on official constellations, and Pippa tried to make animals by stringing together the brightest stars.

When they ran out of guesses, they drank in the universe in silence. The peace was glorious. Erin spotted Uranus and thought she'd found Neptune, but Saturn was the real prize. Of course, she couldn't see its rings without a telescope, but she'd seen them before. She trusted herself to remember exactly how they looked.

Later—who knows when?—they opened the caravan windows and turned in for the night. Listening very hard, Erin could hear animal noises.

She felt small in a very nice way. She was snug in her caravan, and right that second, there was almost nowhere else she wanted to be.

She hadn't felt that way in forever.

BEFORE SHE LOST BOTH OF HER GRANDPARENTS

BEFORE SHE LOST BOTH OF HER GRANDPARENTS

Grampa held his new telescope steady as Erin searched the sky for Saturn.

"Got it," she said.

"You sure?"

"I *am* twelve."

Her Grampa let go, and for the first time, she saw Saturn's rings, clearly separate from the planet itself. "Can you imagine if it were as close as the moon?"

"Nope," Grampa said. "If it were as close as the moon, we'd be in trouble."

"The rings?"

"Not quite. But the moons would be a problem."

"I wish we had multiple moons," Erin said.

She could stare at Saturn forever. It seemed otherworldly, like something out of science fiction. Though she was seeing it with her own eyes, she could hardly believe it was real.

"Saturn is helium?" Erin asked.

"And hydrogen," Grampa said.

"It's getting chilly for me," Grandma Tea said. "Erin, mind if I try out your cello?"

"Go for it," Erin said, her eyes firmly affixed on Saturn.

"Can I bring you two anything?"

"Ice cream!" they said in unison.

Tea said, "It's freezing out here."

"It's summer," Erin and Grampa said before erupting in laughter.

Grampa eyed the moon through his smaller telescope. "Full moon tomorrow night."

"I know! But the moon will always be there. I'm all about Saturn. This is amazing."

FIFTY-SIX

Felicity and Hamish took their morning constitutional in light rain, and Pippa headed for the beach, leaving Erin in the caravan alone with Pippa's guitar.

Please, fingers, don't fail me. It had been a long time—a very long time—since she'd played. Turns out when you have a knack for strings and embark on intensive cello lessons, you can't play guitar anymore. There just isn't time.

She played a little, warming up her fingers after years of neglect. Guitar was more intimate than cello.

Strumming chords and fingerpicking, Erin was eleven years old again.

Her grandparents had been devout James Taylor fans and had filled their cottage with his music. James Taylor's voice was pure, and his music was beautiful, thoughtful, and personal.

"Sweet Baby James" had sold Erin on guitar. When Grandma Tea sang, whole scenes materialized in Erin's imagination.

Sadness welling within her, she reverted to the Red Hot Chili Peppers and tried desperately to conjure up some muscle memory for "Under the Bridge." She'd played it a thousand times. It had taken her ages to learn, but it was in her brain—in her fingers—somewhere. She picked through the rough parts of the beginning.

It took her an hour, but she found it again. God, she loved playing guitar. Making music using her own fingers was personal. The music felt like it was hers. She could make her own music or accompany songs or pick up almost any song she wanted.

She'd forgotten that amazing feeling.

Somewhere between intensive cello and intensive swimming and intensive summer courses and an intense relationship, Erin had lost herself. She had stopped knowing what she wanted. She no longer knew what made her happy.

Still strumming, eager to find the notes, Erin's tears flowed. And if that wasn't a song, she didn't know what was.

The guitar in Erin's hands was friendlier than her cello. She didn't need sheet music, or a director, or an orchestra; it was just her and the guitar. She could sit on the floor or sling it over her shoulder and walk away with it—if it ever stopped raining.

"Is that you?" Felicity climbed into the caravan, spotted Erin's tears, and pulled up a chair. "What's the matter, love?"

Erin couldn't admit she didn't know who she was, let alone what really made her happy. She was lost.

Erin said, "I used to play this song for my grandmother. When I was young. Sometimes, when it was raining at their cottage, we would sit on their screened-in porch for hours. She was so patient with me. She never expected me to be anything larger than myself."

Felicity nodded.

"She died," Erin said. "My grandfather, too. He died just before Christmas."

"Is that why you came to us? Out of grief?"

"Not exactly." The emotions bubbled within her. She stared at her fingers and strummed.

"In May, my whole life fell apart. I had these dreams, and they just . . . weren't going to happen. So we tried to fix it. You wanted to host a student, and . . ." Erin drew a deep breath and her face contorted into an ugly cry. "My mom made me come. I didn't want to, but it was a solution. And now, I don't know. I loved Grandma Tea more than anything in the whole world, and she's gone. I don't know who I am anymore. I loved playing guitar, but I stopped. And sitting here, playing, it's like I'm meeting myself again."

Felicity's wrapped her arms around Erin and rested her chin on the crown of her head.

"And I'm so sorry about what I said in Queenstown. I was really proud of my performance, but then I talked to my mother and I wasn't and . . . I'm so sorry. You have been so kind. And you listen to me. And . . ." Sobs heaved out of her.

Felicity held her close and let her cry.

"Hank says to always do what makes me happy, but I don't know what that is anymore."

Felicity held her at an arm's distance. "Hank is a bit hedonistic, but he's not wrong. Now that you're looking for happiness, you'll find it again."

Erin wiped her eyes and nodded. "I thought I was growing up, you know? Adults can't just swim all summer and play guitar all winter. I started to move toward adulthood—great medical school, great job, great life—but instead of growing into my adult self, I've lost myself completely."

Felicity hugged her again. "You go looking, Erin. I'll get tea."

Felicity selected dishes while Erin picked through tunes.

Pippa came in to change her clothes. "I love hearing you play, Erin."

"Thanks."

"Haven't you been outside today?" Hamish asked.

"Not yet. But it's about time I had a walk."

"Tea first?" Felicity asked.

———

After simple sandwiches and crisps—which Erin still referred to as potato chips—it started pouring. Pippa engaged the family in the world's longest game of Uno. Hamish danced a little jig when he won, and Erin begged off a second game.

"I'm off on a walk."

Felicity said, "Still raining, love."

"I know. I think I might like a walk in the rain."

She had nothing on her mind, no destination, and no motive. And that was perfect. The wet hills were calling her name.

Mud squished around her sandals as she walked away from the ocean. Muddy grass was no problem, but soon her shoes couldn't grip anything and her palms landed in mud. Determined to make it, she clawed her way up the hill, grabbing at a rock that looked suspiciously like a rocket.

Scrambling uphill was simpler when the ground was dry. And she needed tramping boots.

Erin laughed as she slid down the hill.

After five tries, she changed course and returned to the beach. Spring break was long; the mountains would keep.

FIFTY-SEVEN

Her penultimate full day in Pohara, Erin woke to an empty caravan and an urgent text.

Litha: 9-1-1 Call ASAP.

Erin walked through drizzle and morning greetings to find a quiet spot on the rocks between the caravan park and the beach. She loved this view.

Drawing a deep breath, fear welled in Erin's stomach. What could be so urgent? Maybe someone had died. Maybe it was juicy gossip. Or Lalitha was pregnant. Or Ben had gotten someone pregnant.

Erin held her breath and called her friend.

"You can come home!" Lalitha boomed.

"Uh, hello?" Erin said.

"Waterson let me keep my phone on deck during practice, just in case you called. So, it turns out the Quigleys—the parent Quigleys—were having a nasty divorce, and the dad was in California and the mom brought them here, and the courts forced her to return to California. So they're gone!

And you can come back. And I will gladly relinquish my captain's mane to you."

"Li, I—"

"You did the thing! You have the championship. Now you can have a captainship and we can finish our senior season together!" Lalitha screamed, "We're getting the team back together!"

Swimming with her girls. Her sun-drenched solo bedroom and huge tub. Her Fiat.

Her schedule.

Her cello.

Her empty house.

"I can't," she whispered.

"What?"

"I said I can't, Li."

"What do you mean, you can't? Mitchell said you can come home any time. You did the thing! Come home! Come swim with me!"

Erin missed Lalitha, but she was on the cusp of something bigger. New Zealand was changing her—or revealing parts of herself she didn't know existed.

"I love you, Li," she said. "I need to stay. I *want* to stay. I'm . . . unwinding, I think?"

"Is this about Hank?"

"It's about me, Li. I need to be here right now. I have some things to figure out."

"You're serious?"

"Serious. I'm working some things out right now."

Lalitha's silence spoke volumes.

"Lalitha, this is good for me. I promise."

"We're so much better with you. I told everyone you would come back to save us."

"Honestly, Lalitha, I think right now I need to save myself."

"What does that mean?" Lalitha asked.

"Not sure yet. I'm trying to find happiness."

Lalitha said, "Waterson wants me back in the pool. I need to go. Are you sure about this?"

"I'm sure. I promise. Have fun."

"You too." Lalitha made a kissing sound before hanging up.

Erin caught up with everyone's posts and pics from the night before. Good-Time Girl—Gloria—had posted a pic of Jade's profile on a pillow. The climbing crew must be visiting her in Dunedin.

Everyone was preparing to return for term four. From Australia and Auckland and the cliffs of the North Island, they all would converge on Christchurch in two days.

FIFTY-EIGHT

Felicity had left a note in the caravan, because of course she had. *Sun's up! We've gone swimming. Slip, slop, slap, wrap if you go out.*

She definitely would go out. Erin and Pippa had walked the length of the beach twice. The family had kayaked the bay in sun hats and life vests. Erin had lost herself in the glorious night sky many times. She'd buried Pippa up to her waist and fashioned a mermaid tail out of sand. She and Pippa bought ice cream from the canteen and made music together after dusk.

Pippa had given Erin a second childhood, and sleeping almost outside for days had cleared Erin's head.

She dressed and walked to the edge of the caravan park to stare out to sea. She was not at all inclined to return to Wheaton early. This was where she needed to be—where she wanted to be—right now.

The bright morning drew her away from the sea and upward. Sunshine had dehydrated her hill (mountain) and she hiked straight up on all fours.

She might not reach the peak in an hour, but she would try.

Thirty minutes in, that wasn't going to work.

This particular mountain was adjacent to another. They crisscrossed, creating a high valley. Erin wondered whether the geographic feature had a name.

For a good hour, she hiked and climbed toward the nearest peak. Each time she expected a peak, she crested another hill and kept going.

Eventually, finally, the ground leveled off and she walked between peaks towering above her. Turning around, peaks occluded her view of the caravan park; she could see only nature. High on the world, she saw the ocean kissing a sliver of beach far in the distance.

Wind rustled trees as she turned inland. She closed her eyes to listen to leaves beating against one another. Instead, she heard a ping from her pocket.

Hank.

Hank: Weather turned, so we came back a day early. You?
Erin: Back tomorrow.
Hank: Climbing?
Erin: Kind of climbing right now.
Hank: ?
Erin: Standing between two mountains, listening to rustling leaves.
Erin: As if the mountain is talking to me.
Hank: Now YOU have been reading Thoreau?
Erin: No.
Hank: Whitman?
Erin: No.
Hank: Some other transcendentalist, for sure.
Hank: Fresh air is good for your soul.
Erin: You're going a bit too far.

Hank: Nope. Serious.
Hank: Had a crash hot caramel slice on holiday.
Hank: Thought of you.
Erin: Did you save me a bite?
Hank: I thought of you as I devoured it. That counts.
Hank: See you tomorrow?
Erin: If we get home early enough.
Hank: Hope you have punnets for the drive.
Erin: Not funny.

Erin silenced her phone, closed her eyes, and listened to the wind. It soothed her.

She hadn't been alone in nature for years. When was her last time foraging for berries or hunting for hornets' nests? Why had she let go of the calm and the breathing and the things she loved?

Rustling trees compelled her further into the canyon, which beckoned her into its maw and away from civilization.

She went willingly. Happily. Breathing and listening.

Fresh air fed her soul; Hank was right. Hank was right about a lot of things. Erin grinned. She couldn't wait to tell him about this.

FIFTY-NINE

Darkness descended as Erin made her way back to the caravan. She spotted Felicity's green light and slowed. Nearly back to civilization, she needed another moment to herself. She gazed at the night sky; she could see forever.

Way before Erin was born, NASA had sent *Voyager 1* into space. Everyone made a big deal when it left the galaxy thirty years later. Thirty years! Gazing at the stars, Erin saw light-years into the future. Many stars had died already but would appear in the night sky her entire life.

What a complicated universe. Nothing she did could alter it, so why shouldn't she do what she wanted? The universe didn't care whether she went to Columbia. The universe didn't care whether she went to college at all.

So, really, all that really mattered was what she wanted. If only she knew exactly what that was!

It was the second week of October. She had two months to figure it out.

SIXTY

Erin was certain of one thing: she wanted to be a better rock climber. Sunday, they returned to Christchurch too late to climb. Hank would spend the week catching up on work projects, but they'd agreed to climb outside the following weekend.

In preparation, Erin spent every afternoon at The Roxx, where auto-belay machines enabled safe solo climbs. Monday was fine, but Tuesday and Wednesday were rough. She pushed through, and by Saturday she felt sure she wouldn't embarrass herself climbing outside. Her progress might even impress Hank. She hoped.

Saturday morning, she packed a little bag with sunscreen and a hat. She was on the slip, slop, slap, wrap bandwagon. Mimicking Marama's prep for Castle Hill, she'd bought six caramel slices from Horton's Bakery; Hank loved caramel almost as much as she did.

She couldn't remember what he'd eaten at Castle Hill, except Marama's chicken salad. She packed bottled water, four sandwiches, and several pieces of fruit. This time, she was pulling her weight.

She tucked her phone into her bag just as he knocked on the door.

"G'day!"

She was growing quite fond of his crooked smile. "Hi!"

"All set, then?"

"I am." She followed him to the driveway and was stunned to see Gloria already in the car.

Erin climbed into the backseat, her heart sinking.

Hank buckled up and explained where they were headed. Gloria and Hank reminisced about their recent trip, and Erin wanted to shrink into oblivion.

She didn't vomit during the drive, but she wanted to gag herself. *What am I doing here?*

In the Port Hills, they hiked to the rock face, which looked like giant bubbles forming out of a huge boulder. Gloria and Hank set out their equipment, using a language Erin still didn't speak: tapers, trads, bight, jugs, pitch, carabiners.

Carabiners she now knew. All the climbers carried their keys and chalk bags on those metal rings.

While Hank and Gloria continued their private conversation, Erin tried on Hank's sister's shoes again. *Still so tight.*

"It's going to be a while," Hank said. "I'd take them off if I were you."

Gloria started up the rock face with dozens of silver trapezoid things. Every few feet, she stuck a trapezoid into the rock face and threaded her rope through it. If she fell, she'd have a long way down.

That's what Gloria meant when she said this was a far greater challenge than gym climbing.

Ten minutes later, after Gloria had reached the top of the rock, Hank followed. They disappeared over the top of the wall, leaving Erin alone among quiet trees.

She probably wouldn't have tried rock climbing if her Wheaton friends had asked. Then again, they would have known not to ask because she was always busy. Were there rock faces in flat Illinois? Mountain biking? She had no idea. When you bury your head in the sand—or the chlorine, as the case may be—you miss a lot.

Hank peeked over the edge and rappelled down the rock.

"What were you two doing up there?"

Hank gave her the side-eye. "Don't worry. We're being safe."

Erin blushed.

Hank got very close to her face. "What do you think we were doing up there?"

Erin bit her lip.

Gloria returned to the ground, and Erin asked, "You two do this often?"

"In summer we do. You want to do the honors?"

Gloria and Hank had attached the top rope to something above. Erin tied a figure-eight knot and roped in as Hank had taught her.

"Let me check them," Hank said.

Erin scowled.

"Don't be offended! We all check each other's knots. It's not like checking your rugby equipment. This is dangerous stuff."

They all checked one another's harnesses and Hank declared Erin's knots safe. "Go for it."

Erin approached the rock and grabbed on.

"Erin?"

Hank and Gloria were expectant. It took her a second to remember. "On belay?"

"Belay on."

"Climbing?"

"Climb on."

Her little extra climbing sessions had done wonders for her grip strength, but she still couldn't get a good hold on the tiniest rock fragments.

Erin tried to be grateful as Gloria gave excellent directions for her feet. *What else were they doing on top of this rock?*

Two-thirds of the way up the rock, Erin's hands gave out. "Take!"

"Got!"

Erin sat back in her harness and rubbed her fingers. After a minute or two, she grabbed the rock. "Climbing!"

"Maybe take another minute," Hank said. "You've been working hard. Have a break."

She glared at Hank, who hadn't been studying her ass.

He said, "Turn 'round. Look out."

She spun around, and there it was: rolling hills, mountains, and the sea all rolled into one gorgeous and stunning New Zealand view. Had she seen a photo of this, she wouldn't have believed the colors. The sparkling ocean was too blue. Twenty-nine shades of green stretched toward the distant, majestic mountains. Houses dotted a nearby hill, much like the Queenstown houses on stilts.

Queenstown. When she was desperate to swim and desperate to win and her schedule was full. Not fulfilling, but full. Of lifting and practice and that urge to win. It seemed like a lifetime ago. Why had she spent that entire weekend getting her head in the game? The game was out here.

As Hank and Gloria chatted, Erin was alone, hanging from a rope, looking out at the world.

Like Queenstown, Christchurch was simply awesome. Tears sprang to her eyes. She'd almost missed this. If her head had been in the pool, or her sheet music, or her computer desperately trying to get into Columbia, she would have missed New Zealand.

Erin had been missing out. She whispered, "This is the most beautiful moment of my life."

She glanced down at Hank and Gloria, who chatted nonchalantly. They were lucky. They lived in the most gorgeous place in the world.

And so did Erin.

There was something more real about how she was living these days. This sublime outdoor playground was real. Amazing. And she felt a part of it. She felt stronger than ever before. She was living.

Erin turned back toward the rock and swung two feet to the left. She found holds for her feet and reached up to find two easy knobs for her hands.

"Climbing!" she yelled again, and up she went.

Like swimming, she was on her own, but climbing was a whole different thing. Swimming was always more physical than mental. Rock climbing was both. Erin stretched herself to reach the next hold. Sometimes there was a surprise, but mostly she had to hunt. It was the world's smallest, trickiest game of hide-and-seek.

She surveyed the landscape once more on the way up. She had seen many beaches in her life—figure an average of two a year since she was born—and none of them compared to this. The flowers' fragility and water's fluidity mingled with mountains' magnitude to create a scene of overwhelming beauty.

"You feeling hungry?" Hank asked.

She was. She was hungry for all of this.

And slightly hungry for food. "I'm almost at the top. I can be quick."

Hank said, "I can be patient."

Erin made quick work of the rest of the climb. Instead of descending, she sat on top of the rock face, perhaps seventy-five feet up. She had a bird's-eye view of this whole, gorgeous world: beaches to explore, caves to play in, more mountains to climb. She wanted to eat it, to make it part of herself and hold onto it forever. There was so much to do and so little time. This was a great office. She wanted to spend her life in the earth. In nature.

She said, "Falling."

"Fall on."

He hugged her when she landed at the bottom.

"Thanks for bringing me," Erin said. "Even if I'm crashing your party."

Gloria and Hank looked at each other, and Hank burst out laughing.

"What?" Gloria asked.

To Erin, Hank said, "I'm not Gloria's type."

Gloria looked from Hank to Erin. "You know I'm with Jade, right?"

Erin had no idea.

"Hank is like my little brother."

"Big brother," he said.

"Relax, shorty." Gloria's expression turned serious. "Jade's parents don't know, so keep it quiet."

"Of course." Erin couldn't stop grinning. "As long as we're confessing, Gloria, I've been following you online since June. Not in a stalker way."

"I thought you moved here in July?"

"I did, but I didn't want to leave home, and online you seemed like someone I'd like to hang out with. Like maybe it wouldn't suck to be thousands of miles away from everyone

I knew. You were like the friend I dreamed of helping me endure this adventure."

Gloria frowned. "Am I living up to that?"

"That and more," Erin said.

SIXTY-ONE

It was dark by the time they dropped Gloria at Jade's house. Erin, who had climbed up for the view a half-dozen times—once at dusk—was beat, but Hank seemed fine as he drove to her house.

In the driveway, she thanked Hank profusely for inviting her.

"Hey, I'm so glad you're enjoying it. We're outside on top ropes almost every weekend, if you want to join."

"Maybe."

His face clouded over.

Erin said, "I mean, I'd love to, but I need to learn to belay. I kind of feel like I'm not pulling my weight. Literally."

That crooked smile. "It's always like that in the beginning. Belaying's easy, but it's not worth your time if you're not going to stick with it. We'll get you trained up."

He leaned over the gearshift. She expected a kiss, but instead he whispered, "What did you think of the view?"

"Suspended in midair, the view was the most beautiful moment of my life."

"It was sneaky, taking you there. I knew you'd see it and

be in awe. Last autumn we went to that exact spot several Sundays in a row. Gloria started calling it church."

And she was right: seeing the majesty of New Zealand was like seeing God. Or like seeing the world for the first time. It got really dark there; what would the stars look like if Erin were suspended fifty feet in the air?

Erin asked, "Do you ever climb at night?"

"No." He looked out his window, then back at her. "I don't see why we couldn't. I'd want to set the ropes in daylight. We'd need proper lights. Maybe some night gear. I'll look into it."

Erin stared into his deep brown eyes.

He didn't kiss her.

"Thanks for a great day," she said.

"I hope you'll come again."

"Absolutely. Any time." She opened her door but couldn't force herself to get out. "I hate being the worst climber. I want to be strong."

"You are strong, Erin."

"Yeah, but you guys . . ."

"We *guys* have been climbing for years. It's not all about strength. It's about experience, and you'll get there."

Erin stared at the flimsy aluminum garage door. "I don't want to be a deadweight."

"Erin, you do what you can do. I do what I can do. Whatever you can give, that is enough. If we went swimming, you would outswim me in a heartbeat."

They looked at each other for a long time. Still no kiss.

"I want to be better."

"You will be."

"But I'll never be better than you guys. I will always be the worst person on the rock."

"We aren't trying to best each other, not really. We horse around and challenge each other. But we don't do it to be the best. We do it because it's fun."

Cooler air rushed in through Erin's open door. Hank's chocolate-brown eyes looked through her.

"You're right, Hank. It's fun."

He held her gaze. "So you'll come again?"

"I will."

"And you'll climb with me at The Roxx instead of scooting out just before I arrive?"

Her mouth hung open.

He said, "Climbers are tight."

"But nobody knows who I am."

His grin grew. "People know. Come with me Monday and I'll stay for Felicity's tea. Pippa will be delighted."

"Okay."

"Thanks for a great day."

"Thank you."

She could live inside those eyes, to say nothing of the hand gripping the gearshift.

"Good night, Erin."

"Good night, Hank. See you Monday."

She was maybe a little too aggressive with the door, but she didn't care. It was like a date, right? Practically their second—third—date.

What was wrong with him? *What's wrong with me?*

Hank was not Ben. Ben had been the obvious choice. He was going places. He would be a college athlete. He got great grades. Everyone—the whole swim team, the entire straight, sane female population of Wheaton— wanted Ben, and he had chosen Erin.

Hank was different. On paper, he was not her type. On

paper, she wouldn't give a tattooed construction worker the time of day.

But Hank made her think. He opened up a new world, and not something superficial like the names of constellations. Hank was interesting. Thoughtful. And that stuff about Thoreau? He also was smart. For the first time, Erin's eyes were open. Smart people could make their lives about something other than academics and advanced degrees. That was the real surprise.

Looking at the whole life thing, Hank was far wiser than she. Or, at the very least, he had gotten there sooner. He saw through her. He saw into her, to parts of herself she was only starting to understand. She wanted more of that.

Always ask for what you want and always do what makes you happy.

She wanted Hank. She liked who she was when she was with him. More than that, he had helped her figure out what happy meant. For her.

Before she could change her mind, she pulled out her phone.

Erin: If you're not too far away, can you come back to my house?

Hank: No worries.

She sat on the front stoop for a thousand years before walking to the end of the driveway. No headlights. She paced between number 33 and number 37. She couldn't go inside yet, because if he came back, she'd have to explain the whole thing to Felicity. She needed him to come back before she went inside.

She'd wait forever.

She didn't need to. He pulled in, with half his truck hanging in the sidewalk, and rolled down his window.

That beautiful, crooked grin under chocolate eyes. "Forget something?"

She stuck her head inside his truck and kissed him. Firmly. He didn't kiss back.

"Oh my god." Wide-eyed, Erin bit her lip. "Oh my god. I am so sorry. Good night."

Erin ran up the driveway, her shadow shrinking on the front door. She kicked off her shoes outside and slipped into the house. Pippa crafted something on the dining room table as Felicity made tea.

"Hi, Erin! How was rock climbing? Are you hurting?"

Erin burst into tears. "Not feeling well." She ran to her room, hurting badly. She felt like the biggest idiot on the face of the earth.

Someone knocked on her door.

"I'll be fine in the morning, Felicity."

More knocking.

"I already had tea!"

The knob turned. *Get the point. Seriously.*

"Erin?"

Hank opened the door a crack.

Groaning, she buried her face in her hands. "I'm fine, I promise. I'm fine. I'm sorry. Just. Forget it ever happened. Please."

He slipped inside, turned on the light, and closed the door behind him.

Hugging her knees, Erin grabbed her pillow to cover her wet nose and face. "Really, I'm fine. I'm sorry. It will never happen again."

Gently, Hank pulled the pillow down from her face.

She hated excuses and easy letdowns and whatever else he was going to say.

But she loved his stupid jagged smile.

Oh my god, stop smiling.

Hank sat too close to her on the bed, his scent—a mix of chalk and mint—swelled in the tiny room. "Mulligan?"

He kissed her softly, then intensely, running his fingers over her back and up through her hair.

In some spaces of life, being intense was just fine.

Better than fine. Perfect.

"Pippa!" Felicity's voice outside the door stunned them. "Give them some time alone. They'll come out when they're ready."

Erin and Hank shared a glance before pressing their lips together again.

An hour later, they came up for air.

"So, when you called me back here, I put a wad of gum in my mouth. I know you and bad breath," Hank said. "Or I thought I knew you. I knew we'd be talking close but wasn't anticipating the kissing."

Mmmmm. "You should anticipate kissing."

"Sweet as."

He kissed her again. He kissed her for a long time.

A rap on the door pushed them apart again. "Erin? It's Pippa's bedtime, love."

Erin scooted a foot away from Hank. "Come in. I'll walk Hank out."

Erin and Hank walked past Felicity and Pippa. As they entered the living area, Erin heard Pippa say, "Ooooooh. Does she like him?"

Erin walked Hank to his car. "I like this thing. Asking for what you want."

"You didn't so much ask as take it. Though I have no complaints. See you soon?"

"See you soon."

She pushed him up against the car, kissing him hard on the mouth again. *Thank goodness for tall fences.*

"You keep surprising me, Erin," he said.

"I could say the same for you."

"Maybe we'll surprise each other again tomorrow."

"After tea."

"After tea, before tea. Both, I don't care."

"See you then."

Hank kissed her again, quieter this time. He sucked at good-byes and sometimes was flighty, but he was very good at a lot of very important things.

Erin lingered outside long past Pippa's bedtime. Before Erin crawled into bed, because nothing ever felt real until she told Lalitha, she texted her the news.

Erin: I think Hank and I are going to be a thing.
Erin: And I initiated it!

SIXTY-TWO

At tea Monday night, Pippa pushed her food around her plate, completely disengaged from the conversation.

Felicity said, "She's caught wind that Ashley is having a birthday party and she wasn't one of the few invited."

"I thought Ashley was your best friend," Erin said.

Pippa was quiet. "She is. I guess I'm not hers."

That distinction was painful at any age.

Erin said, "When is this birthday party?"

"Saturday, from eleven to three at Ashley's house." Pippa propped her head with her hand while eviscerating her peas with a fork.

Erin said, "And all your friends will be there."

Pippa sunk lower in her chair.

"If all your friends are busy, let's have a sisters day. And I can have you all to myself."

Pippa stared at her. "To do what?"

"I dunno. You tell me."

They negotiated over dinner, and by the time they started homework at the dining room table, they had a plan: swim at Pioneer Pool and have lunch at a café.

Halfway through Erin's Italian homework, Felicity broke the silence.

"Erin, Hank's here."

When she saw him, she couldn't stop smiling at his charming, crooked teeth. "Hey."

"Hi. I wanted to talk. I could have called but . . ." He dug his toe into the blue carpet. "I like seeing you."

Felicity excused herself. Pippa's eyes focused squarely on her book, but her pen wasn't moving; her ears were on Erin and Hank.

Hank said, "I thought maybe we could spend the day together. Doing something alone. Saturday? Climbing? Picnic? Swimming lessons?"

Hank here was no Ben. Ben had been slick and suave and had made reservations for their first date.

"I wish I could say yes," Erin said.

Pippa hopped between them. "She already has a date with me!"

Erin wrapped her arms around her would-be little sister. "She's right. We're having a sister day."

"Bring her along!"

Pippa's body went rigid.

"Sorry," Erin said. "Sisters only." Just as Erin needed time alone with Hank, Erin understood Pippa deserved time alone with her.

There would be time for Hank later.

Hank grinned. "All right then. Can't blame a bloke for trying."

Pippa vibrated with excitement. "I win!"

"Today we have homework. I'll walk you out."

She and Hank stood just outside the front door.

"Homework?" Hank said.

"Some. Pippa's kind of having a rough week. I'm here for moral support."

"I'm sure she appreciates it. So, when are you going to teach me butterfly?" Hank asked.

"Sometime, I promise." She wrapped her arms around Hank's waist and kissed his soft, warm lips. He tasted like peppermint.

"More gum?" she said.

He blushed. "I was hopeful."

They kissed under the porch light for a long time.

"Sunday?" Erin asked.

"I'm here for guitar Sunday afternoon. Morning?"

"Yes. And climbing Thursday."

"I can pick you up after school, if you like. Any time."

"I now have a very expensive bike I plan to use every single day to amortize the cost," she said. "Tomorrow I'm at Marama's house for the afternoon. They're having trouble with Roa again."

"Yeah, I'm trying to help, too. He's pissed every night now."

"Why?"

"No reason."

"People don't just get mad for no reason."

"He's not pissed off, he's pissed. You know, from drinking the piss."

"Ew."

"Beer. Piss is beer. Drink too much and you're pissed. Drunk."

Erin giggled. "I'm so sorry. It's not funny, but it's hilarious."

"Okay," Hank said. "Wednesday, then?"

"Wednesday."

She walked him to his car, where they kissed for another long time.

"Back to homework," she said.

"Catch you later, Erin."

She turned toward the house and straightened the line of shoes outside the door. They didn't have a plan for Wednesday, but they'd figure it out.

Pippa was still grinning when Erin slid into her chair. "We're still on?"

"Of course!" Maybe Erin would've been a different person if she'd had a sister all along. "If there's only one thing you learn from me, Pip, it's that you should never trade time with your girlfriends for time with a guy."

Pippa beamed.

"What?"

"You think of me as a friend, not just a sister?"

Erin said, "I don't even know which of those is better. You, my love, are both."

Erin had always paid attention to how people made her feel, but for most of her life, she had wanted people only to feel that they liked her. Giving her full attention to Pippa made Pippa feel special, and making Pippa feel special made Erin's heart soar.

BEFORE SHE SPIED SATURN
BEFORE SHE SPIED SATURN

At eleven, Erin admired her grandmother's ring and the light it scattered across the ceiling.

"Your Grampa gave it to me when I turned seventeen, and when you turn seventeen, we will give it to you."

"Really?" Erin asked.

Tea nodded. "And perhaps, someday, you'll have a grand-daughter who would like it when she turns seventeen."

"Thanks, Grandma Tea. Thank you so much."

Grampa flung open the door and stumbled into the house.

"You are the most important person in the world to me," Tea said.

"Hey now," Grampa said, through heavy breath. In an instant, Tea's hand was over his heart.

"Are you okay?"

"Fine. I'm fine. But I thought I was the most important person to you? Never mind. I was running; the Boutwell boys and their friends are fixing to race to Summer Island."

"Someone get a new Jet Ski?" Tea asked.

"They're swimming," Grampa said. "I thought our Fish might give 'em a run for their money."

Grinning, Erin ran out the door, Grampa and Tea close behind.

"Hold up! Wait!" they cried to the Boutwell gang.

Grampa and Tea followed the race in their motorboat. When it was over—once Erin had beaten the brothers to Summer Island—they gave her a lift back to the house.

"I wouldn't have missed that for the world," Tea said.

SIXTY-THREE

Erin had spent half her life in pools, but Pippa wanted to swim, so Saturday morning the bus dropped them at Pioneer Pool. Its lazy river, wave machine, and pool toys were a stark contrast to Erin's lap pools.

Pippa was in heaven. They paddled in inner tubes to the lazy river and held hands while the current pushed them in circles. An alarm wailed and Pippa gave their inner tubes to what Pippa called *little girls*, though they couldn't have been much younger than she was.

Pippa pulled Erin to the wave pool, where rough water churned swimmers into human soup. When the waves ceased, Pippa instructed Erin on the rules of Shark.

Erin closed her eyes until the count of ten and turned to find Pippa near a waterspout. Erin dove and headed for her, and she was eight years old again, with the freedom of unbound hair, water rushing over her scalp. Restrained by swim caps for the past ten years, she had forgotten that feeling.

She loved it.

She used to love swimming, playing in the pool, being

underwater. *Going swimming* used to mean *going to play in a pool*.

Pippa squealed as Erin's shark hands nipped lightly at her heels.

"Be the shark again!"

"In a minute. First I want to show you my favorite game." She led Pippa to the deep end. "We're going to be mermaids. First, we'll go under, and you can try to restyle my mermaid hair. Okay?"

In goggles, Pippa moved Erin's curls around in the water, but they weren't to her liking. Seven or eight times, they dove so Erin could endure Pippa's styling in the warm water.

Pippa popped her head out of the water and Erin stood next to her.

"Okay, here's the challenge about being a mermaid: you have to keep your feet together at all times. Otherwise, your tail will split and you'll become human. Be a good mermaid! And be quick! An octopus is after us!"

Erin dolphin kicked to the shallow end. She loved swimming freely.

She'd lived in her grandparents' lake. The mermaid kicks had come later.

Mermaid kicks. Dolphin kicks?

Erin stood in the shallow end. Her favorite pool game had been a clever ruse to train her. And had her swim instructor invented Mermaid Hair so she would linger underwater? Expanding her lungs and holding her breath underwater was far easier when she had a task.

Was her whole life a complicated manipulation toward winning?

She enjoyed competitive swimming; pushing herself was a huge rush. But playing in the water—what she'd called swimming as a child—was fun. She'd stopped swimming for fun when she started racing.

Where had the fun gone, and how could she reclaim it? Fresh air might do wonders for her brain, but Erin needed something to do wonders for the rest of her.

SIXTY-FOUR

When Erin and Hank finally were alone together, he drove her to the distinguished wop wops. On their way, they'd passed a pig farm complete with little pig houses.

"We're nearly there," Hank said as the ratio of houses to cows transposed.

"Did you know my counselor at Ilam recommended you for guitar lessons? She sent a whole list, and you were on it."

"And you never called?"

Erin shrugged. "I thought it would be weird. Hey, what do you hear from Gloria?" Erin asked. "I haven't seen Jade around. Is something going on?"

"Sounds like it's getting serious, actually. They holed up at Gloria's house this weekend instead of climbing. That's a big deal."

"Does she tell you everything?"

"Do you tell Lalitha everything?"

"Touché. So that's why you went alone to the movies during my outing with Pippa."

"Indeed. But don't pity me. I had buttered popcorn for company."

Hank pulled into a gravel driveway and they bounced toward a tiny yellow house with a huge yard in the middle of the flat nowhere.

"Should I be concerned about what Lalitha knows about me?"

"Absolutely not. I adore you, so she adores you. She is fiercely loyal. To me."

"All right then," he said. "Home at last. Come on in."

Hank's house was smaller than the Wakefields': two bedrooms, one bathroom, a living room, and a galley kitchen.

"Used to be my parents' place. When I started working, they shifted to their bach, so now it's just me."

Erin had a million questions about how he'd gotten there and why he lived alone and how he afforded it, but there were more pressing matters.

She kissed him gently, then roughly, and pulled his shirt over his head. She spied his tattoos as he wrapped his naked arms around her, but there would be time discuss those later.

Erin pulled off her own shirt. "Is this okay?"

"Of course. Of course."

"Do you have something?"

He was confused for a second. "Rubbers, ya. Give us a sec."

She stood half-naked in his living room, feeling only desire. Hank returned and slipped off his pants.

While they were rolling around on the floor, Erin said, "Do you like this? Is this good?"

"The best," Hank said.

SIXTY-FIVE

One early November Monday, Erin walked into another gorgeous lunch period: big blue sky and dry grounds drenched in sunshine. Say what you will about freezing nights and wet mornings, but Christchurch had its act together by afternoon.

The guitar trio was singing "Under the Bridge" again. Or trying to.

Erin beelined to their little circle. "Ruby, I can show you a trick, if you want."

The Māori guy said, "What? You wanna have a go?"

"Sure. I'm Erin."

"I remember. I'm Hemi." He pulled the strap over his head and held his guitar to her.

Erin flexed her fingers "It's a bit of a stretch here." She played it through three times until she got it right. "Sorry, I'm rusty. So, both hands are doing two things at the same time. I learned it by spending ten minutes doing the hammer-ons with the left while I did the fingerpicking. Then I swapped and did the hammer-ons and fingerpicked with my right. Then I started over with the pull-offs. It took me weeks to get it right."

She played it again.

"Right on," he said.

She played it once more and didn't really want to give the guitar back. "What's next?"

"'Revolution #9.'"

She pulled the strap over her head. "Sorry. Don't know that one."

Hemi didn't reach for the guitar. "'All of Me'? John Legend."

She shook her head again. "Learned too long ago for that."

"Simon and Garfunkel, 'Sound of Silence.'"

"No, but I know 'Feeling Groovy.'"

"Sweet as. Erin, this is Rico. You know Ruby."

"Hey."

Rico didn't know the chords, but he knew all the lyrics. Ruby harmonized with Erin's chords, which was awesome. Hemi's voice was crystal clear. The moment was a throwback to childhood summers when Erin and Grampa played guitar and Tea harmonized when she could. Tea knew all the lyrics, because she knew everything. She was the crafter and the baker and the builder and she knew all the mom stuff.

Erin missed Grandma Tea so much her heart hurt. Tea had loved Simon and Garfunkel and all the Beatles tunes. She knew every song from the fifties and sixties, and she could sing anything. On rainy summer nights, they played, and played, and played.

That had been exactly what she loved doing, and exactly the people she loved doing it with.

Maybe her life didn't fall apart when the Quigleys arrived in Wheaton. Maybe her life started falling apart when she switched to cello and started intensive study. When she stopped enjoying music and it became work.

Today, she'd focus on what she wanted and what made her happy. And she'd start with Hank.

SIXTY-SIX

Erin saw Hank nearly every day. They climbed at The Roxx before dinner, or he came for dinner and stayed to hang out. He introduced her to Spencer Beach and the Botanical Gardens and punting on the Avon. When she lauded the merits of retail therapy, he introduced her to Re:Start, an open-air mall comprising shops in shipping containers. She shared her artwork from term three and, once, snuck him onto Ilam's campus to see her current watercolor.

Together they explored the demolished Central Business District and talked at length about the big earthquakes. Hank confessed that he still had trouble sleeping all these years later. Erin had felt a few quakes since the bike fiasco and had come to regard them as part of Christchurch. They happened, and she moved past them.

Erin reveled in Christchurch's freedom and fresh air. And, many nights in the wop wops, she reveled in Hank.

The third or fourth time they had sex, Erin paused the kissing to again ask: "Is this good for you?"

"I wish you'd stop that," Hank said.

Erin recoiled.

"Don't get me wrong—I like it. I like everything. But

you're always asking if I'm okay or happy or feeling good. What do *you* like?"

"It's all fun."

"What's all fun?"

"I like being with you, out in the world or in here, naked."

"And when we're naked, what do you like best?"

"Making you feel good."

Hank rubbed his eyes. "But why?"

"It makes me feel good?"

"Now we're getting somewhere. Giving me pleasure makes you feel good? Well giving you pleasure would make *me* feel good. Take something for yourself here, Erin. What can we do to make you feel good?"

"I do feel good."

Hank shook his head. "Nah. This is a team sport. I want you to get as much of your own pleasure as I do."

Flustered, Erin said, "I don't know how to do that."

Running his hand up her thigh, Hank smiled. "So let's figure it out."

SIXTY-SEVEN

Hank played tour guide anywhere Erin wanted to visit, so Saturday morning he drove her to Akaroa.

During the twisting ninety-minute roller-coaster ride, Erin kept her eyes on the shifting horizon and kept her breakfast in her stomach.

Hank parked a few feet from the bay. "Morning tea?"

"Coffee."

Holding hands, they walked to a tiny café overlooking a small, black beach where children teased seashells from the sand and dodged tiny waves lapping at the shore.

Akaroa was a volcanic crater filled with seawater surrounded by mountain.

The bay was large enough to seem majestic but not so large that Erin couldn't swim across with a bit of effort.

"Well, this is gorgeous," Erin said.

"You're thinking about swimming, yeah?"

"Considering it."

"Bring your togs?"

She eyed him. "Swimsuit?"

"That's the one!"

"Not today. Maybe next time." Erin gazed at the

mountains across the water. "This reminds me of my favorite place in the world. My grandparents' cottage was similar. No mountains, but lots of wild blueberries and strawberries. I lived in the water. I kind of dove in the first day, then swam and floated my way through June, July, and August."

Hank smiled. "Sounds like my parents' bach. On Taharoa. You'd like it: swimming, take the boats out, lie about in swim tubes."

"Is there a dock?" she asked.

"Small one, eh."

"Rafts?"

"It's not white water!"

"No, like an inflatable canvas thing you lie on in the water."

"Air mats?"

"Probably?"

"Yes. We have air mats."

"Sounds like a dream."

His face turned serious. "Boxing Day, the day after Christmas, I leave on a tiki tour up to the North Island. Come with me."

"I'm sorry, a tiki tour?"

"Like, meandering. I don't really have a plan. Probably camp roadside. Taharoa's a bit of a hike."

"Do you do that a lot? Just wander aimlessly?"

He smiled. "I do."

"I'd be happy to wander aimlessly with you, but my flight's booked for the twenty-third."

"Tell you what," Hank said. "Next time you're here, we'll go."

"Deal."

Oh, how she hoped there would be a next time.

SIXTY-EIGHT

Erin had wanted to visit Akaroa to buy souvenirs for her parents and Lalitha but was cynical when Hank directed her to a craft fair.

In New Zealand, craft fairs weren't stay-at-home moms knitting afghans and crocheting pot holders; here, artists sold gorgeous art. One woman displayed hand-smocked dresses that looked machine made. A glass-blower sold mouth-blown chess sets.

A husband-wife team designed jewelry delicate enough for boutiques. Erin chose earrings and two necklaces for her mother and a bracelet for Lalitha.

For her father, she found a single pair of 100-percent wool socks and a pair that was half possum. Mitchell was just the sort of guy who might delight in the novelty of possum in his socks. The guy who returned Erin's change was American.

"It's my wife's shop. She's kiwi. I'm from Ohio."

"Chicago," Erin said.

His wife, clearly kiwi, butted in. "Ah, Chicago. Winter in Chicago was piss awful. I haven't thought about that in yonks."

Her husband said, "We met in Chicago ten years ago when she was on O.E."

Hank said, "That's her overseas experience. Most kiwis get away for a year or two, then come back."

"I know the feeling," Erin said. "Okay, so tell me, what is with the possum here?"

The American shrugged. "It's what we've got. Use wool. Use possum. New Zealand doesn't have a cotton industry, so you either import super expensive stuff or buy what kiwis can make here."

"Practical, though, isn't it? Clothes fade on the line, so you're going to have to buy new. And manufacturers don't have three hundred million people to sell to. So, there's low end and high end. Nothing in the middle. No Gap. No Banana Republic."

Erin loved the word *banana* on a kiwi tongue. "So glad I ran into you. I have been wondering about the possum for months."

"Cheers," they said in unison.

Erin circled the remaining artists. She hadn't planned to buy for anyone else, but a thick crocheted tea cozy shaped like an owl would be perfect for Lalitha's tea-obsessed parents. Erin would forever be apologizing for the carpet stains that lingered in Lalitha's mom's observatory.

"Thirty-seven and twenty," the artist said.

Erin would miss kiwi's accents. *Sea-vin. Tweentee!*

She accepted her change and told Hank she was done. "After all this time, your money still cracks me up."

"How's that?" Hank asked.

Erin fanned a rainbow of paper—pink, blue, orange, red, purple, green. Each denomination was physically a little larger than the last, so the ten was longer and wider than the five, but shorter and stubbier than the twenty.

"It's like Monopoly money. Have you seen ours?" She

pulled out the American bills sitting idly in her wallet. "All green, all the same size, fitting neatly into my wallet.

"Fine for you, innit? But what if you don't know your numbers?"

"Maybe if you don't know your numbers, you shouldn't be handling money."

Hank couldn't counter that. "What about people who are blind? Colors don't matter to them, but they can tell by size whether they're using the right note. Or whether someone is trying to cheat them."

Now Erin had no counter. She studied the New Zealand bills. Every bill had a bird on the back—no kiwis—and royalty on the front.

"And who is this woman?"

"Kate Sheppard."

"Past . . . president?" Erin asked.

"Women's suffrage."

"Voting rights for women. Pretty recent, then?"

"Nah, nineteenth century. New Zealand was first in that race."

Stunned, Erin stared at her money again. History wasn't her thing, but she knew women hadn't been able to vote until the flappers. Nineteen twenties, maybe?

What else could New Zealand do better than the States?

SIXTY-NINE

One sunny Friday in mid-November, everyone celebrated Show Day, which meant no one had to work. Erin had taken a hard pass on Pippa's invitation to what sounded like a county fair, and instead found herself lying next to Hank in his hammock. His left leg hung over the side, so every few minutes he rocked them gently.

Waiting for Gloria and Jade, with whom they were heading to a beach bonfire, Hank said, "I could live in this hammock. For a while. I could be happy here for a whole holiday."

He closed his eyes.

"I badly want you to meet Lalitha."

"You think we'd get on?"

"I know you would. And Marama, too. Honestly, I think Litha's jealous of both of you. You're in my time zone. You both get me in person. On more than one occasion, she's referred to my time as 'sloppy seconds.' She knows how much I like you."

He smiled.

"Hank."

Eyes open.

"Can I ask you something?"

"Anything"

"For the first three months I knew you, I was not interested. And then I got to know you. You're kind. And you're smart. Clearly. And well-read. So, why did you leave school? I get that New Zealand needs people in construction, but you're smart enough to go to school."

"Yeah, but it's not what I want. I like using my hands and working outside."

"Going to college would keep your options open."

"That's not a good enough reason to go." He rolled onto his side to face her, not smiling. "I could be in year thirteen right now, but for what? Pass my exams and go to more school. For what? Engineering? Architecture? More school? More school, so I can sit at an office for the rest of my life."

"But you could have a much better life!"

Those deep chocolate eyes stared at her blankly. "Better how? I'm happy."

"Everyone is always so happy here. My bus driver, my teachers, the people who work on the roads are smiling half the time, even in the rain. Checkers at the grocery store. They can't really be happy, can they? Are they just complacent?"

"It's just where they fit, Erin. I'm great with my hands. I love working outside. I was finished with sitting in a classroom all day."

"But you're so smart. You should use your brain to make something of yourself."

He rolled onto his back, staring at the remarkable, cloudless sky. "I am something. I'm a very, very happy bloke. I can support myself and have pretty much everything I need."

"Get a better job and you could have great vacations and a much, much bigger house."

"Yeah? So tell me about your life back in Chicago. Tell me about this much, much bigger house."

Feeling defensive, she said, "It's fabulous. Four bedrooms. Four full and two half baths. All our baths except the second guest room's have extra-wide tubs." She described the basement exercise room, the flat-screen TVs, and the dining room that sat twelve.

"How else is your house in the States different than here?"

"There's just more room! The third floor was my playroom as a kid, and now it's where I practice cello and hang out with . . . people Saturday nights. I have a huge walk-in closet."

"Your parents have one, too? I assume they didn't give you the best room in the house."

"Their suite takes up the whole back of the house. Bedroom, walk-in closet, and a great bathroom with separate shower and Jacuzzi."

"And where do you spend your time in the house?"

"My room or the third floor. The basement if I'm watching movies."

"And where do your parents hang out?"

"Dad reads at the kitchen table after dinner, usually until bed. Mom works on the sofa if she's working. Or watches TV in the living room."

"So you three spread out all over the house, so you never see each other at all. If I got a big job with big pay—which doesn't really work here like it works in the States but, you know, sake of argument—I get this huge house, and for the few waking hours when I'm home, I will have more space. And when I go on holiday—and I haven't a shit show of going on holiday after I've paid for a mansion—you think I should stay at a hotel alone instead of an RV park. That's not life, Erin."

"No! My parents spend lots of weekends on their law partners' sailboats. See? Money can get you a sailboat."

"Erin, I have a sailboat now."

"You do not."

"I do. Walk 'round the shed."

Erin crawled out of the hammock and circled his shed to find an old sailboat—not a sunfish, but a genuine sailboat.

Hank laid his hands on her shoulders.

"You snuck up on me," she said.

"Sorry. I know I came down too hard on you. I'm not saying owning things is bad! I'm just saying there's a trade-off between buying everything you want and trading away your life to get them. I don't want to work sixty-hour weeks. I don't want to work Saturdays. I already have lazy Sundays at home and several holidays a year. Why would I want a four-bedroom house like your parents? Where two bedrooms go unused ninety-nine percent of the time? I want to live. I want to work enough at something I'm good at that helps people and lets me pay for the things I need and the things I really, really want—which is mostly exploring, anyway. Enjoy living. I want to see the whole world as truly as possible. I want to find the things that make me happy and enjoy them as long as I can. . . . And, Erin?"

Those eyes.

He was quieter. "I want the same for you."

She kissed him, holding onto the back of his head because he might go away at any time.

He wanted a life of happiness for her. A lifetime of happiness. That was the kindest wish anyone had ever made for her. If Ben had said anything remotely like that, he would have gotten into her pants instantly.

And that was the thing, wasn't it? Here was Hank,

absolutely sincere. Not even considering getting into her pants at this moment.

Erin said, "So, where do we go from here?"

"Always ask for what you want, and always do what makes you happy. That's a start."

"You've said that."

"And also, I need you to reserve December twenty-second for me. The whole day."

"The whole day? What are we doing?"

"It's a surprise. A Christmas prezzie. An experiential gift."

Two car doors slammed, and Erin emerged from behind the shed.

Gloria yelled, "Come on, you wanker! Let's get a move on. Sorry, Erin. I didn't mean you were a wanker."

Hank ran around the shed. "Nope, she is!"

And they were off, again.

BEFORE SHE LEARNED HOW FAST SHE WAS

BEFORE SHE LEARNED HOW FAST SHE WAS

Mitchell and Claire had departed before breakfast, complaining about the double bed. For years, Claire had implored her parents to buy a house big enough for everyone to spread out.

Clad in bathrobes, Erin and her grandparents devoured sausage and pancakes drowned in syrup.

"Let's relocate you from the pullout sofa to the guest bedroom," Grampa said. "We can do anything you want, all summer."

"Swimming!" Ten-year-old Erin tore off her bathrobe to reveal a velour swimsuit.

"Is that it? Are we going to swim all summer?"

"Boating!"

"Don't get him started," Tea said.

Grampa laughed. "I had an idea. What if we have a midnight paddle into the middle of the lake and go stargazing?"

"Yes!" Erin said.

Grandma Tea said, "I've added it to the list. What else?"

"Hiking! Music! Ice cream! Daddy Frank's!"

"Should we take the boat to Daddy Frank's today?" Grampa asked.

"Swimming!" Erin said.

"You are a fish, my sweet granddaughter. Give us a minute to get dressed."

Grandma Tea whipped off her bathrobe to reveal her own swimsuit. "Time waits for no man. Let's go, Fish."

"I have been outsmarted," Grampa said as his two girls ran to the dock's edge and dove in.

SEVENTY

Sunday afternoon, something tugged the edges of Erin's brain.

Choosing Columbia had been a combination of things, really: she was a legacy candidate, their acceptance rate was two percent higher than Harvard and Yale, and it was still on the East Coast. Columbia had a great swim team, but not so great that she couldn't get on it.

For years, her laser-focus on Columbia had forced her into AP classes, orchestra, and varsity swimming. She would parlay her every effort into an Ivy League acceptance letter, and parlay that undergraduate experience into a good med school, so she could parlay that into a six-figure salary and respected position in a teaching hospital.

But why?

Great medical school, great job, great life.

But she didn't want that life. She really, really didn't. She didn't want to spend eight more years in school, so she could spend eight more years locked in hospital residencies, fellowships, and whatever else it took to succeed. She didn't even like biology.

Erin: Li, do you think I'd be a good doctor?
Litha: Of course! You are a beast.
Erin: Right. This is a real question.
Erin: Would I be a good doctor?
Litha: Yes. You will stop at nothing to succeed.
Litha: (I can't tell what mood you're in. Is that the right answer?)
Erin: Do you think I'd be a happy doctor?
Litha: What, exactly, is going on down there?
Erin: Crisis, I think.
Erin: I don't think I want to be a doctor.
Litha: Biology and anatomy would be steep hurdles for you.
Erin: Right?
Erin: WTF was I thinking?
Litha: Probably that you could do anything you put your mind to.
Litha: And you could.
Litha: But should you?
Erin: I'm thinking no.
Litha: I'd love to dwell in existential crisis with you.
Litha: But Teddy's parents are out of town.
Litha: So we have the house to ourselves.
Litha: So bye. ☻
Erin: Make him wear a raincoat.
Litha: Shhhhhhhhh.

Erin loved knowing her friend was happy. And she loved how well Lalitha knew her. Erin hated biology, and would undoubtedly hate another anatomy class, to say nothing of needles, catheters, and bodily fluids.

"I don't want to be a doctor." Admitting it aloud gave it power.

"Did you say something, love?" Felicity poked her head into the girls' room.

Erin stared at her but couldn't focus.

"I was going to ask you to tea, but your mind is leagues away. You look like you're in crisis."

Erin was in crisis. "I am trying to determine the essence of a person."

Timidly, Felicity sat on the edge of Erin's bed. "That's quite deep, eh?"

They said nothing for a few minutes.

"Is this about Hank?"

Erin guffawed. Hank certainly had led her here, but this wasn't about him at all. "No, it's about me. I have been spending so much of my life working toward the Ivy League—looking good on paper—that I hardly know who I am anymore. I need to sort through what everyone else wants from me, and what people expect of me, to figure out what I want. At this point, I don't even know."

"Why don't you join us for tea, and determine the essence of a person afterward?"

"Yes. I know for sure I'm hungry." They walked toward the kitchen. "Felicity? Are you happy?"

"I am very happy."

"But what things would make you happier?"

Felicity bit her lip, thinking. "I don't need anything else. All I really want are long and happy lives for all of us."

Through the huge windows, Erin spied Pippa and her pals jumping on the trampoline. She said, "Life is slower here. Smaller. Your houses. Your cars. Your boats. The things that make kiwis happy are different."

"Happiness is happiness," Felicity said.

"Yeah, but, so Hank has his boat, right? My parents'

partners' boats are much bigger and pristine. They can live on them for a week if they want."

"And how often do they live on those boats for a week?"

"Never, I guess. But they could."

Felicity said, "There's a difference between what you need in a boat and what people want in a boat. Same with houses. Same with everything. The closer together your wants and needs are, the happier you'll be."

"How do I know you're not saying I should own less stuff simply because you own less stuff."

"I'm asking which stuff you actually need to be completely yourself."

That was food for thought.

"And something else," Felicity said. "You're talking about *things* here. Things will never make you happy. There's always something bigger or better or newer. Life isn't about that. Look at our neighbors who lost their homes during the quake. It was devastating, but they're living on. Life is about what you enjoy doing and who you enjoy doing it with."

They stared at each other, Felicity smiling warmly.

"Does that make sense?" Felicity asked.

"Yes, Mum." Erin caught herself, panicked, then smiled. "Felicity, sorry. Yes, it makes sense."

SEVENTY-ONE

Hours later—after tea and a bit of homework—Pippa snored lightly while Erin's mind raced.

Always ask for what you want, and always do what makes you happy.

In Ilam's front office on her first day, there'd been a poster: INTEREST + APTITUDE + CAREER. Four months ago, Erin's "interest" list would've been completely different. It would've been a list of expectations forced upon her. What did she want?

She whispered, "I do not want to be a doctor."

But what do I want?

Wide awake, Erin crept into the dining room with her backpack. She wrapped herself in blankets and opened her steno pad. In all caps, she wrote THINGS I WANT.

What was so exciting she would want to do it every day for the rest of her life?

She had fun with guitar, but that wasn't a career for her. She loved rock climbing and swimming, but they didn't make a life. She loved, loved physics and astronomy, but where would they lead her? Life as an astronomer? Working for NASA? An astrophysics professor?

Claire always said those who can, do—and those who can't, teach.

Erin *wanted* to excise her mother's voice from her brain.

She did want astrophysics, but Google said astronomy and astrophysics were almost exclusively graduate programs. She could start with physics.

That narrowed the field.

It would be nice to swim, but . . . there was no but. She wanted to swim competitively. Big schools were out, because she was good but not that good.

That narrowed it down.

And where?

Claire and Mitchell loved Columbia because they loved New York, but Erin didn't need to be in a city. In fact, she would love to live near mountains. She would never be a mountain biker, but climbing was awesome.

A quick search yielded dozens of colleges with great climbing walls, and many with climbing clubs. She definitely wanted to stick with climbing in addition to swimming.

She wanted starry nights. Beautiful scenery she could breathe in. Easygoing people. But with interest in and access to good clothes.

She wanted a town similar to Christchurch, but with better fashion and warmer winters.

She made a second list, DO NOT WANT: religious schools, all-girls schools, schools close to Wheaton.

Her list nearly complete, she converted it to a spreadsheet.

The thing is, what she liked about Ilam—what she loved about Ilam, aside from free time at lunch and the fact that she could wake up five minutes before it was time to leave the house—was the lack of constant competition. No one really cared who was studying what, and no one had uttered the word *valedictorian*. Everyone acknowledged people with talent in sports and in art, but they collaborated. Erin liked competing—she really, really liked winning—but in class, competing didn't feel productive.

Columbia had competitive admissions and a reputation for a cutthroat premed undergraduate program. Four years of cutthroat academics would be a nightmare.

DO NOT WANT: a cutthroat undergraduate experience.

She cross-referenced and Googled, removing schools consistently included in cutthroat lists. University of Chicago, Johns Hopkins, and Columbia fit every other bill, but no.

No school had an undergraduate astrophysics program, decent swim team, rock climbing, low light pollution, and a collaborative environment. Cross-referencing the physics program with at least two of the others whittled her list to twelve.

She pored over websites, took virtual tours, and narrowed again to seven. For Cornell, Colorado at Boulder, Wisconsin at Madison, Washington at Seattle, Stanford, Illinois Champaign-Urbana, and University of Arizona—Erin outlined a sincere essay about how study abroad had changed her.

SEVENTY-TWO

Hours later, Erin edited her passionate essay about her life in New Zealand.

All her schools took the Common Application, and Claire's approved essay was uploaded already for all the Ivies.

Since Claire insisted on having Erin's passwords, this would be tricky. Once applications were saved in "ready" mode, only the first hundred or so words were visible.

After the first full paragraph of her Columbia essay, Erin inserted a new one:

To Whom It May Concern:
I respect Columbia, but while you're on my parents' list of ideal colleges, you're not on mine. You've read about helicopter parents? Mine are the worst kind: they don't even have my best interests at heart. As you can read in the surrounding essay—which a professional essay writer edited heavily—I've learned a lot Down Under. Unfortunately, I still am working on standing up to my parents, and doing that from the Southern Hemisphere is unlikely. When I return from New Zealand next month, we will have a heart-to-heart about college and my long-term plans. In the meantime, I hope you will send me a

very nice letter of rejection. I would be unhappy at Columbia, and you would be unhappy with me.

She did that for all the Ivies except Cornell. Cornell needed the new essay.

If admissions officers read every application they received, this couldn't go wrong: either they'd respect her wishes and reject her, or they'd think she was too weak of character to stand up to her parents . . . and reject her.

She couldn't lose.

Erin was banking on the fact that she'd get in somewhere decent where she actually wanted to go.

Please let me get in somewhere decent.

Cornell was Claire's least favorite Ivy, but if Erin got in there, everyone would win.

And, if it wasn't an Ivy, so what? Claire didn't go Ivy for undergrad . . . and she thought herself perfect.

Erin emailed Claire: "Because I'm a lopsided candidate, I've widened my scope of safety schools, just in case."

Claire would think that was a great idea. She hoped.

Morning dawned and Hamish joined Erin in the kitchen. "Up early, Erin."

"You too," she said.

"Right on time for me."

Erin worked while Hamish started coffee and toast. She'd condensed her entire college search into twelve hours.

Doubting herself, she doubled-back to her long list and Googled madly. One website let her compare up to five colleges on twenty-nine key issues and find colleges most similar to Cornell.

Her cursor hovered over the "international" box. How far from Wheaton was too far?

Hamish slid a cup of coffee toward Erin and offered her toast with jam.

"Thanks," she said.

"Felicity told me what you're working on. I'm impressed."

Erin smiled. "Thank you, Hamish. That means a lot."

"I know it's been hard. You think we're backwards. Or opposites."

"The Antipodes, they call it," Erin said.

"Yes."

"Actually, Hamish, I looked it up, and your exact anti-pode is in Spain."

"Never been."

"Where I lived, in Wheaton? That antipode is in the middle of the ocean, so, I think you got the better deal."

"Erin. Focus. I know it was piss awful in the beginning, but I think we found our way."

"I think we did. And now I'm trying to find mine."

"Best of luck," he said.

"Hamish, can you recommend any universities in New Zealand?"

"'Fraid I don't know much. Canterbury's the only one I've visited. I'm off!"

Erin browsed the University of Canterbury's website. Mere blocks from Ilam High, it was the third best university in New Zealand. And it had an undergraduate program in astronomy.

Holy crap.

Sipping her coffee, Erin studied the application, which was due in twenty-four hours. While completing the form, she contemplated strategies for selling the program to Claire.

And Lalitha. Lalitha would kill her.

But this felt right. Without a tour, without talking to

anyone or reading student interviews, she knew she wanted it. Badly.

Erin emailed her Wheaton and Christchurch guidance counselors about forwarding her transcripts to Canterbury, zombied her way through a shower, and hopped onto her bike. At the roundabout, she felt reassured: this was the right thing. Riding her bike woke her right up.

And she was awake.

And she felt good.

SEVENTY-THREE

Erin mentally composed an email to Lalitha all day. Lalitha would be pissed. Claire might be easy by comparison. That afternoon, while she waited for her friends at The Roxx, she texted Claire her Plan B.

> **Erin:** Mom, I had a brilliant plan.
> **Erin:** I'm applying to University of Canterbury in Christchurch.
> **Claire:** No.
> **Erin:** Just hear me out.
> **Erin:** Colleges are going to admit me (or not) based on everything that's happened already. They're not taking next semester in Wheaton into account. Spending a semester at the University here can only improve my résumé.
> **Claire:** So you would come back to a real college in September.

Erin let the *real college* comment pass; she couldn't afford a fight right now.

Erin: Yes, but it gets better! If I don't get into a good school in the States, I could apply this May as a transfer candidate. Transfer applicants have a much higher acceptance rate.

Claire: Good point!

Claire: How long ago was the application period?

Erin: Even better news! It ends tomorrow.

Claire: Great. You should've done this weeks ago! Get on top of it and let me know how I can push it along.

Erin breathed deeply as Marama pulled into the parking lot. Erin smiled and raised her index finger to indicate she needed a minute.

Erin: Relax, Mom.

Erin: Copied and pasted all my application materials into their application last night.

Erin: Already asked Mrs. Brown to forward my transcript.

Erin: When I get home tonight, I'll submit it.

Claire: Fine.

Claire: I hope you don't have to transfer. Med schools might think that looked like . . . exactly what it is. Like you weren't good enough to get in on your first try.

Erin: I'm covering all the bases.

Claire: Fine.

Claire: What's their acceptance rate?

Erin: I'll do a lot more research and email you tonight. Have to go now. Meeting friends.

Claire: This is important, Erin. FOCUS.

Erin: I am focused.

Claire: There are a million tomorrows for friends. Focus on this until it's done.

Erin: Right, of course. I will, Mom. Bye.

Erin powered off her phone. "My mother is crazy."

"Aren't they all?" Marama said.

"Mine is freaking out because I want to apply to University of Canterbury."

"You mean ours?"

"Yours. Ours, yes."

"You see?" Marama said. "This is the problem in our country: people swing through and never want to leave!"

"Sorry," Erin said.

"It's okay. I love you. You can stay." Marama wrapped her arms around her friend.

Erin squeezed her. "I hope so."

They changed in the bathroom and buckled their harnesses. Hank and Gloria arrived as they were roping in.

"Guess who wants to be kiwi?" Marama said.

"Whazzat?" Hank said.

"She's going for Uni. Submitting her application tonight." Erin hadn't expected Hank to flinch.

"Climbing," Marama said.

Erin's voice was quiet. "Climb on."

Hank stared at Erin as Marama scrambled up the wall. Belaying Marama was the perfect excuse to not look him in the eye.

"Hello?" Hank said.

"Hi," she whispered.

"Were you going to tell me about this?"

"I decided literally hours ago."

"You shouldn't change your life because of me."

Erin fought to contain her laughter. "I definitely am not doing this for you, Hank." She looked at him for a split second, then back to Marama. "You are wonderful, don't get me wrong, but I'm doing this for me. The University of

Canterbury is one of few I've found to offer an undergraduate program in astronomy. And I feel good here. I'm doing it for me. It's what *I* want. I think it will make me happy."

Erin bit her tongue to stave off tears.

"I can't argue with that." Hank kissed her on the cheek. "I'll change and be out. Hey! Does this mean you'll join us at the bach on Boxing Day?"

"I wish. Flight's still the twenty-third. First term starts in February."

Believing it was a sure thing, Erin realized she had internalized her mother's judgment of colleges. In the back of her brain, she didn't think of the University of Canterbury as a *real college*.

But it was. And what if they rejected her?

SEVENTY-FOUR

To quell any urge of refreshing her mail for the next ten hours, Erin sent an email from her computer two minutes before the family left for Ilam Primary. Even if Lalitha replied immediately, Erin would not check her mail for hours.

Pippa's long-awaited Kapa Haka performance was casual. Young children sat on the floor before rows of adults in chairs. Toddlers ran rings around the auditorium and babies cooed. This was a family affair.

Pippa's group took the stage in black lipstick and grass skirts that rattled as they walked. Masculine costumes included a bare chest with only a short black cape on top. Color block tops with thick shoulder straps completed the feminine costumes.

An adult in a similar costume said, "Waiata-ā-ringa."

The crowd quieted as the group started singing a cappella. Pippa's hands fluttered at her sides as her smile reached Erin. Erin didn't understand the language, but she understood the dance was of happiness and peace.

The adult on stage said, "Haka," and students bunched together on stage. One student shouted and others responded. They stomped loudly; this was a battle hymn. A serious, fierce face replaced Pippa's grin as she clenched her fists at her sides.

Erin's body tensed until the song was over.

The adult said, "Whakawātea," and the group spread out on stage. Pippa—Pippa!—collected her guitar from the back corner. She strummed a note, tapped her guitar twice, and the students sang.

Pippa became a calmer version of herself, chin held high as if she had accomplished something important. Erin knew Leonard Cohen's "Hallelujah," and the Māori version was equally effective: Erin breathed deeply as peace settled within her.

Afterward, Erin had a single text from Lalitha.

Litha: If it makes you happy, it can't be that bad. ❤

Erin nearly cried. She was going to be okay. She was on her way to happiness.

Now out of her costume, Pippa ran to hug Erin before introducing her to friends.

Felicity had made fairy bread—buttered bread covered with nonpareils—and it was gone in an instant. Pippa loaded her plate with sweets from other families.

She munched a biscuit. "At the start of next term, we get to learn poi!"

"What's that?" Erin said.

Pippa stood and looped her arms in front of her face. "It's a Polynesian ball on a string. When you suss it properly, it's beautiful. Every time I try it, I make a tangled mess."

"Well, I look forward to your poi," Erin said. "I could tell you enjoyed that. I loved watching you dance."

Pippa beamed.

BEFORE SHE WAS FISH

BEFORE SHE WAS FISH

On Grandma Tea's birthday, Erin wore a dress over her swim-suit. She stood in the middle of the cottage and asked her grandparents to share the sofa.

"First, happy birthday, Tea. I'm nine, so you're turning sixty-nine," Erin said. "Sixty-nine is the same right-side up and upside-down, which is cool. And it's the solstice, natu-rally. Also cool. I know we're doing your favorite hikes today. I even found a new blueberry bush a couple weeks ago and have kept it secret until today. I brought presents from home, but I want to give you this one first."

Rapt, Erin's grandparents waited patiently while she tuned her guitar.

"I'm going to need some help."

Her Grampa stood to help her.

"No, no, no. I'm fine here. You'll know what to do. Ready?"

She strummed the first few notes of "Sweet Baby James" and Tea's eyes sparkled.

They sang right on cue.

Erin got flustered in the middle, but they made it through slowly. Her grandparents applauded when she was done.

"I was expecting 'Happy Birthday'!" Grampa said.

Grandma Tea hugged Erin tightly. "Thank you, my girl."

"I learned half of his songbook," Erin said. "And played 'Carolina in My Mind' all over Door County during spring break as protest that we didn't actually go to North Carolina."

"Good for you," Tea said. "I couldn't be more proud."

SEVENTY-FIVE

In the Southern Hemisphere, the end of school butted right up to Christmas, so Erin's classmates graduated surrounded by Santas clad in fur, plastic evergreen trees, artificial snow, and twinkle lights.

Twinkle lights were less charming when the sun set at nine.

Hank's Christmas present to Erin was experiential—a word she thought was him saying *experimental* incorrectly—and a surprise. As requested, she'd reserved the entire day of December twenty-second.

Erin, who envisioned a long drive culminating with a rock climb at dusk, woke well before the crack of dawn.

Hank rapped quietly before 5 a.m., and Erin tucked her present to him into her little bag; she hoped it was as meaningful to him as everything he'd given her.

She threw in some of Felicity's biscuits, too. Felicity had left a note: *Enjoy your day! See you tomorrow!*

Erin loved her. She loved her for not waking up to manage the moment and for leaving a note that made her feel loved.

Erin opened the door to find Hank holding a stainless-steel cup. "Coffee?"

She kissed him before sipping the hot coffee. "Want to come in for a minute?"

"Nah, can't. You ready?"

"Swimsuit on. Tramping boots, fleece, jacket, activewear, hat." She stepped onto the stoop and, on second thought, ran back inside. She flipped over Felicity's note and scrawled: *Thanks! Have a great day working in the garden. I'll see you tomorrow morning. Love, E*

Hank rested his hand on her knee as they drove eastward. Erin took in the quiet, dim roads and trees. Light edges of the huge sky hinted that day would soon dawn. Peaceful, Christchurch felt the way home should feel. The comfortable, easy feeling of her grandparents' cottage. Calm. Serene. Like the lake on crisp mornings.

"So, where are we headed? Sumner Beach?" she asked.

"Close."

She wasn't sure what was close to Sumner. "Clifton? Redcliffs?"

"Your guess was close. We're not going close to Sumner."

Erin couldn't stifle a yawn.

"Would you rather be in bed?" Careful, cautious Hank kept his eyes on the road, though yes, she would enjoy another lazy afternoon wrestling in his bed. Since that first kiss—which felt like ages ago—they had enjoyed each other for long hours on end.

She expected some naked time today.

The air thickened slightly as they approached the ocean.

"You're taking me for a day at the beach?"

"Sort of."

Hank parked next to a playground that overlooked a beach so vast they couldn't see either end. "Have you been to New Brighton?"

She hadn't.

"It's one of my favorites. Surfing's no good, but the beach goes on forever. And if the weather turns, the library's right there."

Hank handed a small bag to Erin and kept the larger one for himself. They trudged toward the water, Hank glancing between the sea and the beach several times until he'd found the perfect spot. He dropped his bag and laid out a blanket.

On the blanket, Erin kissed Hank's neck. He turned and lost himself in her for several minutes.

"So, why the beach?" she asked.

"You said you'd never seen a sunrise over the ocean."

"Or anywhere."

"Over the ocean is the best. It'll be up in—" He checked his phone. "Seven minutes." He ran his hand from her knee to her hip and kissed her lightly. "I don't want you to miss it."

It was already bright enough to see everything. The sky was more beautiful than any painting she'd ever seen; streaks of pinks and purples and blues and grays laid atop each other, a colorful textured collage over an ocean of blue on blue on blue.

It was perfect. Just perfect.

A sliver of burnt orange poked into the horizon and slowly became a full circle. Mesmerized, Erin said, "I never imagined it rising so fast."

Hank whispered, "I've always been fascinated by the sun like this. Only on the horizon can you look directly at the sun without damaging your eyes."

Spectacular morning colors faded quickly as the sun took center stage. Hank slid his arms around Erin's torso and they lay on the blanket.

"Thanks for giving me the whole day," he said.

"Thanks for giving me my first sunrise."

"You bet." He kissed her sweetly, then less sweetly, and they rolled around on the blanket until a huge brown dog bounded onto them, trying to get in on the action. Its human called it away and more people peppered the beach, so they sat looking outward, fingers interlaced, for a long time.

Erin hadn't much silence in her life before New Zealand. Before Hank. They talked plenty and did other stuff plenty, but he often left her alone with her thoughts. That was a gift in and of itself.

"Thanks," she said.

He kissed her. "Good morning. Swim?"

They peeled off their clothes and walked to the chilly water's edge.

"Better to do it all at once." Erin walked into the ocean and dove under.

Hank said, "Not sure I'm ready for that."

"You'll be cold until you get your head wet. You could face the shore and fall backward."

Hank dove under and came up shrieking.

"Are you okay? Don't tell me it was a jellyfish."

"No, it's cold as a witch's tit!"

Laughing, Erin wrapped her arms around his neck. He kissed her and she dunked him.

He emerged a moment later. "Now you're in it!"

Erin dove and swam hard out to sea. Minutes later, she checked on Hank, who was swimming far behind her.

"It's not a fair fight!" he yelled.

Erin rolled onto her back, floating in early morning light.

"I'm not that great a swimmer," Hank said when he reached her.

Instantly alert, she said, "Don't panic."

"Not panicked, but I'd like to touch sand on occasion."

"Let's go in. Gently."

Slowly, they swam toward shore. Erin kept a keen eye on Hank until they reached a depth where he could touch bottom

"Sorry," she said. "I wasn't thinking. Is this better?"

"All good."

SEVENTY-SIX

After an hour of swimming and diving, they wrapped themselves in towels.

"Coffee?" Hank asked.

They bought coffee and pastries from a café on the beach. While the barista worked her magic, a chef handed Hank a jug of the previous day's seafood chowder. "Don't open it until you get where you're going. Should stay warm for a few hours."

Hank said, "Sweet as."

In the car, Hank said, "I brought you a fantastic present."

She dug in her bag before Hank handed her an ice cream punnet.

He said, "See? I know you!"

She bopped him on the head with it. "Just drive."

They circumnavigated Christchurch before winding through the Southern Alps. Erin admired the scenery, admired Hank, and focused on the horizon as required. In late morning, they stopped at Arthur's Pass, a national park off a well-traveled road.

Hank pointed at a trailhead. "This is when you need your

layers. Wrap your jersey and your jacket around your waist. You'll want them before lunch."

Erin screamed as a vulture perched on her mirror. Its huge, green tail twitched slightly as it settled and cocked its head to study her. Pecking the rubber around her window, each monstrous jab disheveled its thick, gray feathers.

One of its friends tap-danced on the car roof. Two more stared from the grass. They were behemoths, determined to break into the car and devour them both.

"Fucking keas," Hank said. "They're the worst of New Zealand." He slammed the car door on his way out to scare the birds . . . but keas don't scare.

Hank swatted at the one on Erin's mirror before physically pushing it away. It fought back, and he released a low, deep moan, spreading his arms out and dancing like a lunatic.

That worked, but when Erin emerged from the car, she ran to the trailhead. The keas perched in front of the car, taunting her.

Hank caught up. "You know they can get out of the parking area, right? It's not like they live there. You may be walking into a forest full of 'em."

She shrugged and hiked on, shaking off those particular keas. Arthur's Pass was very New Zealand—mountains, water, tramping—but everything was more pronounced with Hank. She would forever remember him looking over his shoulder to ensure she was okay.

She was okay.

The terrain could be rocky, but spending time with Hank was easy. The conversation was easy. The silence was easy.

She chose him.

They hiked for two hours, stopping to ogle interesting flowers and trees. Their extra layers migrated from waist to torso as they gained altitude. Even in summer, mountain air chilled Erin.

Off the path, they found a sublime view and set up lunch: the thermos of chowder, ceramic bowls, genuine silverware, jugs of water, and more sweets than any two people required.

Hank's back must have been killing him.

Sitting across from each other, it was practically a formal dinner, their legs crossed on a blanket in the middle of nature. Erin followed a deep breath with a satisfied sigh. With nothing to do and nowhere to be, she felt free.

"Thanks for this."

He gazed down at the valley. "I feel like we got a late start. The South Island has a lot of great stuff."

"Yeah."

"Seriously. Today was your first trip to New Brighton. This right here is the best chowder around, and this is your first bowl. You have so much great stuff to discover."

"I hope to come back and discover it all."

"If you come back, I'll make a list."

The cooling chowder lingered on Erin's tongue. By the third bite, she believed it was the best. Like the night sky, and like New Zealand, the chowder grew more nuanced with time. And it was packed with seafood.

She held a spoonful toward Hank. "What do you think this is?"

"Gurnard, maybe? I don't know my white fish."

He knew his chowder, though. And dense, crusty bread. Maybe soup was the answer to cold New Zealand winters, too. Erin could eat this chowder forever.

Or at least until Hank lay on the blanket. Bellies full, they pushed the sweets aside and discovered each other again. Between the trees, under the sun, in the middle of nowhere, even chilly mountain air couldn't deter them from losing some clothes.

An hour later, Hank's stomach growled. "Caramel bars in the chilly bin."

Erin shrugged her shoulders and grinned. "Chilly bin. That's the cutest one yet." She opened the cooler and pulled out two caramel bars.

Hank polished off his and said, "We should get moving soon."

Erin wanted to spend the rest of her day with him. Here.

"I have a present for you," she said, withdrawing the parcel from her bag.

Hank turned it over in his hands. "Is it a self-help guide on how to speak American?"

"Better," she said.

He ripped off the paper and stared at the very old copy of *Walden*.

"So, my Grandma Tea, who I loved more than anything in the world, wrote her thesis on Thoreau and feminism. This is one of her copies of *Walden*."

Tears welled in Erin's eyes as Hank thumbed through the pages.

She wiped her sleeve across her face. "Literature was never really my thing. I've always been a scientist. I was so thrilled when I learned one of Mercury's craters was named Thoreau and Tea thought that was great. She and I met in the middle of art and science."

Erin wiped her eyes again. "She was wonderful. I miss her so much."

"I think you should keep this."

"I've thought about it. I really want you to have it." She opened the book to a well-worn passage. "See all her notes in the margin? I sometimes look through her books and imagine we're talking about them together. She was passionate about books and nature and music and art."

He gazed at her with sad eyes. "I love it. Thank you."

"Thank you," she said. "For everything."

They held hands for a few minutes, gazing at the sky together. Erin shaded her eyes from the sun.

"Let's just stay here all day."

He kissed her. "Any other day, we could. But I have something really, really important for you. I promise."

He pulled her to standing and wrapped her in a bear hug. "You're amazing. Want to lead down or follow?"

SEVENTY-SEVEN

In the parking lot, Hank shooed the keas away and they were on the road again.

"I'm having fun, I promise," she said. "But it sort of feels like we're spending the day in the car."

"We just spent two hours getting lucky on a mountain."

She couldn't help smiling. "But otherwise, we're spending the day in the car."

"Google maps says under ten hours in the car today."

"Now I know why you needed me on the longest day of the year."

Grinning, Hank took a different way down from Arthur's Pass. "Fact is, half our driving will be out of the sunlight. So, we're only really wasting five hours of sun. And we're already half done."

She loved that he was a planner. He could have packed a single suitcase for five months away. He definitely wouldn't have packed the clothes that sat unused in Pippa's closet these past few months.

They passed a sign for Hokitika.

"Oh! Felicity was just there!"

Hank nodded.

"Arts and crafts village, right? Felicity went for Christmas presents and art. Are we doing an art walk or something?"

He said, "It's not about the town."

Hank drove straight to the ocean, waved at it, and headed south. They drove for miles, parallel to the surf, their road separated only by a thin strip of farmland. Not two hundred meters from the beach, herds of cattle grazed in the rare flat land of New Zealand.

"Did I tell you someone was herding cows in the road when we drove down to Queenstown? It was hilarious."

Hank said, "Yep. Happens a lot, especially in the wop wops."

At Hokitika, they turned inland toward Hokitika Gorge and Hank said, "Solid ninety minutes in the car, and you haven't chucked. I'm impressed."

"There's still time."

Hank parked in a tiny lot and checked his watch for the ten millionth time. "Two hours, that's it."

"I'm not in a rush. Are you in a rush?"

He said, "We have one more stop, and we can't be late."

That deadline was a shame, because the gorge was, in fact, gorgeous: impossibly blue, still water pooled between boulders in a forest of evergreens. Mountains loomed all around as if this gem were here just for them.

"We don't have time for both swimming and hiking. What's your pleasure?"

She'd had enough hiking at Arthur's Pass. "Let's swim."

"Down to your togs, then!" Hank ripped off his shirt, jumped off a boulder, splashed into the water, and screamed. "Dicey! It's frigid."

Erin stood at the water's edge for an eternity.

"Come on in!" Hank said. "It's like ripping off a plaster: best to do it all at once."

"I'm not falling for that."

"Come on. I did it for you!"

She ran toward the water and cannonballed two feet from him. Her head broke the water and she screamed, "Jesus!"

"Nope, still Hank."

"It's freezing!" She pulled herself up onto a cool rock.

"You prefer the hike, then?"

"Not now. Now I'll freeze no matter what we do."

"Back to the truck, then?"

She wrapped up in her towel while Hank dove underwater a few times. Hopping into the truck would warm her up for sure, but they'd only just arrived. And she knew Hank had other ideas. "It's a long drive for a quick peek at a blue gorge."

She peeled out of her suit and dressed in dry clothes.

Hank rubbed his hair and trunks with her towel. "It's a short walk, really. Let's go for it."

———

From the swing bridge, the electric blue water was mesmerizing.

"How is it so blue?" Erin said.

"It's glacial water, for one. The rock flour makes it opaque."

She hadn't noticed it was opaque, didn't even care when she jumped in—that's how compelling the blue was.

"I feel like your country is constantly playing a game of one-upmanship with itself."

He laughed. "It's a South Island thing. If you come back, we'll take you to the North Island. It's a whole different story: cities and ten-lane highways and crowds."

"I think. I think I might be a South Island girl."

"I certainly hope so." He kissed her for a long time. "Warming up?"

"Starting to. Back to the car?" She raised her eyebrows.

His watch. "We're nearly out of time. Let's make our last stop, and then maybe some time in the car?"

Erin couldn't imagine anything more pressing than pressing their bodies together. She locked her arms behind his neck. "Let's just stay here. Right here. South Island. Gorgeous gorge."

He pulled back. "Nope. We need to finish the story, and it doesn't end here."

Hank pulled a pair of socks and a jersey from the backseat. Wearing them, she tucked up into a ball and warmed up. A half-hour later, they drove through the quaint town of Hokitika and parked near the shore. Hank leapt from the car, grabbed his blanket, and dragged her onto the beach.

"Here we go." He spread out the blanket and lay on his belly, facing the water. "Quick. Quick!"

Erin stretched out next to him and followed his gaze, over shadows cast by tiny sand hills and onto the water. The wind had picked up, so whitecaps broke near and far. The sea appeared green and black, and broke into white frothy caps. An inch above the horizon, the orange sun threatened to take a dip.

Oh.

Sunset was like a larger-than-life rainbow, without the green . . . unless she counted the sea's deep green. Erin and Hank lay in silence as the sun dipped its toes into the ocean and slid in.

The sun had set over the ocean trillions of times. While she'd lived intensely in Wheaton, waves had crashed onto this shore. Waves crashed, mountains loomed, shells washed in and out with the tide. Since before she was born. Since before anyone was born!

The gorgeous sunset would repeat tomorrow and the next day, regardless of where she was and what she was doing.

She whispered, "Sunrise over the ocean. Sunset over the ocean."

Hank said, "The Tasman Sea, but you get the idea. No matter where you go, or what you do, I hope you will remember spending the longest day of the year with me."

"Thank you."

As darkness descended around them, Erin rested her cheek on her hands, facing Hank.

"Naked swim?" he said.

"Can we do that?"

"Course we can do that."

Near the water, they dropped their clothes and ran into the chilly sea. For an hour, they frolicked, naked, under a crescent moon in the deep charcoal sky.

"Thank you for giving me the day," Hank said.

In neck-deep water, Erin wrapped her arms around Hank and kissed him as if it were the last time. "I'll never forget this."

Erin wanted it to be true. In less than twenty-four hours, she'd be gone—for a while, at least. And she desperately wanted to hold onto the part of herself she'd found in New Zealand.

Forever.

SEVENTY-EIGHT

The next morning, Erin found Felicity in her bedroom.

"Felicity?"

She looked up from her book. "Yes, love? How was your day with Hank?"

"Wonderful. Just—it was amazing. How was your day?"

"Great. Pippa ran with her pack all day, naturally. That's how summer is: see her for brekkies, see her for tea, and she's off the rest of the day."

"I love that," Erin said. "My summers were like that, a long time ago."

Felicity smiled. "And I got heaps done in the garden. I was thinking you'll miss the feijoa if you don't come back in January."

"Feijoa?"

"It's the tree beside the swing set. Lovely fruits."

Erin stared at Felicity, trying to convey with her eyes everything she couldn't yet say.

"What did you need, love?"

Erin stared at the blue carpet that now felt like home. How could she leave?

"Erin?"

Ear-in.

"I was wondering whether you would give consent for me to get a tattoo."

Felicity paused. "How do you think your parents would feel about that?"

"That's the thing. I want one to remind me I don't need to follow their path. I have to go back for now, at least. But I don't have to continue the rat race. I don't have to push myself into things I don't particularly enjoy. A tattoo will help me hang onto the peace and headspace I've found here."

Felicity took two deep breaths. "You know, tattoos are harder to hide on swimmers."

Erin swallowed hard. "I'm not sure I care about that."

"Tell me what you're thinking."

"Well, I have already thought about my mother and, you know, the rest of my life. I could hide it on my butt, but then I'd never see it. And the whole point is to see it all the time. Below my navel, in the bikini area, is certainly an area she wouldn't find it but, you know?" Erin blushed, thinking of Hank. "Someday, someone else might find it and it's not for them, either."

Felicity nodded. "When I was on my O.E., I went out with this bloke. I was in England. His name was something royal. Charlie? George? It hardly matters anymore. Anyway, we were getting . . . intimate. And his knickers were black with the name Amy in pink cursive all over them. Bad time to discuss it."

"No!" Erin might miss Felicity—being Felicity's daughter—more than she'd miss New Zealand itself.

Felicity said, "So, not the bikini line. Good decision. Where, then?"

"I was thinking of getting it wrapped around my middle finger, where almost no one would see it, but I would, every day."

"Under your ring?"

"Yes." Erin twisted the ring so its diamonds scattered sunlight across the ceiling. What if Claire confiscated the ring when Erin landed? All these months gone, and Claire had never mentioned it. Erin felt confident in her case for keeping it.

"Legal age of consent in New Zealand is just sixteen. I couldn't stop you if I wanted to."

They held each other's gaze for a long minute. Erin whispered, "Do you want to stop me?"

"I don't." Felicity's smile was kind. "I think you're a different girl than the one who landed here almost a half year ago. You've shown your true self. I agreed to take care of you and provide for you, and even in the beginning I was going to do that. But, over these last five months, you've impressed me. You are a smart young woman. You're choosing your own way and making decisions that, frankly, I didn't expect when I met you."

"So you think it's a good idea."

"Nope. I don't think it's a good idea. I'm delighted to be tattoo-free. But I trust you. I trust that this is the right decision for you. I trust it's what you want. And it's your body."

"Thank you."

Felicity pulled out her bookmark and returned to her novel.

"Felicity? Could you drive me?"

SEVENTY-NINE

It hurt more than she'd expected, and she was grateful for choosing something small. Her tattoo artist, Jo—a tiny woman with one arm bare and one tattooed—warned that finger tattoos didn't always have the staying power of tattoos on other areas of the body.

"You'll need an artist to touch it up every few years."

Erin was adamant: it had to be under her ring.

Jo recommended Erin get the tattoo on her right hand, since a wedding band might force Tea's ring to her right hand.

Erin had nodded her agreement, but as the needle pierced her flesh over and again, she almost wished she'd let Jo talk her out of it.

Almost.

Two hours later, she admired her right hand. New Zealand's islands ringed her middle finger; no matter what happened, they would be part of her forever.

EIGHTY

Hank picked up Erin after her last tea with her kiwi family.

They wound up naked on his sofa again, and an hour later retired to his hammock in very little clothing.

"You never taught me the butterfly."

"We need to do it in a pool."

"Sounds naughty."

They giggled, and Erin realized how much she would miss his smile, his deep brown eyes, his hands.

"I don't want to go."

"You can teach me when you come back."

"I mean, I don't want to go, ever."

"Life goes on," Hank said.

"All the time." Erin expected a shooting star to punctuate the moment, but the deep starry sky didn't change. "I hope to be back soon enough. I just feel so good here, especially when I'm with you."

He kissed her forehead. "I know what you mean. You make me feel good."

"You make me feel . . . like myself. Like it's okay to be myself."

They dissolved into warm kisses, their hungry bodies entangled.

Between kisses, Erin said, "I got a tattoo this morning."

He pulled back. "You're joking."

"Nope. I did it."

He was almost giddy. "Well, what is it? Where is it?"

She bit her lip. "Maybe you should go looking for it."

"Sweet as." He kissed her navel and up her torso, between her breasts. "Well hidden, eh? I'll keep looking."

It took him an hour of stimulating searching to find it.

EIGHTY-ONE

Pippa bawled at the airport. "You'll always be my sister."

Erin, who had never wanted a sibling, was suddenly losing one. She kissed Pippa on the head.

"I'll try to come back as soon as I can. If I come back for college, we'll see each other all the time."

"Yeah!" Pippa said.

"And you'll move back in with us?" Hamish asked.

Erin looked from Hamish to Felicity. "If you'll have me."

Her words hung in the air for an eternity before Hamish spoke. "You're part of our family, Erin. And you're welcome back any time."

Erin nodded.

She hugged them all, and the whole family had wet eyes.

Hank's eyes were dry when she got to him. Erin whispered, "Thanks. This has changed my life."

"I hope your life is happy," he said.

Felicity snapped a picture of them together and promised to email it.

Erin stood back with her phone to snap photos of Pippa and the rest of the family. Hank snapped a photo of Erin with them.

"Could you take a video?" Erin asked.

"Of what?"

"Just start rolling."

He touched the screen and Erin turned to her family, hugging them again. She told them and how grateful she was, and that she'd miss them.

Hamish said, "It's been good. For all of us."

Felicity said, "I'm so proud of you."

Erin took three steps back and waved. Hank panned from Erin to her family.

"I love you!" Pippa yelled.

Hank touched the screen again. "Got it."

After one final hug, Erin walked toward the scanners.

There's a difference between knowing you're loved and feeling loved. Erin's little video would go a long way toward making Erin feel loved every time she watched.

She placed her bag on the belt and waited as security personnel escorted an elderly man in a wheelchair. Staring at her hands, Erin spun her grandmother's ring and moved it toward her knuckle. She loved how her tattoo made her feel: strong, self-aware, and truly independent. At last, Erin felt she belonged to herself.

Actually, that feeling had always been within her; she just had to come to New Zealand to rediscover it.

And that feeling was hers, forever.

–LOGUE

Erin dove off the dock and swam underwater, the lake water a cold comb raking her hair. She propelled herself onto her canvas raft and relaxed her muscles.

Music danced across the water, so they'd be leaving in an hour. Erin rested her arm over her eyes and soaked in the warmth. Basking in sunlight, Erin imagined herself at nine.

Nine-year-olds had more freedom. Nine-year-olds had more fun.

She still needed to pack, but her luggage could wait. For now, Erin reveled in her own happiness.

AUTHOR'S NOTE

Unlike Erin, I loved New Zealand years before we met. Before moving to Christchurch, I conducted heaps of research. I knew about the 2010/2011 earthquakes. I knew everything would be smaller, the pace would be slower, and my life would be different in myriad and unexpected ways. And it was. And it was fabulous. I would move back again in a heartbeat.

Also, Vogel's bread is the best bread.

I'm sure I idealize and romanticize my life in New Zealand, and I'm fine with that.

There exist a few discrepancies between Erin's Christchurch and *actual* Christchurch:

I created Ilam High, but Ilam Primary is real. It is the most wonderful school I've ever known. Ilam's faculty and community welcomed us during our scant year in Christchurch, and I cannot thank them enough. I miss that community.

There are no direct flights from California to Christchurch, but Auckland airport wasn't part of Erin's story.

To the best of my knowledge and view from Google Earth, there are no docks on Lake Taharoa.

There is no cell service in the hills of Pohara. And many other places in New Zealand. It's glorious.

The Roxx is now closed. Go climb outside.

To suit Erin's calendar, I altered New Zealand's tides, phases of the moon, and planets visible in the night sky.

Like Seattle, Christchurch is awash in rainbows. They weren't part of Erin's story, but have been a dazzling aspect of my own.

Stay strong, Chch; my heart beats with you.

ACKNOWLEDGMENTS

My favorite cartographer created the map of New Zealand featured here. Thank you, Karen Rank.

I, too, had a New Zealand relay team. Thank you Jill Wellman (who's the perfect neighbor), Vienna Galagher (whose friendship surprised me), Donna Blakely (whose entire family is a joy), and Annie Horton (who anchored me). I miss you all.

Without other people performing their jobs spectacularly, I could not do this job I love. Thanks to everyone in my community, but especially Jennifer Anaya, Tessa Boutwell, Nancy Broaders, Tetiana Dunets, Nicole Frail, Natalie Jacqua, Andrea Somberg, Karlee Taylor, and Sylvie Taylor.

My critique group keeps me in line. Thank you Kristina Cerise, Elisabeth Fredrickson, Mary Jean Lord, Meg Pasquini, Peggy Sturdivant, Ruth Teichroeb, and Lauren Ziemski.

Though I learned the word *sublime* from my favorite sixth-grade teacher, I didn't truly understand the concept for nearly twenty-five years. Darleen Carey, thank you for every invaluable lesson, especially the importance of editing with red pencil.

Early readers provided guidance. Thank you Katie Anthony,

Alison Bazeley, Donna Blakely, Heather Booth, Anique Drouin, Gretchen O'Connell, Sarah Quigley, and Renita Stuart. And very special thanks to Kylie Jabjiniak, whose insight was crucial.

I'm grateful to finally have colleagues. Thank you, Cupcake Writers; you are lovely and amazing.

Without a timely writer's residency at Chez Cerise, I could not have made deadline. Merci.

Elena, Katie, and Marisa. Namaste.

My family copes with irrational questions, irregular schedules, unruly piles of paper and books, and a frequently distracted Me. Thank you Charles, Charlotte, Eleanor, and Katherine; you're the highs of my life.